Buying the farm . . .

"Are you sitting down?" Amy asked when Piper picked up.

"Why?" Piper, who'd been standing to check her supply of canning jars, didn't immediately reach for a chair. Though she was surprised to hear from her assistant that day, Amy's tone wasn't warning of deeply upsetting news, such as anything happening to Aunt Judy or Uncle Frank. It did sound serious, though.

"My dad was called out early this morning."

"Oh?" Piper decided to ease over to one of her tall stools after all. Anything involving the sheriff was bound to be bad.

"It's Raffaele Conti." Amy said. "He's dead."

Piper sucked in a breath. "Conti's dead?" she asked, hoping that death had been from perhaps a sudden heart attack. That would be terrible, of course, but still not as terrible as —

"I don't know how yet," Amy said. "But Conti was found in Gerald Standley's dill field."

"The dill field!"

"Right in the middle of it." Amy said. She then blew away the last of Piper's hopes. "He was shot."

License
to Dill

MARY ELLEN HUGHES

BERKLEY PRIME CRIME, NEW YORK

THE BERKLEY PUBLISHING GROUP
Published by the Penguin Group
Penguin Group (USA) LLC
375 Hudson Street, New York, New York 10014

USA • Canada • UK • Ireland • Australia • New Zealand • India • South Africa • China

penguin.com

A Penguin Random House Company

LICENSE TO DILL

A Berkley Prime Crime Book / published by arrangement with the author

Berkley Prime Crime Books are published by The Berkley Publishing Group.
BERKLEY® PRIME CRIME and the PRIME CRIME logo are trademarks of
Penguin Group (USA) LLC.

For information, address: The Berkley Publishing Group,
a division of Penguin Group (USA) LLC,
375 Hudson Street, New York, New York 10014.

ISBN: 978-0-425-26246-7 *5599 9782*

PUBLISHING HISTORY
Berkley Prime Crime mass-market edition / February 2015 *3/15*

PRINTED IN THE UNITED STATES OF AMERICA

10 9 8 7 6 5 4 3 2 1

Cover illustration by Chris O'Leary.
Cover design by Sarah Oberrender.
Interior text design by Laura K. Corless.

For Joshua and Jordan, with love.

Acknowledgments

Writing a story that involves pickles, Italians, soccer, and murder meant calling on the expertise of a wide variety of people. My thanks always go out to the countless excellent cooks who've shared their pickling know-how with me through the years. Maria Luna Baker generously helped me with the Italian phrases, and if mistakes slipped in, they're all mine. Having a pharmacist in the family is extremely handy when writing a murder mystery, and my sister, Barbara Gawronski, once again answered the call. Advice on the ins and outs of soccer came from my husband, Terry, who has also become something of an expert in murder—from a theoretical standpoint, of course. He's been invaluable in helping me develop deadly scenarios and in spotting tiny holes in plots before they become craters.

I'm very grateful, of course, to my editor, Faith Black, and the wonderful team at Berkley Prime Crime who make sure this book is the best it can be and who do so with such grace. Thanks, too, to Kim Lionetti, agent extraordinaire.

Acknowledgments

Once again, many thanks to the team of Annapolis-based writers whose suggestions helped move a raw first draft to its fully cooked and seasoned state: Ray Flynt, Lynda Sasscer Hill, Becky Hutchison, Debbi Mack, Sherriel Mattingly, Bonnie Settle, and Marcia Talley. It's been a great ride, guys, that I hope will go on for quite a while.

1

Piper Lamb walked over to the front window of her shop, Piper's Picklings, for about the twentieth time that morning.

"I've got to stop this," she muttered, "or I'll wear a groove in the floor." Scott Littleton was arriving that day. Typically, her ex-fiancé had neglected to give her a precise time, but he'd be showing up after months of travel about the globe to "find himself." Piper didn't know if he'd run across the real Scott Littleton during that time. But she did know he'd find a very different Piper Lamb from the woman he'd once been engaged to.

Piper was certain there was little trace of that unassuming girl who had worked at an unfulfilling job in the New York State tax office, and who had waited much too long for a foot-dragging fiancé to agree on a date for their wedding.

Nor did she bear any resemblance to the Piper who had once regularly deferred to her fiancé's opinions on things that affected her own life. The very thought now made her cringe.

Since she'd returned to Cloverdale, the upstate New York town where she'd spent many happy childhood summers with Aunt Judy and Uncle Frank, Piper knew she'd become a self-sufficient and competent businesswoman as well as a person who spent her days doing what she loved. In her case, that happened to be running a shop that offered customers everything they'd need for deliciously pickling or preserving every vegetable and fruit on God's green earth, as well as happily doing a fair share of the same herself.

Scott, however, seemed convinced she'd been simply occupying herself with a little hobby to keep from missing him too much until he decided to return. No matter that she'd explained multiple times by phone, text, and e-mail that she considered their relationship over and had moved on to a new life. For an intelligent person, Scott apparently had difficulty absorbing that information. Would saying it to him face-to-face make the difference? She hoped so. But why, then, did the thought of seeing her ex-fiancé for the first time in months make her so nervous?

Piper walked back to the window, telling herself that this time she was looking out for Mr. Standley, who was due to bring her a fresh batch of dill. Gerald Standley owned a farm outside of Cloverdale, just as Piper's aunt and uncle did. But Standley had branched out beyond the usual crop of vegetables to include dill, and had become Piper's main source of the tasty weed. You couldn't get much fresher than "picked that morning," and Piper felt extremely lucky to have a Gerald Standley nearby.

She loved driving by his farm and seeing the three-foot-tall stalks with their feathery heads waving gracefully in the breeze. Thinking about the tasty pickles she would eventually season with them got her adrenaline pumping, which only convinced her that she had been right to leave the safe but dreary career of numbers and tax forms for the simpler but oh-so-much-more enjoyable life she now had.

One part of the enjoyment—a significant part—was Will Burchett. Piper had begun seeing Will a few weeks ago, and though she was uncomfortably aware that half of Cloverdale was planning what to wear to their wedding, Piper intended to take things slowly. She'd spent much too long mired in her relationship with Scott to want to tie herself to anyone else in a hurry, though Will was a definite temptation. The more she saw of the tall blond Christmas tree farmer the better she liked him, so much so that she worried about how he would take Scott's sudden appearance on the scene.

Which was why she probably should have warned the man. And she'd meant to. Piper looked at the phone. She should pick it up and call Will right then and give him the whole story—that Scott, the ex-fiancé she'd told him about, had decided not to return to his job in the state's attorney's office in Albany but was seriously considering settling in Cloverdale. She stared at the instrument, planning her words, but the sudden honk of a truck's horn pulled her gaze to the window. Gerald Standley had driven up with his delivery of fresh dill. Piper left the phone and hurried to the door, promising herself she'd call Will the minute her visitor left.

"Good morning, Mr. Standley," she called, holding the

door open for the farmer as he made his way toward her shop with a crate packed full of wonderfully aromatic dill.

"Morning, young lady," Standley responded. "You're looking mighty perky today."

Piper smiled. It was Gerald Standley's standard greeting, and she had no doubt he'd deliver it even if she stood propped on crutches, suffering from the flu, and covered with red blotches. Standley, on the other hand, did look pretty lively. As he set the crate down in her back room, Piper asked him why.

Standley straightened to look at Piper with surprise. "Why, haven't you heard about the big soccer match coming up?"

"Um, no, I haven't," Piper admitted. "You mean a match at the high school?"

"Young woman," Standley said with mock indignation, "this just might be the match of the century!" He grinned, and softened his statement. "At least for Cloverdale. And no, it's not Cloverdale High School's team, though a few did play on the team before they graduated. This is a brand-new group, drawn from top Cloverdale players as well as surrounding areas. In other words, we have an all-star team!"

"Impressive. And who will they be playing?"

Standley's face shone with excitement as he reverently whispered the words. "A semiprofessional team from Italy." Which told Piper it was, in his opinion, the best thing that could have ever happened to Cloverdale, perhaps in his lifetime. She tried to look properly impressed.

"That's wonderful," she said. "But how did that come about?"

"The Italian team is touring," Standley explained as he

took off his cap and swiped his forehead with his sleeve. "They're doing exhibition matches, and they don't play just anybody. This was arranged months ago, and our all-star team had to meet top standards. Which, after plenty of good, hard work, we did. It's going to be great, just great!"

Piper remembered that Uncle Frank had once mentioned that Gerald Standley helped coach the Cloverdale soccer teams for years, both boys and girls.

"Gerry's plumb crazy about the game," Uncle Frank had said. "He played it himself in school, and he's volunteered for all the teams his daughter played on growing up. When Miranda moved on to other things, he kept right at it. Cloverdale High is lucky to have him pitching in."

Piper, who'd played soccer at age seven or eight and remembered it mostly as running around the field and pretending she knew what she was doing, nevertheless was delighted for Mr. Standley. "When is the match?"

"Actually, it's a tournament—best of three matches. They'll start this weekend, only two days from now!" Standley's eyes sparkled. "The team—Bianconeri—arrives tomorrow."

Piper, who had started thinking that the tournament might be a useful distraction for keeping Scott out of her hair once he arrived, smiled delightedly. "That's terrific. Go Cloverdale!" she said.

"Cloverdale rocks!" a voice answered from the front of the store. Piper recognized it as that of Amy Carlyle, her young, part-time helper who'd arrived for her shift. Amy walked into Piper's back room, tying back her thick red hair as she did. "Hi, Mr. Standley. Ready for the big match?"

"Ready as we'll ever be, most likely, though it never hurts to get in more practice. I'd better get going. Have to make a few more deliveries before heading over to the field." He slipped his cap back onto his thinning but still dark hair, and straightened his light jacket over a trim frame. All that soccer play along with plenty of hard work in his fields obviously kept the man in great shape, Piper thought. Only a few wrinkles hinted at his forty-something age.

"Break a leg," Amy said. "Wait, no! I mean, knock 'em dead! We'll be cheering you on."

Gerald Standley waved his thanks as he hustled out.

When Piper heard the door close, she turned to Amy. "You knew about this big tournament?"

"Of course! Everyone does. It'll be the event of the year for Cloverdale."

"It's news to me."

Amy grinned. "You had a few other things on your mind lately. Any word from the ex yet?"

"Not a peep. I'm hoping he's changed his mind."

"Not me. I'm dying to see the guy. Is he as cute as Will Burchett?"

Piper knew Amy was teasing but answered loftily, "I like to think a man's looks are the least important quality to consider." As she said it, though, she was aware of how Will's bright blue eyes had bowled her over the first time they met. "Besides, who knows what Scott looks like after tramping through every kind of climate and condition as well as eating strange foods for months."

"Oh, he won't have changed that much. It's not like he was marooned on a desert island." Amy had started unloading Gerald Standley's dill, getting ready to separate and chop bunches for freezing, drying, or immediate use. Her culinary skills were matchless and Piper daily considered herself blessed to have the girl's assistance—for as long as it lasted. She knew the twenty-one-year-old's long-term goals were to own her own restaurant. But for now she gathered experience by also working part-time as an assistant chef at Cloverdale's finest restaurant, A La Carte. Amy's boyfriend, Nate Purdy, also conveniently worked there, but providing the musical entertainment.

Eager to change the subject, Piper asked, "How's Nate doing?"

Amy smiled. "He's doing great. He's written a few new songs and plans to record a demo. But we were talking about Scott. You still haven't hung up that gorgeous wooden plaque he sent you from Thailand. Has Will even seen it? What does he think of Scott's coming here?"

Piper winced. "I'll find out as soon as I tell him." Amy's lips formed a silent O. "I know, I know," Piper said. "I should have. Go ahead and get started on the dill. I'm going to call him right now."

Piper went out to the customer area of her store and pressed Will's speed dial number but almost immediately caught sight of Aunt Judy out front, climbing out of her blue Equinox, and quickly hung up. Piper usually loved seeing her aunt, but she hoped this visit would be brief. As she went to the door, her white-haired, slightly plump aunt caught sight of her and waved. Aunt Judy turned to lift out a large paper bag from her car, and Piper hurried out to take it from her.

"These are the green tomatoes Uncle Frank promised you," Aunt Judy said as she reached back for a second bag.

"Great! I wanted to make some green tomato relish. A few customers had never heard of it. This'll give them a chance to try it out."

"I've made it for years," Aunt Judy said. "And I helped my mother make it when I was a girl, just as you helped me when you were little."

"I remember." Piper led the way to her back room, thinking about those days in Aunt Judy's big farm kitchen. The first summer she'd been sent there by her archaeologist parents as they headed off to a weeks-long, child-unfriendly dig, Piper had sullenly resisted, convinced she wouldn't like it. But Uncle Frank and Aunt Judy had quickly won her over with fun things like tractor rides, but especially with Aunt Judy's cooking. Piper, who'd never done anything before with food other than eat it, found she loved helping her aunt can, pickle, and preserve much of the fresh-picked produce from Uncle Frank's farm. Now Piper was doing it herself, and able to make a living at it!

"Hi, Mrs. Lamb," Amy said, turning from her work with the dill.

"Good morning, Amy," Aunt Judy said. "I'm afraid I've brought you more work."

"Bring it on," Amy said cheerfully and continued her rapid chopping of a large bunch of freshly washed dill leaves. "Are you and Mr. Lamb going to the soccer tournament?"

"Oh yes." Aunt Judy set her bag on a counter and stepped back, dusting off her hands. "Gerry Standley's been talking about it for weeks. We wouldn't dare miss it." She turned to Piper. "What about you? Have you made plans to go with

Will? Or has Scott's visit . . . ?" Aunt Judy's voice trailed off uncertainly.

"I don't have any plans for the tournament other than sending Scott in that direction on his own. Might as well get the message across right away that he's not going to be able to pick things up where he left them six months ago."

"Oooh," Amy said, shaking her head. "That could backfire. Scott could take it as a challenge. That might make him ramp up his efforts to win you back."

"He can take it any way he wants. As long as he takes it out of my presence." Piper knew she sounded tougher than she felt. Deep down, she worried about her own reaction to seeing the man she'd once been in love with. She'd been doing so well with Scott not around. Would she be able to hold strong with him nearby?

The toot of a car's horn sounded from out front, drawing Piper out from the back room, followed closely by Aunt Judy and Amy. The first thing she saw was a red convertible Volvo, the exact model Scott had sold before leaving on his soul-searching journey. The driver's door opened and someone climbed out. Piper held her breath. She heard the door slam shut and a man stepped into view, looking toward the shop.

"Oh!" Aunt Judy cried. "It's Scott!"

Piper found herself nodding dumbly. It was indeed Scott. And he looked absolutely great.

2

Piper felt herself rooted to the spot. Aunt Judy glanced at her, then moved on past to greet Piper's former fiancé.

"Scott," Piper heard her aunt cry at the doorway. "How nice to see you again!"

Piper was aware of Amy's stepping discreetly back into the workroom, though she left the door open. Piper knew she should take a step forward but couldn't seem to will herself to do it. She watched as Scott gave her aunt a hug then looked toward Piper. This was silly, Piper told herself. If she was such a self-assured person she should start acting like one. She therefore held out her hand and moved forward, intending to keep her greeting cool and distancing. It didn't work. Scott rushed forward, crying, "Lamb Chop," the pet name she hadn't heard in six months, and engulfed her in a breath-stopping hug. When he attempted a kiss, Piper strong-armed him back.

"It's nice to see you, Scott," she said, pushing space between them.

Scott looked startled, then glanced back at Aunt Judy and seemed to take her presence as the reason for Piper's reticence. He stepped politely back, which gave Piper a chance to look him over in more detail.

He'd acquired a tan, something Scott rarely managed while working long hours in Albany. It gave him a rugged, outdoorsy look that was augmented by the safari jacket he wore. He appeared more muscular, and his brown hair was longer and flopped boyishly over his forehead. But the biggest change Piper saw was an excitement in his eyes, which she didn't flatter herself was due to her. Yes, he was clearly happy to see her, but she saw something deeper shining through, as though he were much more aware of the world outside himself than he had been before.

"Your travels seem to have agreed with you," she said.

"Piper, you have no idea the things I've seen. I have so much to tell you!"

"That would be really interesting. We'll have to get together sometime when I'm not working." Piper stepped casually behind her counter, putting more space between them. "How long will you be in Cloverdale?"

Scott spread his arms wide. "As long as I like. Maybe the rest of my life. Of *our* lives."

Piper groaned internally. "Scott, you need to understand—"

At that moment the door to Piper's Picklings opened and

a young woman stepped in—Gerald Standley's pretty, blond daughter, Miranda.

"Oh!" she said, glancing around. "I thought my father was here."

"Miranda! Good to see you!" Piper said, delighted with the interruption. "Your dad was here a few minutes ago. He said he had more dill to drop off before heading over to the soccer field."

"Hi, Miranda," Amy called from the back room, apparently able to keep track of the goings-on up front quite well.

"Miranda, dear," Aunt Judy said, "this is Piper's friend, Scott Littleton. Miranda's father," she explained to Scott, "is handling the big soccer tournament this weekend, something we're all excited about."

"Soccer! I went to a couple of fantastic matches when I was in Italy."

"That's where the visiting team is from!" Miranda cried. "Maybe you saw them? Bianconeri?"

Scott wrinkled his brow. "Doesn't ring a bell. They're all good, there, though. I swear soccer's in their genes."

"Oh, don't say that." Miranda laughed. "Dad's team doesn't have much Italian blood in it. He hopes they'll make a good showing." She grinned. "Actually, he'd love it if they'd kick their butts. I've never seen him so excited."

"He's coaching?" Scott asked.

"More assistant-coaching, which he's done for years. Dad's happy to do just about anything to stay close to the game. Everyone connected to Cloverdale soccer knows my dad."

"And loves him," Aunt Judy added.

Miranda smiled and nodded. "Well, I'll try to catch up with him at the field. See you at the games?"

"Absolutely!" Amy, who'd come to the back room doorway, responded along with Aunt Judy. Piper simply waved cheerily as Miranda took off.

"Well!" Aunt Judy said, turning back to Scott. "What are your immediate plans? Do you have a place to stay?"

Please don't invite him to the farm, Piper prayed silently.

"I do," Scott answered, and Piper exhaled. "With the iffy flight connections I had, I wasn't sure when I'd get here, so I booked a room at the Cloverton. Good thing, since I rolled into town around two this morning. I can't even guess what time zone my sleep clock is in. But I'll catch up quick. I always do. Anyway, I thought I'd get to know the town a bit and see if it can use another lawyer."

"Oh, we can definitely use a good lawyer," Amy said, which earned her a strong look from Piper. "I was remembering that awful guy Nate almost hired," she defended. "But then again, he was in criminal law. Maybe you'd do something else?"

Scott grinned. "Criminal law is exactly my field. I was a prosecutor up in Albany. But I doubt a small town like this has much crime—"

Oh, you don't know the half of it, Piper thought.

"—so I'll probably aim for doing a little of everything," Scott finished. "Contracts, wills, whatever comes up."

"Well, that sounds just lovely," Aunt Judy said, then, hearing a cough from Piper, added, "though Cloverdale just might seem a little mundane after all the exotic places you've just seen."

"Not at all!" Scott proclaimed. "I believe my travels have taught me to truly appreciate the simple things in life." He glanced around Piper's shop. "Such as what you've got here, Lamb Chop. Love it! Good, solid, down-to-earth basics for working with food. Preserving while adding spice. Wonderful!"

Piper couldn't help but be pleased at that, and she beamed.

"Lamb Chop?" a male voice questioned. Will Burchett stood in the open front doorway, looking from Scott to Piper and back again.

"Will!" Piper cried in surprise. "Will, I was just about to call you."

It was Scott's turn to look from Piper to Will and back.

There was an awkward pause, which Aunt Judy once again smoothed over. "Will, this is Scott Littleton, who's just arrived from—where did you actually arrive from, Scott? China?"

"China, Japan, and a smattering of islands along the way till I landed on the West Coast. After that it was full steam ahead for Cloverdale and back to Lamb Chop, here."

"Please don't call me that, Scott."

"*Back* to Lamb Chop?" Will asked. He was looking fairly tanned himself, especially in contrast to his blond hair, and possessed his own brand of outdoorsyness. Piper guessed from his jeans and roll-sleeved checkered shirt that Will had come straight from his Christmas tree fields.

"No," Piper said. "Not 'back,' simply here. Scott and I are going to have a talk concerning that, very soon."

"Great!" Scott said. "How about closing up shop and we go somewhere for a nice long lunch."

"Scott, I don't just close up shop at the drop of a hat," Piper said. "This is my livelihood now."

"Okay. I'll scout around town this afternoon and we can have dinner. What time do you close?"

Will cleared his throat. "I'm afraid Piper and I have plans for tonight. Assuming"—he looked at her—"they're still on?"

"Yes, of course they are, Will." She turned to Scott. "I'm sorry, Scott, but you didn't give me much notice." Seeing his crestfallen expression, Piper softened. "Tell you what. If you come back in about an hour, we can go out for a quick lunch while Amy's here. But it'll have to be quick."

Scott brightened and glanced at his watch. "Be back here at twelve." He gestured toward the street. "It'll be like the old days, riding in my Volvo C70. This one's a rental, but if I can get a decent law practice going here, I'll be looking to buy a replacement." He grinned. "There are some things in life you just can't give up. See you later!"

As Will watched Scott trot out the door and hop into the Volvo, he asked, "Law practice? Here?"

Just then two women customers pushed their way into the shop.

"Tonight," Piper promised Will before turning gratefully to answer one of the women's questions. Being able to talk about pickling and preserving was a huge relief, temporary though it might be. Will left—in what kind of mood Piper couldn't guess—and Aunt Judy toodle-ooed, obviously intuiting that Piper needed a little space. Piper waved back but expected space was likely to be a precious commodity in the next few hours.

~~~~~~~

Piper took Scott to the Clover-Daily Deli, which served up great sandwiches in record time but offered tiny tables and stiff, hard-bottomed chairs at which to enjoy them—a major reason most customers chose carryout and the very reason Piper picked it, as she hoped to keep her time with Scott to a minimum. While they unwrapped their choices and popped straws into their drinks, Scott shared his early impressions of Cloverdale, all of which were glowing.

"I love it here, too," Piper said, taking a quick sip of her lemonade. "But don't imagine it's Utopia. There's plenty of wonderful people—with my aunt and uncle at the top of the list. But just like any place, you'll find some bad along with the good." She was thinking about the situation Nate had recently struggled through, when he came very close to being charged with murder.

"Oh, I know," Scott said airily, sinking his teeth into his steak and cheese, smothered with onions. His eyes lit up. "Wow!" he said after chewing and swallowing. "I'd say any town that can offer fast food this amazing must have plenty more 'good' to look forward to."

Perhaps her choice for lunch hadn't been as clever as Piper thought.

"Scott," Piper said, getting right to the point. "You're certainly free to live anywhere you want. But you should understand that settling in Cloverdale doesn't mean that you and I will go back to where we once were. If you remember, I returned my engagement ring—"

"Yes, but—"

Piper raised her hand. "Returning the ring wasn't just a

temporary gesture, a 'putting things on hold' while you traveled about. It truly meant our engagement was over. And it's still over. Finished. We are no longer a couple."

Scott stayed silent for a while, chewing on that idea as well as another bite of his steak and cheese. Knowing him as well as she did, Piper could see the cogs spinning. Where they were leading him, though, she could only guess.

"So you really meant those texts and e-mails?"

"One hundred percent."

Scott puffed his cheeks and exhaled. "Well," he said with a weak smile, "it looks like your own, much shorter journey—from Albany to Cloverdale—brought about some pretty significant changes."

"It has. But I'm happy where I am. I hope you can be, too."

"Oh, I'll be okay," Scott said. "I'm not the same supercharged guy I once was. My travels have changed me, too. Maybe you don't see it yet, but I hope in time you will." He reached for her hand, holding it with both of his. "I still want to settle in Cloverdale. I hope we can be friends?"

"Certainly," Piper said, patting Scott's hand with her free one in a friendly, platonic way before gently sliding her captive hand back.

Their conversation shifted to more neutral topics as customers crowded in, and they eventually parted on amicable terms. As she headed back to her shop, Piper heaved a huge sigh of relief.

She still had to face Will that night, though, and that was going to be harder. Piper had been at fault for not preparing Will for Scott's sudden appearance, so the first thing she did as they sat down for dinner was apologize profusely.

"It wasn't fair to let you be blindsided like that. I'm truly sorry."

"Accepted," Will said with a small smile. "So," he said, opening up his napkin, "you had lunch with Scott?"

"I did. And I was able to make it clear that he and I are no longer a couple." Piper hesitated, trying not to squirm. "But he still plans to settle in Cloverdale."

Will frowned. "Well, I suppose that's his right."

Piper nodded.

"Think you'll run into him much?"

Piper had thought hard about that. Will had become special to her, but she didn't want to make promises that implied a certain level of commitment. She just wasn't ready for that. "Scott and I parted as friends," she said. "I won't be searching him out, but I expect us to remain on good terms."

Will was silent for a long while then nodded. "Okay. If I had my druthers, Scott Littleton would take off again for Timbuktu, or better yet, Mars. But I can deal with him setting up a law office in Cloverdale. I'll even wish him success that will snow him under with enough work that he barely has a minute to drive anyone around in his shiny, retractable-top Volvo C70."

Piper grinned and reached her hand across the table. Will covered it with both of his, where she was more than happy to leave it—at least until she needed it to eat.

The next morning, Piper made an early shopping trip to TopValuFood before opening up Piper's Picklings. She quickly found and paid for milk, bread, a few frozen items, and, of course, chocolate, and was loading the bags into the trunk of her car when she saw a large bus drive by with "Bianconeri" painted on its side.

"That must be the Italian soccer team," Mrs. Peterson said as she climbed from her own car nearby. "I'll bet they're heading for the high school."

Piper nodded, then checked her watch. She had a few minutes to spare. After hearing Gerald Standley and the others talk so excitedly about this visit, she was curious to see the Italian team in person. She hopped into her driver's seat and started up.

As she pulled into the high school's parking lot nearest the soccer fields, Piper saw she wasn't the only one eager to meet the visiting team. The school itself was not in session— she'd overheard mention of professional days for the teachers—but plenty of students had given up their morning sleep-in to welcome (and ogle) the Italian team. Gerald Standley stood at the forefront as part of a small group of official greeters. Piper guessed the group was made up of the coaches and school administrators. She wouldn't have thought it possible, but Standley looked even more excited than he had the day before.

She watched from the edge of the crowd as the occupants of the bus moved about, gathering gear, then one by one stepped out to noisy welcomes. Hands were shaken, shoulders clapped, and greetings in Italian and English traded as they passed through the crowd.

Miranda Standley, along with several other young women, stood ready to hand each player a goody bag from a large basket, and quickly became surrounded by the athletic and highly attractive young men.

The last to exit the bus were two older men. Piper assumed the first, dressed in a matching black-and-white team warm-up, was the coach, and he waved, speaking exuberantly in Italian and English as he made his way out.

The second man paused on the last step and looked about him, an odd smile, almost a smirk on his handsome face. He was dressed in casual but not athletic clothing—a polo shirt, slacks, and a light jacket—although he looked trim enough to play. Judging by the streaks of silver in his thick, dark hair, Piper guessed his age at forty-five to fifty, and she wondered if he were the team manager.

"Conti!" she heard Gerald Standley suddenly call out in surprise, and from his tone it didn't sound like a welcome one.

The man on the step looked about for the source of the call and spotted Standley. His smile widened, but to Piper it looked self-satisfied rather than joyful. "Standley," he said. "I wondered if you'd be here."

Piper saw Gerald Standley's face darken. He stared hard at the man he'd called Conti, then turned and pushed his way off through the crowd. Piper was surprised at the action, even more so when she looked back at the man who'd apparently caused it. Conti remained on his step, standing a full head above everyone below and seeming to relish his position. With obvious pleasure, he watched Standley walk off until the embarrassed remaining members of the welcoming group, along with the affable Italian coach, drew him from the bus and into the crowd.

Chatter and bustle resumed, but Piper stood silently by. What had turned the mood of the day so downward for

Gerald Standley? Who was this Italian man Conti, and how did Standley, a dill farmer who never traveled farther than Manhattan for the annual Christmas pageant at Radio City Music Hall, happen to know him?

She shook her head. Too many questions to ponder as her newly purchased milk grew warm and her shop awaited opening. She predicted that an answer or three or four would be offered during the day as word of the morning's excitement spread its usual small-town way through Cloverdale. As she headed back to her car she knew the only remaining question was how long it would take.

3

~~~~~

It took, by Piper's watch, exactly one hour and thirteen minutes for the first person to pop into Piper's Picklings with "news" of the incident at the soccer field. That person happened to be Emma Leahy, a generally no-nonsense woman in her sixties who'd heard about it from her next-door neighbor. That neighbor's teenage son had apparently been on the scene. As she listened to Emma's version, Piper began to have serious doubts about the teenager's ability to process information. Either that, or there was a future ahead of him in fiction writing.

"The minute the Italian team arrived, the coaches started shouting at each other," Emma claimed. "One of the Italians actually swung at our men, and it would have turned into a terrible brawl except that Jared and his friends stepped in."

Ah! Jared wrote himself in as hero and graciously included his friends.

"There's a tiny bit of exaggeration there, Mrs. Leahy," Piper said and shared her own, eyewitness version. Emma Leahy seemed disappointed with the less dramatic account but took it with good grace. She ended up purchasing a set of decorative glass canning jars for her Christmas jellies and went on her way.

The next "newsperson" to stop in was Erin Healy, one of Amy's good friends. "Did you hear what happened at the high school?" Erin asked, looking distressed, but in her own quiet way, with her already-large brown eyes opened wide. Before Piper could answer, Erin shared an account that was nearly as off-kilter as Mrs. Leahy's, minus action from teenage heroes.

"One of the Italian coaches turned up his nose at our facilities and immediately called the tournament off. Mr. Standley was so upset he started having chest pains, and they had to carry him into the school and call an ambulance. The whole thing's turned into a terrible mess!"

"Last I saw of Mr. Standley," Piper said, "he was walking away from the Italian team's bus under his own power. A little upset, but as far as I could tell, in good health. I'm pretty sure the tournament is still on."

"Oh, I'm so glad! But what was Mr. Standley upset about?"

"I don't know. There was nothing obvious, like insults traded or anything like that."

"Well, then that's very odd." She gave Piper an impish smile. "Another mystery?"

"If it is," Piper said, shaking her head, "I expect it will be solved very soon. Once, that is, all the misinformation gets cleared up." Piper reached for a jar on the counter behind her. "Will you be seeing Ben today? He asked if I had any plum sauce, and I set this aside for him."

"I was going to stop by his office, so I'll be glad to drop that off." Erin's cheeks turned a becoming pink. "Ben's been experimenting with Chinese cooking. I think he wants to make mu shu pork for us using the sauce."

"Sounds good." Piper had watched Ben's near obsession with Amy gradually fade as Erin quietly made clear her own interest in him. It helped that Amy was obviously head over heels for Nate and he for her. Piper herself didn't quite understand the attraction of Ben, who, she felt, took himself and his auxiliary police volunteerism far too seriously. But if Erin thought he was wonderful, that was all that mattered.

In the next few hours, visitors continued to pop in to Piper's Picklings and offer increasingly dramatic versions of the happenings at the school, and Piper had no doubt hers wasn't their only stop. She offered occasional corrections to lessen the spread of wild rumors but had yet to hear a reason for Gerald Standley's odd reaction. Then, around midafternoon, as Piper tidied up a shelf, humming along with a lively Gilbert and Sullivan tune coming from her radio, Gil Williams, proprietor of the new-and-used bookstore next door, stopped in.

"I've been invited to a dinner tonight," he said. "A last-minute fill-in to even up the table, no doubt, and am in need of a hostess gift. Can you suggest something tasty from your stock?"

Piper smiled at the thought of this genial, sixty-something neighbor being a last-minute fill-in. With his voracious reading habits, Gil Williams was such a font of interesting tales, all related with such wit, that she was sure he must be the most sought-after dinner guest in town.

"Any idea of what they might be serving?"

"None whatsoever. The tastes of these particular friends are quite eclectic."

"Hmm. Then maybe something your hosts can enjoy later on would be best." Piper pulled out a jar from the jellies and jams section. "What do you think of a raspberry jam with mint and lavender? Amy and I cooked this up about a month ago. Besides raspberries, it has Granny Smith apples, fresh lavender blossoms, and a touch of lemon juice."

"I think it sounds like I should take two—one for my hosts and another for myself."

Piper grinned and took down a second jar. As she bagged them, Gil said, "I presume you've been getting the same flood of comments on this morning's incident at the school that I have?"

Piper sighed. "Absolutely. And I've had to set plenty of informants straight since I happened to be on the scene myself."

"Well then! Perhaps you can confirm or deny that the meeting of the two teams came to blows?"

"Denied." Piper related what she had observed, that Gerald Standley appeared to recognize one of the Italians, possibly the team manager, and had called out his name in shock and with definite distaste. "The Italian," she said, "seemed unsurprised to see Mr. Standley. In fact, he looked amused when Standley stomped away."

"Hmm. You said Gerald called out the man's name. What was it?"

Piper thought for a moment. "Conti." When Gil nodded, she asked, "Why? Do you know him?"

"I think so. It was many years ago, at least thirty, but I think he must be the same man. Gerald Standley hasn't had problems with very many people."

"No, I wouldn't think so. He's been wonderful to deal with as my dill supplier, and I've heard others say only good things about him. So who is this Italian?"

Gil sank onto a tall stool Piper kept handy for customers. He adjusted the brown, elbow-patched cardigan that often served as his work uniform and said, "Raffaele Conti was an exchange student here in Cloverdale back when he and Gerald were both in high school."

"Oh," Piper said, mulling over what that might mean.

"I remember," Gil said, "because, for one thing, it was quite unusual to have an exchange student in our small town. But Conti himself caused his own stir during the year he was here."

"Who was his host family?"

"The Andersons. They've since moved to California where their daughter now lives. She was away in college at the time, and I suspect Tom and Joy were feeling a bit of empty nest syndrome. They probably thought having a teenager in the house again would help fill the void, but I don't think they were prepared for what they got."

"Sounds intriguing," Piper said. "What exactly did they get?"

"Well, as I said, it was many years ago and the details have faded. But despite coming across as a rather charming

26

fellow, Raffaele tended to generate plenty of negative feelings. I do remember the boy was quite good at soccer and was initially welcomed onto the school team. But he managed to alienate his teammates fairly quickly."

"In what way?"

"The trouble apparently came from his expecting star treatment, along with being a bit of what they called a 'ball hog.' Maybe a *lot* of one. His teammates—and Gerald Standley was one—didn't consider themselves slouches in the game and I'm sure weren't enamored of being treated as simply backup support to this newcomer."

"Didn't their coach put a stop to it?"

Gil ran fingers through his thinning white hair, returning it to its usual semiwild look. "He should have, definitely. But Conti was scoring a lot of goals, from what I understand, and the team was winning more often. That can be more important to some men than preserving team morale."

"That was a long time ago," Piper said. "Would Gerald Standley hold a grudge over something like that for thirty years?"

Gil Williams shrugged. "There likely was more to the story. I've told you what I picked up from various townspeople, but I wasn't exactly a confidant of the teenage set."

He stood up and tucked his bagged purchase under his arm. "Well, let's hope Gerald and Raffaele can put aside any lingering differences for the next few days."

Piper nodded agreement, but as Gil left her shop, the memory of Gerald Standley's anger-filled face stirred significant doubts. But, she mused, pushing those disturbing thoughts away, the tournament was only for a weekend. The teams would play, the town would have its excitement, and all would be back to normal soon.

An image of Scott's face then popped into her head, and she remembered how thoughtfully he had mulled over her pronouncement of their changed relationship. It gave her an uneasy feeling. Piper's own, painstakingly created normal had already been disturbed by her former fiancé's unexpected arrival in Cloverdale, which brought back her concerns about Conti.

Raffaele Conti and Scott had both stirred things up in Cloverdale, rather like a gust of wind blowing through an open window. Papers fly about when that happens, and they can't always be put back in order. Piper pondered that for several moments, but decided all she could control was her own actions. And hope for the best from those around her.

4

~~~~~

Friday night, Will picked up Piper shortly after she'd closed up shop to head over to the first soccer match. If Will had suggested the idea a few days ago, Piper might have declined, soccer never having been high on her list of entertainments. But with all the drama buzzing around the teams' first encounter, she was not about to miss seeing how it would play out—on the sidelines as much as on the field. As they rode to the school stadium, she shared the background information she'd learned from Gil Williams about Gerald Standley and Raffaele Conti.

"So they're rivals from way back," Will said.

"Well, they were on the same team but maybe rivals for the top spot. Though I don't see Mr. Standley as someone craving the spotlight, do you? They definitely didn't get along, for whatever reason, and the bad blood between them was enough to linger all these years."

Will pulled into the stadium parking lot, and Piper caught sight of a familiar mane of red hair. Amy was heading for the gate on the arm of her musician boyfriend, Nate. Piper pointed them out, and Will tapped a friendly toot on his horn.

The couple looked back and waved, Amy calling, "A bunch of us are sitting together. Come join us."

"We'll be right there," Piper answered. She reached back into Will's green van for the tote she'd packed full of snack food, and Will grabbed the cushions he'd brought along to soften the steel bleacher seats. They then worked their way through the gathering crowd to catch up with their friends.

Erin and Ben were already seated and had saved, along with Ben's sister, Megan, a generous space around them. Megan, Erin, and Amy had been friends since kindergarten and still managed to do most things together. Amy and Nate settled next to Megan, and waved Piper and Will to the seats directly in front.

Piper had at first felt very much the older adult with the trio, having, at twenty-nine, at least eight years on them as well as being one of Amy's part-time employers. That had rapidly changed, especially when they'd worked together as a team during the recent difficulties heaped on Nate. Now she simply enjoyed being with them all—even Ben, in whom she could see signs of softening from his by-the-book ways, probably due to Erin's growing influence.

The crowd was rapidly filling up the medium-size stadium, the match having drawn interest far beyond Cloverdale's boundaries. Will alerted Piper when he spotted Aunt

Judy and Uncle Frank arriving, and she called and pointed to two seats she'd saved in front of her using her bag and Will's cushions. The two worked their way over and gratefully settled in, replacing Will's and Piper's items with their own versions of the same.

"Isn't this exciting?" Aunt Judy said, rearranging her multiple bags and jackets. "I heard that a television crew from Albany is here to cover the game for tonight's news."

"Darn. We should have come in costumes," Megan said from behind Piper. "We would have gotten some major screen time when the camera panned the crowd."

"What kind of costumes?" Erin asked.

"Tigers, of course. For the Cloverdale Tigers."

"But our team isn't all from Cloverdale," Amy pointed out.

"But the game is *here* in Cloverdale, isn't it?" Megan argued, never one to relinquish a point easily. That was one of the few things she had in common with her older brother, though Piper had often seen her roll her eyes and toss her long blond hair impatiently at some of his more didactic statements.

"Do you *have* a tiger costume?" Will asked with a grin.

"No, but if I'd thought of it early enough I could have come up with one."

"Costume wearing is not advisable for outdoor, nighttime events," Ben put in, using his auxiliary officer voice, which Piper knew grated on Megan's nerves. "They can all too often—"

"Sandwiches, anyone?" Aunt Judy called out, effectively ending Ben's lecture in the making as several voices responded at once, accepting or declining.

More food was pulled out of various totes and shared around, and Piper's spears of dill pickles were quickly snapped up. Piper was so busy distributing, eating, and talking that she didn't notice the teams had arrived until the crowd around her reacted. She looked up to see the Cloverdale All-Stars team trotting out onto the field in their orange and black uniforms. The crowd cheered loudly, and Piper heard voices around her call, "Oh, there's Dan!" or "Go, Billy!" along with many other players' names. When the Italian team—Bianconeri—trotted out in their black-and-white uniforms they were greeted by equally enthusiastic applause.

The two teams lined up to face the crowd, and a master of ceremonies—Cloverdale's mayor, Tom Whitaker—gave a brief speech about what an honor it was for the town to host the event, welcomed the Bianconeri team, then introduced the coaches. Coach Vince Berner of the Cloverdale team waved to much applause. When Gerald Standley was introduced as assistant coach, he was greeted enthusiastically as well, though he barely acknowledged it with a modest wave before stepping back.

When the Italian coach was introduced, he took the microphone to say a few words in heavily accented but lively English about how happy he and his players were to be there. Piper glanced around for Raffaele Conti, who she'd since learned was the team manager, and finally spotted him at the sidelines. He was speaking into a microphone held by a reporter whom Piper recognized from WABY as they both faced a camera. As she watched that scene, she was distracted by a commotion to her right.

"Excuse me. Pardon me. Oops, sorry about that." Scott

was inching his way along the row of spectators in front of her.

"Any room to squeeze in here?" he asked cheerily, coming to a stop beside Aunt Judy.

"Oh, of course!" Aunt Judy began gathering up jackets and sliding closer to Uncle Frank, causing Uncle Frank to move closer to the people next to him, who grudgingly gave up a little room.

"What's he doing here?" Will whispered to Piper, who could only offer an innocent shrug.

"Hi, there!" Scott said, turning around, the backpack hanging from one shoulder causing the man next to him to duck as it swung toward his head. "Whoops! Excuse me," Scott said and slid the pack safely down. "I had a hard time finding you all. Good thing you wore that bright red sweater," he said to Piper. "I always liked that color on you."

"We're glad you made it, Scott," Aunt Judy said. "You'll get to know our town a little better, since just about everyone's here. We're all excited about this tournament."

"Down in front!" a deep voice called from several rows back as the game was apparently getting started. Scott waved good-naturedly and sat down, repositioning his backpack and digging into it as he did.

"I picked up a few things on my way over," he said over his shoulder and pulled out a plastic container. "Sushi roll, anyone?" He opened the container and held it up invitingly, saying to Piper, "The ones in the middle are spicy tuna. You still like them, right?"

"I'll have some," Megan said. Scott stretched it her way as she reached over Piper's shoulder.

"You like sushi?" Will asked Piper.

Megan picked out a single roll, then offered the container to Erin and Ben, who both shook their heads. Amy and Nate each took one before Megan handed the plastic box to Piper, who looked at the tempting food, unsure what to do. She actually loved sushi and hadn't had any for weeks. She'd never suggested to Will that they visit the one restaurant in Cloverdale that offered it, knowing his taste in food was fairly cautious—he'd only reluctantly sampled her pickled zucchini on their earliest meeting (and been pleasantly surprised). So the subject had never come up between them.

Would taking one of Scott's sushi rolls be read as a signal of some kind by one or both of the men? Oh, what the heck, she decided. She was going to have one, and they could fight it out if they wanted. Piper chose a delicious-looking tuna roll and thanked Scott, passing the container back to him.

"I'd love to try one," Aunt Judy said, which surprised Piper. Uncle Frank passed, which didn't surprise her, and Scott grabbed one for himself, glancing back at Piper with a grin that could have been taken to mean so many different things that Piper didn't want to even think about it.

The crowd cheered as the Cloverdale goalie blocked a kick, and Piper turned her attention back to the game. However, it soon wandered back to Raffaele Conti. The television crew had moved on, and he was strolling along the sideline, watching the players but also talking animatedly to those around him. Piper leaned toward Aunt Judy and pointed him out, giving his name.

"Gil told me he lived here years ago as an exchange student," she said. "Do you remember him?"

Aunt Judy stared for several moments. "Why, yes. Yes, I do!" She nudged her husband. "You remember Raffaele, don't you? Back when Gerald was in high school? That's him!"

Uncle Frank looked over at Conti, recognition gradually dawning. He nodded. "Hasn't changed much."

"No," Aunt Judy agreed. "Except for the touch of gray in his hair, which only adds distinction. He was always a good-looking boy."

"I've seen him around at my hotel," Scott said. "The whole team's staying at the Cloverton."

"Are they?" Aunt Judy said, looking at Scott with interest. "I hope they haven't been rowdy."

"No, not at all. In fact, I shared a table with a couple of the players at breakfast. Practiced a bit of my Italian, though I have to admit my Spanish is a lot better."

Piper heard Will cough, but when she glanced at him he seemed absorbed by the game.

"Very friendly guys," Scott went on. "And one of them, Frederico, I think his name was, seemed quite taken by that girl who came into your shop the other day, Piper."

"Miranda?"

"Right. Apparently there was some kind of welcoming party. Frederico had a lot of questions about her, which I couldn't answer, of course, except to say that she's the daughter of one of the coaches. That's right, isn't it?"

Piper nodded. Miranda was indeed the daughter of the Cloverdale assistant coach, Gerald Standley. Did Miranda return Frederico's interest? Piper wondered, and if so, how would her father feel about that? Probably a nonissue, she decided, since the team would be moving on in a few days.

She glanced back at the sideline. A bigger issue, she thought, might be the fact that Raffaele Conti was now speaking with Gerald Standley's wife, Denise, and from the look of it, in a rather flirtatious way. If Aunt Judy thought Conti hadn't changed much over the years, Piper guessed she would say the same about Denise Standley, who had a decidedly youthful appearance with her slim figure and pretty face.

Denise Standley didn't appear to be flirting back and instead leaned away from Conti. She took a step back as though ready to leave, but Conti moved forward, taking her elbow as he continued talking.

Where was Gerald? Was he seeing this? Piper glanced around, but before she could find him, Scott pushed his box of sushi her way once more.

"Another spicy tuna?"

The Cloverdale team scored a goal and the spectators rose en masse with a roar. By the time things settled down, Raffaele Conti had joined his team's coach beside their sidelined members, and Denise Standley stood with her husband, Gerald, near their team bench.

Miranda Standley appeared in a line of girls in gold and black cheerleading outfits, all shaking pom-poms. They led the crowd in a rousing cheer full of rhythmic claps and stamps, and Piper smiled and relaxed.

All, she felt sure, was fine. *At least*, she added, *for the moment*.

5

The Cloverdale All-Stars lost, the game ending with a heartbreaking, last-minute score of 4 to 3. But during the postgame analysis exchanged during the walk to the parking lot and beyond, the team's supporters agreed that Cloverdale had made an excellent showing, had identified the weaknesses of the Bianconeri team, and would come back with a strong win the following night.

In that optimistic mood, Piper and her friends belted out several rounds of the fight song over foaming mugs of beer at O'Hara's, enough so that when she opened up her shop on Saturday morning, Piper found that the tune had taken up residence in her brain. In an effort to dislodge it, she clicked on her radio, hoping for something a little less rousing to sip her coffee to.

Instead of music, however, a lively male voice flowed out

of the speaker. Piper recognized it as belonging to Chet Morgan, host of a morning talk show that originated in Rochester but which often covered local events in nearby towns, including Cloverdale. She was about to switch the station when her phone rang, so she went to answer the call.

"Good morning, dear!" Aunt Judy, a lifelong morning person, cheerily greeted her. "I just wanted to let you know I picked up your cold pack last night. You left it under your seat." Aunt Judy and Uncle Frank had declined the invitations to join everyone at O'Hara's after the game, pleading fatigue, and had lingered at their seats to chat with a friend as the others left.

"Ah! I forgot all about that cold pack! Thanks, Aunt Judy. I remember taking it out of my tote to get at the food and never thought about it again."

"I can drop it off later today if you'll need it soon," Aunt Judy offered.

"No need. I have another. If you're coming to tonight's game, use it for your own bag of nibbles."

"I will. Will you be there, too?"

"Definitely! I can't miss seeing if Cloverdale will even the score with that band of marauders."

Aunt Judy laughed. "You make the Bianconeri team sound like a bunch of pirates."

"They were called worse last night at O'Hara's. All in good spirit, of course."

"Of course. Well, I'll let you go. See you tonight!"

Piper hung up, smiling as she thought of the good time of the night before. Much to her surprise she had enjoyed a sport she'd previously lacked enthusiasm for, even when playing it herself. It was amazing what a difference good players could make, such as the semiprofessional Bianconeri facing the college-level Cloverdale All-Stars.

Of course, some of her interest had come from the people on the sidelines. After the drama she'd witnessed between the team manager, Raffaele Conti, and Gerald Standley during the Italian team's arrival, and then learning of the history between the two men, she couldn't help but keep a curious eye on the two, who never came within twenty feet of each other.

Then later, as she and Will were driving out of the parking lot, Piper caught sight of Gerald's daughter, Miranda, chatting with one of the Bianconeri team members. She'd wondered if that was the "Frederico" that Scott had mentioned, the one who'd expressed a strong interest in the pretty young woman after meeting her at the welcoming party. All Piper could say for sure was that the Italian player was very attractive with his dark curls and athletic build, and that Miranda didn't appear to be in much of a hurry to move on.

Chet Morgan's voice coming from her radio snapped Piper back to the present, and she stepped over to change to her favorite semiclassical station. As she reached for the dial, though, she heard Morgan welcome his guest for that morning—Raffaele Conti. Piper raised the volume instead.

After a brief description of the ongoing tournament, Morgan began his interview. "Mr. Conti—"

"Raffaele, please," Conti interrupted. "And let me say, too, how delighted I am to be here, Chet." Conti's accent was slight but enough to add a definite spice to his speech.

"Raffaele, then," Morgan responded cheerfully. "Congratulations, first of all, on your team's win last night."

"Thank you! It was a close fight, but I am happy we managed to persevere." Instead of stopping there as Piper expected, he then added, "But I'm not surprised."

"You're not?"

"We are Bianconeri. Italians! Our young players have football, or as you call it here, soccer, in their blood."

"So you feel the Cloverdale team had no chance against your team?"

"Well . . ." Conti laughed deprecatingly. "Cloverdale has very good players, very good." His tone seemed to suggest otherwise to Piper, which Morgan apparently picked up on, too, as he wisely decided to move on.

He asked Conti about the makeup of his team, and Conti discussed several of his players in glowing terms. When he mentioned Frederico Esposito, Piper thought he might be the player she'd seen Miranda talking to. Conti called Frederico his top player. They then discussed the Bianconeri team's upcoming schedule, after which Morgan touched on Conti's background.

"I understand this isn't your first time in our area, that you actually spent some time here as a youth?"

"Yes, yes, that's right." Conti said.

"And that you played soccer while you were here?"

"I did. Of course, it wasn't anything like playing back in my hometown in Italy, but it was very interesting. I like to think I brought something to that high school team."

"I'm sure you did. I did a bit of checking in our archives, and it looked like you were the star player for Cloverdale High School back then."

"Well . . ." A noncommittal chuckle.

"How does it feel to be back now? Have you run into old friends?"

"Yes, yes, of course. Many. It's been good, very good."

Piper had seen Conti talking with only Denise Standley during the game, and she appeared uncomfortable and anxious to move on.

"And the town, has it changed much?"

At that, Conti laughed broadly. "In some ways, of course, yes. But after all these years, it still needs to work on its pizza! Our first day in Cloverdale, we go to Carlo's for the pizza pie. Sounds Italian, right? Well, Carlo, it turns out, has never been anywhere near my country, and what he brings us was, well, it was disappointing, yes, but the worst thing was . . ." Conti cleared his throat. "Let's just say that maybe the health inspector should drop in to take a look around?" Conti chuckled.

"Last night, to celebrate our win, we go outside of town to a place called La Trattoria, where we hope to find *real* pizza along with clean tables—which we did! And who owns it? A German named Burkhart! But I think his mother must have been Italian." Conti laughed heartily, but Piper didn't hear Morgan joining in. Instead he hurriedly thanked Conti for his time and sent the show to commercial.

Piper's eyebrows had arched with Conti's first comments and remained that way through most of the broadcast. Conti surely hadn't won any friends with that interview. She could see why he might want to put down Cloverdale's team— possibly to stir more ticket sales by riling up the local team's supporters. But then to bash one of its restaurants? Piper didn't know if Carlo's pizza was authentic or not, but the place had seemed perfectly clean when Will took her there once. She hoped Carlo, and most of Cloverdale for that matter, hadn't been listening.

The phone rang, and Piper turned the radio down.

"Miss Lamb? You had a question about one of our spices?" It was one of Piper's suppliers; she'd left an inquiry with them the day before. She spent the next few minutes discussing the sources of their ginger along with the price. By the time she'd finished, the Chet Morgan show had ended, and Piper switched to the soothing music she'd sought earlier.

Piper was in her back room, getting a batch of white pearl onions ready to pickle along with Gerald Standley's fresh dill, when she heard her front door open. Wiping her hands on a towel, she went out to find Emma Leahy, who looked highly indignant.

"Did you hear Chet Morgan's show?" Emma asked. Her short salt-and-pepper hair looked to have been raked through with impatience.

"I did, at least most of it. Did it get any worse after they went to commercial?"

"That horrible Italian! Suggesting Carlo's had health code violations? Outrageous! Maybe one of Conti's people called him during the commercial. Who knows? But he spent the rest of the interview trying to fix what he'd said about our pizzeria. To my mind he only made things worse. The man doesn't seem capable of saying anything good without it being some kind of put-down."

"That's how he sounded when he talked about the Cloverdale team," Piper agreed.

Emma Leahy was about Aunt Judy's age, so Piper asked if she remembered Conti from his time at the high school.

"I didn't at first. But then Joanie, my oldest, reminded me who he was when we spoke on the phone. Joanie lives in Pittsburgh now," she explained. "She was at the school the year he was there, but she was pretty heavily involved in the drama club and didn't mingle with the sports crowd all that much. Luckily for her, I'd say now, looking back. She's a sensible girl, but who knows if at that age she might have been overly impressed by the boy." She paused. "Like Denise Standley was."

"Denise?"

Emma nodded. "She was young then, of course, and I'm sure Raffaele Conti must have seemed very exciting to her, you know, coming from another country and all, not to mention his good looks and all the attention he was getting as a soccer star. But she and Gerald had been an item for some time. Joanie said Gerald was crushed when that Italian stole her away. Obviously, they got back together, eventually, but it must have been hard for a while."

"I'm sure it was." Gerald Standley's attitude toward Raffaele Conti suddenly made a lot more sense to Piper. A rivalry over a major spot on the team could be intense but short-lived. But stealing away the love of one's life? That would be much more difficult to forget, Piper guessed, much less forgive.

Emma stepped over to Piper's spice section, saying, "As long as I'm here . . ." and began browsing, eventually picking out a jar of cumin and one of turmeric. "I always seem to find something I need when I'm here," she said. "Your spices are so much better than the supermarket's."

"I'm glad you think so," Piper said as she rang them up. "I go to some trouble to find the best for the price."

After Emma took off, Piper returned to her dilled-onion project. She had peeled about half of the onions when Amy showed up for her shift.

"Hey, I thought I was going to do that," Amy protested cheerfully. She took off her light sweater and tossed it in a corner, replacing it with a clean apron.

"These lovely white things were calling to me," Piper said. "Along with the aromatic dill heads over there."

Amy laughed. "That's what you always say. If it's not pearl onions, it's cucumbers, or apples, or cranberries, or whatever you happen to have! How you manage to sleep at night I'll never know, what with all the 'calling' that must be going on in here." She got busy measuring the vinegar, sugar, salt, and water that Piper would soon simmer her onions in.

"That was a fun time last night, wasn't it?" Amy said as she worked.

"It was."

"And interesting, watching Will watching Scott as he watched you," Amy said with a grin.

Piper rolled her eyes. "I wish the suggestion to head over to O'Hara's hadn't been spread quite so broadly."

"He would have found us anyway," Amy said. She stirred her vinegar solution and set the large pot on the burner to heat. "And, you know, O'Hara's is a public place, just like the stadium. It was funny how he wormed his way to sit right in front of you at the game."

"Hilarious," Piper deadpanned. Figuring it was time to

change the subject, she told Amy about Raffaele Conti's radio interview.

"Wow, that's a shame that he dissed Carlo's."

"I know. I hope the poor guy didn't hear it."

"He didn't need to be listening. He'll learn about it, eventually. He isn't Italian, by the way. Mr. Conti was right about that. His name is actually Carl. Carl Ehlers. And no Italian mother either, as far as I know. But I never saw anything that hinted at a health code violation, and believe me I'm aware of such things. Mr. Ehlers bought the pizzeria a couple of years ago, and he makes a good pizza. But the impression I got from friends who've worked there is that he might be struggling financially."

"Well, I've heard there's no such thing as bad publicity, but I'm not sure it applies to restaurants," Piper said as she scooped her onion peelings into the waste bin. She got an idea. "Why don't we all go there after tonight's game?"

Amy shook her head regretfully. "I'm working at A La Carte tonight, remember? Nate, too. But I can suggest it to Erin and Megan."

"Do that. I think Will would go for it." Was there a way to keep Scott out of the picture? Piper wondered. Carl Ehlers might appreciate one more patron at his pizzeria, but Piper wouldn't mind a bit if Scott instead decided to follow Raffaele Conti's recommendation and head out of town for "authentic" pizza.

From Scott's actions of the evening before, however, Piper suspected the chances of that were slim.

6

~~~~~~

Piper's circle of companions at the game was smaller than the night before. Uncle Frank and Aunt Judy sat beside Will and her, and Erin and Megan had taken seats directly behind. But Amy and Nate were on restaurant duty, and so far there had been no sign of Scott, though Piper wasn't holding her breath that she'd escape so easily. And Ben, instead of sitting with Erin, had donned his auxiliary officer uniform and was busy helping out Amy's father, Sheriff Carlyle.

"The sheriff asked him to pitch in on the traffic control," Erin explained. "But Ben said he'll also be walking about during the game, you know, just looking out for any problems."

Piper knew how seriously Ben, a desk-bound insurance agent by day, took his volunteer activity, enough to give up enjoying the game next to Erin. Becoming an auxiliary officer gave Ben no official powers, but acting as an extra pair of legs and eyes for the sheriff helped stretch that department's limited manpower. Sheriff Carlyle obviously thought highly of the young man's drive and financial stability and had, Piper thought, once considered him excellent son-in-law material. Amy, however, quickly made clear her own thoughts on the matter as she happily settled into a relationship with her struggling musician.

"We're saving Ben a place," Erin said, patting the space between Megan and herself, "in case he can take a break."

"Sandwich, anyone?" Aunt Judy asked the group.

Piper declined, having had time for dinner before being picked up by Will. Erin and Megan shook their heads.

"I'll take one," Will said, and chose a roast beef sandwich from Aunt Judy's bountiful cache. Aware of Will's strong leanings toward familiar foods, Piper wasn't surprised, but she was also working to expand Will's tastes a bit. She'd brought along a jar of the apple and red onion marmalade that she'd cooked up recently to spread on slices of crusty bread along with a bit of cheese. Will had already gamely, though tentatively, tried it and admitted he liked it. So there was hope for the man, though Piper doubted he'd ever give anything like sushi a try—especially after the production Scott made of it the night before.

The crowd settled down, and Piper was reaching into her tote for an apple cider drink when the teams trotted onto the field to enthusiastic cheers. Lacking the welcoming ceremony of the night before, there was a feel of "getting down to business," with the Cloverdale All-Stars and their fans clearly aching to redeem themselves after the previous night's loss.

Gerald Standley took his place on the sideline beside the team's head coach, both of the men wearing grim, determined looks, but Piper didn't see Denise Standley. She might be simply sitting in the stands with friends, Piper knew, but it still was surprising not to see her beside her husband as she'd been during the first game. Knowing now what she did about the history between Denise and Raffaele Conti, Piper hoped there wasn't a personal reason for the glower on Gerald Standley's face.

"Oh, there's Ben," Erin cried, and Piper followed her gaze to see Ben strolling at the base of the stands, thumbs looped over his auxiliary officer belt as he scanned the crowd with an intense "Dirty Harry" squint. Then he spotted Erin, and a little-boy grin lit up his face. Ben waved, then glanced around with an air of embarrassment before resuming his authoritative attitude.

Piper suddenly caught sight of Scott wandering along the same walkway and scanning the crowd. Piper had dressed in grays and browns that evening, hoping to be much less conspicuous than she'd been the night before. She knew she'd agreed to remain friends with the man, but at the time she'd assumed that meant sharing an occasional pleasant greeting as they passed on the street, not spending one evening after another in his company. She held her breath as Scott passed in front of their section and let it out as he continued on by, her camouflage apparently working. Then she saw him walk over to Ben.

No, no, no, she silently mouthed. But Ben became the

helpful (though unofficial) policeman as he raised an arm to point in her direction. Piper's hands shot up to her face as though to shade her eyes. She saw through her fingers, though, that she'd been too late, as Scott retraced his steps and trotted up the aisle toward her.

"Hey, there!" he cried. "We meet again!"

"Hello, Scott!" Aunt Judy responded cheerily. "I wondered if you weren't coming! The game's already started."

Piper was going to have a serious talk with Aunt Judy about her hospitable attitude toward Piper's ex-fiancé.

"I had to hustle," Scott answered her aunt, "since the time with my Realtor ran a bit late."

Piper, who'd noticed Scott once again had his backpack with him, managed a weak smile in greeting. Will grunted, having just ripped a huge chunk from his sandwich with his teeth.

"Mind if I squeeze in?" Scott asked Erin, already swinging down his backpack and easing into the row behind Piper. Erin, ever polite, slid toward Megan to make room, though she looked somewhat distressed to lose the space she'd hoped Ben would fill.

"Realtor?" Aunt Judy said over her shoulder. "How exciting. Living quarters or office space?"

"Office. And," he added, "I looked at a nice little place right down the block from your shop, Piper."

Will choked on his food, and Aunt Judy helpfully pounded on his back.

"You did?" Piper asked, once Will had settled down.

"Right next to an orthopedist's office. Good location, huh? Get patched up by the doc for your accidental fall, then come next door and talk to me about suing. One-stop shopping." Scott laughed heartily.

"Oh, I wouldn't count on much business of that kind," Aunt Judy said, though Piper saw Uncle Frank's lip curl upward just a bit at the comment.

"Just joking," Scott assured her. "I don't intend to be an ambulance chaser. Though in a town this size, I know I'll need to be open to handling a broad range of cases. No specializing."

The crowd roared, and everyone's attention snapped forward. Cloverdale had blocked a Bianconeri attempt at a goal.

"That number twelve on the Italian team is pretty good," Megan said. She then grinned. "But our goalie is better."

"Number twelve," Scott said. "That's Frederico, the guy I was talking to at the hotel."

Piper searched the field for number twelve to see if she would recognize him as the player she'd seen chatting with Miranda Standley.

Megan saved her the trouble, saying, "Frederico! That's who was with Miranda this afternoon. I ran into them near the Italian ice stand in the park. She said she was showing him the town." Megan clapped a hand to her mouth. "Oops, I forgot. She asked me not to say anything. She didn't want that to get back to her dad."

"Why on earth not?" Aunt Judy asked. "What could be more innocent or thoughtful than spending a little time in the afternoon with a visitor, especially when the poor young man is so far from home?"

"I don't know," Megan admitted. "But she seemed to think her dad wouldn't like it. Maybe because he's on the rival team?"

"That seems rather extreme," Scott said, but Piper

thought she could imagine Gerald Standley's feelings, which might stem from his experience with Raffaele Conti. Unfair, of course, to Frederico. She wondered how much Miranda knew of her father's old grievance.

Thinking about Raffaele Conti, Piper scanned the field, looking for him. With no television crew to pull him away that night, she quickly spotted him pacing behind the Bianconeri players' bench. As she watched, he went up to the team's coach and appeared to argue with him. Piper figured a team manager had authority over the coach but wondered if that included overriding strategy during a game, since that's what Conti seemed to be attempting as he gestured toward the field. The coach was shaking his head and his body language telegraphed anger. Eventually he walked away from Conti, still shaking his head.

Will noticed Piper watching the two and leaned closer. "That Conti fellow," he said, "has been stirring up more than one pot since he got here."

"You mean from his comments on the radio this morning?"

"That, yes, but the interview also clued in a few of his old classmates who hadn't been aware that Raffaele Conti was in town. *Female* classmates. They apparently were fairly swooning over him in the hotel lobby this afternoon. You'd think Elvis had returned, from what I was told."

When Piper grinned at the image, Will added, "That might not have been a big deal if Conti handled it better, but he ate it up and flirted right back pretty outrageously. This didn't go down well with one or two of the husbands, as you can guess."

Piper was about to ask which husbands in particular when

an open box of candy with Scott's hand on it was suddenly wriggled between her and Will. "Piper," he said, "look what I got! I stumbled upon an amazing candy shop today when Stan Yeager and I were out office shopping and remembered how much you liked peanut butter meltaways. So I ran in and picked up a box. Help yourself."

Piper saw that the box came from Charlotte's Chocolates and Confections, a shop Piper hadn't yet visited because of its prickly owner, who'd given her trouble since day one. Which was a shame, since by all accounts Charlotte Hosch made totally wonderful fudge and candies. Looking into the box of meltaways, Piper groaned internally. The chocolate-covered, velvety-smooth candies were indeed her favorite sweet indulgence. Though she noticed Will staring ahead stiffly, there was no way Piper could turn down Scott's offer, insidious though she recognized it to be.

She reached into the box with a restrained "thank you," then tried not to moan as the candy touched her taste buds.

Scott grinned, then held the candy out to the others— Erin, Megan, and Aunt Judy each happily taking one. He popped a piece into his own mouth. "Hey, not bad. Maybe even better than that place we used to go to in Albany. Piper, remember when—"

A sudden roar from the crowd thankfully drowned Scott out, and Piper looked onto the field to see the Cloverdale team celebrating a goal.

"Woo-hoo!" Megan crowed, pumping a fist, and Piper kicked herself for missing the big moment. She became determined to pay more attention to the game and less to the temptations around her.

The teams regrouped on the field, and Piper noticed Conti once more berating his coach. He then walked over to one of his players and had a long discussion. A glance toward the Bianconeri coach showed him to be pointedly ignoring Conti while calling out encouragements to his team.

The game progressed, and Bianconeri scored a goal, eliciting groans from the Cloverdale crowd. As consolation, more food was shared within Piper's group. Piper, summoning up her willpower, turned down a second meltaway from Scott but accepted a homemade brownie from Aunt Judy to make up for it.

For the rest of the first half and much of the second, the ball traveled up and down the field with little result. Goals were attempted but blocked, and the clock ticked closer to the end of the match.

"What happens if it's tied?" Erin asked. "Will they go to overtime?"

Several voices around her answered at once, explaining the ten-minute, sudden-death overtime procedure.

"Too bad it can't just end in a draw," Aunt Judy said. "With no one coming out the loser."

Piper doubted Raffaele Conti would be satisfied without a clear win. A glance his way, though, showed him looking surprisingly calm as he stood near his team.

"Ooh-ooh, we have the ball," Megan cried. "Go, go, go!"

The Cloverdale players passed and maneuvered expertly down the field, moving steadily toward their goal. Then they were surrounded by Bianconeri players, who struggled to take the ball back. Piper lost sight of who had what for several moments in the crush of players. Suddenly a whistle blew and all play stopped. The referee ran over and players spread apart, all except one black-and-white-uniformed player who writhed on the field, clutching his leg.

"Who is it? Is it number twelve? Frederico?" Megan asked.

"No," Scott said. "I see Frederico. He's okay."

The group could hear the cries of pain all the way from the field, and Aunt Judy pressed her hand to her lips in worry. They watched in silence as trainers, coaches, and assistants came to examine the injured player, then a stretcher was brought to carry the young man to the side.

"Oh, that poor boy," Aunt Judy cried. "What will happen now?"

"Bianconeri gets a penalty kick. He's claimed a foul," Uncle Frank answered.

"No, I meant with the boy! Did he break something? He sounds in terrible pain."

"Let's wait and see. There's people looking after him," Uncle Frank said. "Right now we're in danger of losing the game."

"Frank!" Aunt Judy said disapprovingly, but the attention of all had refocused on the penalty kicker.

"No, no, no," Megan pleaded softly, and Piper held her breath as the black-and-white-uniformed player ran toward the ball. He kicked hard, the Cloverdale goalie dove toward it, and . . . missed!

"They scored!" Scott said.

"We lost," Will muttered, and Piper heard the groans and felt the deflation of an entire stadium of spectators.

Raffaele Conti, however, was jubilant, as was his entire team. A glance toward the injured Bianconeri player showed even him to be celebrating, having miraculously risen from his stretcher to bounce on one foot. Was the leg he held up, his left one, the one he'd injured? Piper asked herself. She seemed to remember it was his right. Or was she mistaken?

That, however, was the same question a lot of others around Piper were asking.

"That guy took a dive!" she heard someone say in disgust.

"The ref must be blind," another cried. "Our guys never touched him!"

"It's actually fairly common in Italian football to fake fouls," Scott said, leaning toward Piper.

"They're not in Italy now," Will said over his shoulder. "It's a crummy way to win."

"It happens everywhere," Scott insisted. "All kinds of fouls. The saying is 'if the ref didn't see it, it didn't happen.' Or in this case, I suppose it'd be 'if I scream loud enough, the ref has to believe it.' "

Piper didn't comment, but she was surprised to see Bianconeri resort to such tactics, assuming it was true. They were a good team, and the matches were exhibition. Apparently Raffaele Conti hated to lose, no matter what. The Cloverdale coach, she saw, was walking over to shake hands. Gerald Standley, however, could be seen rapidly striding the other way.

The group headed to Carlo's for pizza, as planned. Scott managed to tag along once again, counting, Piper was sure, on everyone's good manners, especially in front of Aunt Judy. It worked this time, but Piper resolved it would be the last time. She would definitely have a private talk with her relatives and friends on the subject and, if needed, a second serious talk with Scott.

The mood, when the group arrived, was much less lively than it had been the night before, though the owner, Carlo, or rather Carl, was definitely pleased to see them.

"Welcome!" The middle-aged, fair-haired but balding, clearly non-Italian "Carlo" greeted them, his smile just a bit strained and overeager. Piper could understand why. The place, unlike the last time she'd been there, was more than half empty. She didn't know if that was due to Conti's remarks on the radio or just a general disinclination of disgruntled spectators to celebrate after the questionable ending to the game. Either way, Carlo's business was obviously affected, and as a fellow Cloverdale businessperson, she empathized.

Once they were seated, she and her group did their best to be as upbeat as possible over their pizza and beers, but it was an effort as the conversation kept returning to the probably faked foul that clinched the game for Bianconeri.

Eventually Uncle Frank gave up, though he'd given it a decent amount of time. "Got a few things to do tomorrow," he claimed, rising and pulling bills from his wallet to leave behind. Aunt Judy gave quick hugs and pats as she eased her way out.

Erin, disappointed that Ben hadn't been able to join them, was next, and Megan soon followed. That left Scott sitting with Piper and Will, a situation that Will tolerated for about thirty seconds before downing the last of his beer. "Ready?" he asked Piper, who nodded.

"Well," Scott said with a downturned mouth as they rose, "I guess I'll just go back to my lonely hotel room."

"Maybe there'll be a few Bianconeri players in the hotel bar to talk to," Will said, pulling out his car keys.

Piper, who would have felt sympathy for anyone else, had none for her ex-fiancé. He was perfectly able to find his own entertainment. "Good night, Scott," she said. "Good luck with your office shopping."

The next afternoon, Piper took advantage of her Sunday closing to do a bit of inventory, working at it in a leisurely way. When the phone rang, she almost didn't answer, thinking it might be a customer query that she could deal with on Monday. But a glance at the caller ID revealed Amy's name.

"Are you sitting down?" Amy asked when Piper picked up.

"Why?" Piper, who'd been standing to check her supply of canning jars, didn't immediately reach for a chair. Though she was surprised to hear from her assistant that day, Amy's tone wasn't warning of deeply upsetting news, such as anything happening to Aunt Judy or Uncle Frank. It did sound serious, though.

"My dad was called out early this morning."

"Oh?" Piper decided to ease over to one of her tall stools after all. Anything involving the sheriff was bound to be bad.

"It's Raffaele Conti." Amy paused. "He's dead."

Piper sucked in her breath. "What happened?" she asked,

hoping it would be of natural causes—perhaps a sudden heart attack, or even a car accident, both terrible, of course, but still natural.

"I don't know many details," Amy said. "But Conti was found in Gerald Standley's dill field."

"The dill field!"

"Right in the middle of it," Amy said. She then blew away the last of Piper's hopes. "He was shot."

7

~~~~~

Piper paced through her empty and shuttered store for several minutes after Amy's call, thinking over what she'd heard: Raffaele Conti, shot, and in Gerald Standley's dill field! It was all too much to deal with on her own. She needed help, so she grabbed her purse and keys and headed out to her aunt and uncle's farm.

Ever since her first summer spent there as a child, Piper had come to rely on the calm common sense that reigned at the farm. Her own parents, while loving, had always been much more absorbed with the past than the present. As archaeologists, of course, that was probably a given. But to an archaeologist's daughter that often meant growing up without a lot of helpful advice beyond "study hard" or "organize your collections." Where were Peter and Sheila Lamb now? Bulgaria, or had they finished up there? Her parents were hard to keep track of, working as they usually did in remote, out-of-touch areas.

But two people in Piper's life who were nearly always available were the ones she was heading for now, hoping they could help her sort out an event that, while tragic in itself, could have grim consequences extending far beyond Conti himself.

Piper took back roads to get to the farm, unwilling to drive past Gerald Standley's dill field and view the clutch of official vehicles she knew would be there. As she turned into the farm's driveway, though, she realized with a start that her aunt and uncle might not be home. In her rush, she hadn't thought to call and check. But the sight of Aunt Judy's blue Equinox parked in its usual place immediately erased that concern.

Piper pulled onto the graveled parking area and heard Jack, the black-and-white mix-breed stray her aunt and uncle had adopted, barking. As she climbed out, he scurried up for an ear rub, his tail wagging furiously. Aunt Judy appeared from behind the house, pulling off gardening gloves, her face solemn.

"We called, but you must have already left," she said. "I'm glad it was to come here." Piper met her halfway and they hugged. "Want to come inside?" her aunt asked.

"I'm just as glad to help you weed if that's what you were doing."

Aunt Judy did a quick check of Piper's jeans and rolled-sleeve shirt—acceptable weeding attire, apparently—and nodded. "That would be lovely," she said. "You heard about poor Raffaele I take it?" she asked, turning to lead the way to the kitchen garden that she kept filled each year with vegetables and herbs for her cooking and canning.

"Amy called," Piper said. "How did you hear?"

"Bill Vanderveer. He was driving by the dill field this morning on his way back from church—he goes early." Aunt Judy tsked. "What a thing to happen on a Sunday morning— or any morning, for that matter."

She found an extra pair of gardening gloves and a trowel in the small shed and handed them to Piper. "My squashes have been running rampant," she said, bringing up a small smile. "It's like they sense winter is getting closer and are getting in as much growing as they can. But so are the weeds. I've been working on this row," she said, pointing to a half-tidied area. "Pick any spot you like. There's an extra basket over there if you want it."

Piper knew the drill, having worked beside Aunt Judy during many a hot summer. She also knew that weeding was one way her aunt dealt with a worrying situation—that, and scrubbing floors—so she wasn't at all surprised to find her hard at work. Piper grabbed a basket, pulled on her gloves, and got down on her knees, thankful at least that the day was mild enough to be outdoors. She wasn't particularly fond of scrubbing floors.

They worked quietly for a few moments until Piper said, "What worries me is where Conti was found."

Aunt Judy looked up. "That's the first thing we thought of, too. Uncle Frank is over there now, on the off chance he can see Gerald."

Piper sat back on her heels. "I can't imagine Gerald Standley capable of any sort of violence, can you? He's always been the good-natured farmer who grew excellent dill. But I was there when Raffaele Conti stepped off the team bus, and I witnessed Gerald's fury at sight of the man. I've also learned some of the history between them. Then there's the way last night's game ended, which upset plenty of people who didn't have nearly as much of a stake in it. Do you think, on top of everything else, that could have pushed Gerald over the edge?"

"It's so hard to say," Aunt Judy said, her brow puckered. "Gerald has always been even tempered about the usual, everyday things. But when it came to soccer? Or his family? If Raffaele Conti crossed the line with both . . ." Aunt Judy shook her head. "But I don't think it's wise to speculate on anything at this point, do you? There's so much more we'd need to know."

"You're right." Piper pulled up a handful of weeds and plopped them into her basket. "For all we know the sheriff may have found evidence pointing to someone else altogether. Or even that it was suicide." Though from what Piper knew of Conti, he was a man much too pleased with himself to commit suicide—especially in a dill field. That didn't keep her from holding on to the possibility, however unrealistic it might be.

Both heads turned as they heard the sound of a motor coming up the driveway. Jack, who'd been dozing in a nearby patch of sun, was on his feet in an instant.

"That sounds like Frank's truck," Aunt Judy said, and she and Piper pulled themselves up—a little less briskly than Jack—and followed him to the front of the house. Uncle Frank was climbing out of his pickup when they got there.

"What did you find out?" Aunt Judy asked.

Uncle Frank shook his head. "Not much." He pulled off his John Deere cap and wiped his forehead with his sleeve. "Conti's rental car was on the shoulder of the road, next to the Standley's field. Looked like it had a flat."

"Might he have been going for help?" Aunt Judy asked.

"Possible, I suppose, but why not simply call for help on his cell phone? Why head into the field? I didn't get to see Gerald or Denise." He looked from Aunt Judy to Piper, then back again.

"I'm pretty worried about them," he said.

Piper stayed at the farm, aware, for one thing, that it was the best place to be for hearing news, at least on a Sunday. Once her shop reopened the next day, she knew she'd get a steady flow of information, some of it even reliable. But for the time being, Uncle Frank and Aunt Judy would hear from their many friends around the town as quickly as there was any news to spread.

Her main reason, though, for staying nearby was seeing that her aunt and uncle wanted her to. A murder occurring nearby was upsetting enough. But the murder of a man they'd known in his youth was doubly so. The connection—at least by location—to a good friend tripled the stakes. Neither Uncle Frank nor Aunt Judy was overly emotional, but Piper could read the worry in their actions. Uncle Frank sat on a stump and sharpened tools that didn't appear to need sharpening, while Aunt Judy pulled at weeds with extra vigor—all between answering calls to their cell phones, which only added to their tension.

"Bill says the body's been taken off, but the sheriff's car is still at the house," Uncle Frank said at one point.

A few minutes later, Aunt Judy reported that Trish Warren had tried to see Denise Standley but had been turned away by a deputy

"Who found the body?" Piper asked.

Uncle Frank shook his head. "Don't know. Maybe someone spotted the car and followed a trail in the field?"

"Oh, I hope it wasn't Denise who found him," Aunt Judy said. "Or Miranda!"

Piper hoped it wasn't Gerald Standley who reported finding the body. She remembered the grilling she'd gotten after finding Brenda Franklin's body some weeks back. The first person on the scene was an automatic suspect, she knew, and Piper hadn't had anywhere near the history with Brenda that Gerald had with Conti.

Uncle Frank's phone rang, and Piper waited to hear what that call would bring. Her uncle's brow furrowed as he listened. "Uh-huh. Uh-oh. Sorry to hear that." His eyebrows shot up. "Really! Uh-huh. Uh-huh. Okay. Thanks, Roy."

He disconnected and looked at the two women, who faced him expectantly. "Roy Linebarger," he explained. "He says Gerald's been taken to the sheriff's office."

"Arrested?" Piper asked.

"Don't know. All Roy saw was Gerald sitting in the back of Carlyle's car."

"Oh, that doesn't sound good. Not good at all," Aunt Judy said, and Piper had to agree.

"There's one other thing," Uncle Frank said. "Turns out there was someone in town we didn't know about."

"Yes?" Aunt Judy prompted.

"A woman. She arrived sometime yesterday, on her own." He picked up the blade he'd been working on before the call and wiped it with a rag. Piper knew he was simply thinking over what he'd heard, but she wished mightily he'd share it with them.

So did Aunt Judy, apparently, as she cried, "Frank! Don't stop now! Who is she?"

Uncle Frank looked up in surprise as though he thought he'd already said it. "Oh! The woman? It's his wife. Conti's wife."

8

~~~

After getting home from the farm, Piper talked with Will by phone. He had already heard the news.

"I feel I should do something," he said, "but I have to drive to Rochester tomorrow to check out new bailing equipment."

Piper knew it was crunch time for Will's Christmas tree farm, when he needed to make sure all his ducks were in a row for his busy November-December season. She wished him a safe trip and promised to update him on the situation when he got back.

The next morning, expecting a busy day, Piper fortified herself with a breakfast of oatmeal and toast topped with her own strawberry jam and, of course, coffee. Lots of coffee.

When she raised the shade on her shop door, hopefully

prepared to face the onslaught of rehashings and minute-by-minute updates of the previous day's events, to her surprise the first person she saw heading toward Piper's Picklings was Erin. Quiet, mind-her-own-business Erin.

This longtime friend of Amy's had flexible hours, Piper knew, working part-time at Dr. Dickerson's office while taking classes at the community college in nearby Bellingham. But Piper was still surprised that Erin, instead of all the more news-spreading townspeople (Piper carefully avoided the word "gossiping"), was the first to arrive on this extremely newsworthy morning. However, given a choice, calm and sensible Erin would have been a strong favorite.

Piper unlocked her door and held it open as the young woman approached.

"You're out early," she said. Erin was dressed for her receptionist's job, having paired a pale yellow sweater, which complemented her brunette coloring, with a dark, knee-length skirt.

"I have to be at Dr. Dickerson's in a few minutes, but I wanted to get this to Amy today." She held out the book she'd been carrying. "It's a library book she asked me to pick up for her when I was there. I know Amy sleeps in after working late at A La Carte, so I thought I'd leave it here. Is that okay?"

"Of course. Come on in. Want some coffee?"

Erin stepped in but turned down the coffee, saying, "I'll get plenty at the office." She paused. "As well as an earful about what happened yesterday."

Piper noticed dark shadows under Erin's eyes. "This is upsetting you."

Erin nodded, grimacing. "I like the Standleys. I got to

know Miranda when we were both in chorus. She was two years behind me at school, but she sang second soprano, like me. We were about the same height, so we were usually next to each other. I like her a lot."

Erin reached over to straighten a pickling cookbook that jutted out of line on its shelf. "And Mrs. Standley," she said, "came along sometimes when the chorus traveled for performances. She was always really nice. I hate to think what they might be going through. People are saying Mr. Standley might be in a lot of trouble."

" 'Might' is the operative word," Piper cautioned. "So far I haven't heard of anything beyond his being questioned, which is absolutely normal and routine, I'd say, when a body has been found on your property."

"I tried to call Miranda, but I can't get through."

"She's probably being barraged with calls right now. Give it a day or so, Erin. Maybe everything will be straightened out by then. Have you talked to Ben lately? Does he know anything more than the rest of us?"

"No, I don't think so. The sheriff had him helping out at the Standley's farm yesterday, but he was mostly there to move curious onlookers along. Today he's back in his office. I'll call him at lunchtime. He might have heard something by then."

"Let me know if he does, okay?"

"I will." Erin saw Piper's gaze shift over her shoulder and turned to see Mrs. Tilley approaching the shop. "I'd better get to work," she said, returning an errant purse strap back to her shoulder. She held the door for Mrs. Tilley, both exchanging polite greetings.

Mrs. Tilley, a regular customer at Piper's Picklings, smiled as she stepped in. "I just wanted to pick up some cinnamon and cloves," she explained and proceeded to pluck the two jars off their shelves. Instead of bringing the spices to Piper to ring up, however, she continued to browse, adding an occasional item—a slotted ladle, then a package of jar labels—to one of the small shopping baskets that Piper kept handy.

Piper could see from the woman's furtive glances her way that Mrs. Tilley was bursting to chat, but as she watched the purchases drop into the basket she was torn between making it easier for the woman or letting her continue to build what might total up to a tidy sale. When she saw Mrs. Tilley circle a display of canning supplies that Piper knew for a fact she already possessed, she relented.

"I guess you heard about the Italian team's manager," Piper said.

Mrs. Tilley's face brightened. "Yes! Wasn't that shocking? I heard he was found in the Standley dill field. Is that right?"

"That's what I understand."

At that moment, Phil Laseter, Cloverdale's retired optometrist, entered the shop. "Ah, Joan! I thought I saw you turn in here. How's Bob?"

"He's fine. Over his cold now," Mrs. Tilley said, her head bobbing.

"Good, good. Remind him there's a woodworking club meeting tomorrow night, would you?" As Mrs. Tilley nodded, he said, "Terrible business out there at the dill farm, isn't it?"

"Oh, we were just saying!" Mrs. Tilley chirped. "I can't get over it, where he was found, and all. Do you suppose Gerald . . . ?" Her voice trailed off.

Piper jumped in at that point. "It may be only a coincidence. Raffaele Conti's car was found with a flat tire next to the dill field."

"She's right," Phil Laseter said. "No use leaping to any conclusions. Though we all know the grudge Gerald held against the man, and—"

"And *nothing*," Emma Leahy proclaimed as she pushed her way into the shop. "That was years ago when they were kids. Don't go hanging poor Gerald over water that's long gone under the bridge."

"I wasn't—" Phil Laseter defended himself, only to be interrupted by Joan Tilley, who was in turn interrupted by Emma Leahy.

Piper could only look on in dismay. Gerald Standley was being tried by a jury of his peers before he'd even been charged with anything. And her pickling shop had turned into the courtroom!

"Ladies! Gentleman!" she called, restraining herself from rapping on her counter with a nearby wooden spoon. When they turned her way, Piper asked, "Does anyone know about Raffaele Conti's wife being in town? I heard she'd arrived sometime Saturday."

"Really?" Mrs. Tilley's eyebrows shot up. "I didn't know that." Phil and Emma looked at each other and both shook their heads, looking equally surprised.

"I never heard anything about a wife," Phil said. "She must have stayed at the hotel. Who would know about that?"

"Well, Don Tucker works the desk at the Cloverton," said Emma. "He should know."

"Good point. Why don't we go and talk to him." Phil turned and headed out the door, followed closely by Emma. Mrs. Tilley was on her way out as well when she remembered the basket of unpaid-for items still hooked over her arm.

"Oh!" she cried, glancing anxiously from Piper to her rapidly retreating friends. Piper could see she wanted to keep up with Phil and Emma much more than she wanted to keep her purchases.

"I can hold those for you, Mrs. Tilley," Piper offered.

"Would you? I'll come back for them. Well, maybe not today. I have to, well, there are things I need to . . ."

Piper sighed silently and took the basket from her would-be customer. "Whenever you can, Mrs. Tilley," she said and watched the woman scurry down the street after the others.

That scene repeated itself several times that morning, with variations, before Amy finally arrived for her shift. When she walked in, stepping aside for two exiting, and still talking, women, Piper nearly cheered with relief.

"Busy morning?" Amy asked.

"Nonstop. But chatter, not sales. Thoughts of pickling, apparently, do not go along with crime, which I suppose I should be grateful for. Oh, before I forget, Erin dropped a book off for you." Piper hadn't checked the title when she took it from Erin, and she glanced at it now. *The Ins and Outs of Running a Restaurant.* "Hmm. Something in the works?"

Amy laughed. "I wish! But not for a good while. It's my

long-term goal. I'm getting the kitchen end down pat, working at A La Carte. I thought it wouldn't hurt to start studying up on the business end."

"Good thinking." As Amy dropped her purse and the library book behind the counter, Piper added, "Perhaps Carl Ehlers could have used some instruction in that department before opening up his pizzeria."

"I know. What he's going through is exactly what scares me. I don't want to sink a pile of money into a place and then watch it go down the drain. A lot goes into making a success of a restaurant beyond offering good food. There's location, figuring out the right prices, good suppliers . . ." Amy shuddered.

"Where is Carl missing out, do you suppose?"

"I don't know." Amy stopped tying the strings of the apron she'd put on to think. "His pizza is great, and I think the waitstaff generally do a good job." She shrugged. "Customers can be fickle, though. One week yours is the trendy place to go to. The next week, who knows? It's like everyone gets the memo, and something sends people elsewhere."

"Something like a comment on the radio about health code violations at your restaurant?"

Amy nodded vigorously. "If you're in trouble already, that sure won't help. Think anyone would want to patronize a restaurant once the image of a bug-infested kitchen is in their heads? I wonder why Conti did that."

"Who knows?" Piper said. But as she walked over to tidy up a display of seasoning jars, Piper thought the more interesting question might be how Carl Ehlers reacted to it.

~~~~~~~~

Amy disappeared into the back room to start cooking up a green apple pectin stock from a batch of Granny Smith apples, and Piper stayed where she was, expecting a fresh onslaught of Cloverdale "news spreaders." What she didn't expect was Scott popping in, looking dapper in a sports jacket and shirt and tie over khakis.

"Hey, Lamb Ch—oops!" He grinned. "I mean, Piper. Guess what?"

"What, Scott?"

"I just signed the papers on my new office. It's the one I told you about, down the block and next to the orthopedist. We'll practically be neighbors! I'm celebrating. Want to go to lunch?"

Piper stared at her ex-fiancé. She'd reached the end of her rope with him and it was time to shake him off it. "Scott, we have to talk."

"Great. I have a nice, quiet place in mind for that, where we can also get a glass of wine to toast my new digs. Sound good?"

"No, not good." Piper glanced outside her windows to see if anyone was heading their way. All looked clear. "I know when we talked the last time that I agreed to remain friends."

"Uh-huh. And friends celebrate with friends, right?"

"You've been pushing it, Scott. Showing up at the soccer games, following Will and me to the restaurants afterward—"

"Following?" Scott looked offended. "Your Aunt Judy specifically asked me to come along."

"And I'm going to have a talk with her, too. Of course she'd invite you along! Aunt Judy has always looked after strays—cats, dogs, and now, apparently, ex-fiancés. Scott, you decided to move to Cloverdale, and that's your call. But you can't just move into my life again. I have some say in that. You have to give me my space."

Scott was silent.

"I know what you've been doing, picking up sushi and my favorite chocolates, and choosing an office close to my shop."

"It's a great office," Scott argued. "It just happens to be where it is."

"Uh-huh. And I can't stop you from settling there. But don't expect me to join you for lunch at the drop of a hat. And don't show up wherever I happen to be, or bring me gifts. We don't have that kind of relationship anymore. What we had is over."

Scott stared at the floor a few moments, then looked back to Piper. "I'll stop bringing you things," he said softly, "if that's what you want. But you can't stop me from caring about you, Piper."

Piper kept herself from screaming in exasperation, *You had your chance and you blew it!* Instead she simply said, "I hope you can move on, Scott."

Scott looked ready to say more when Emma Leahy burst into the shop, something that was becoming a habit with her. Emma always seemed to be dressed in what Piper thought of as gardening clothes—loose denims and oversize shirts over faded tees, often with a smudge of dirt or a grass stain—but she was doing precious little gardening that day.

"We weren't able to talk to Don Tucker," Emma reported. "He wasn't on duty at the Cloverton."

"Don Tucker?" Scott asked. "The guy at the front desk?"

"That's him. We wanted to ask Don about Raffaele Conti's wife coming to town. If anyone knows anything about that, he would."

"Oh, I know about that," Scott said. "I was there when she showed up. What do you need to know? I'd be glad to help."

Emma's face lit up as Piper's fell.

And I was so close, she thought, *to sending him on his way.*

9

"You know, of course, about Conti being murdered?" Emma said to Scott. When he nodded, she said, "A lot of people are assuming Gerald Standley did it, since the body was found in Gerald's dill field and the two had, well, history between them. I, for one, don't happen to think that what occurred between people years ago when they were in their teens is going to cause one to kill the other. A wife, on the other hand, might have much more immediate reasons to kill a husband, wouldn't you agree?"

"Absolutely! I prosecuted loads of domestic cases when I was in Albany. Passions always ran high in those situations."

"That's exactly what I thought!" Emma said. "So, what I want to know is what this wife is like and why she showed up out of the blue just hours before her husband was found dead."

"Well," Scott said, "I can't answer your second question. But I can tell you something of what she's like. Drop-dead gorgeous, for one. Possibly at least ten years younger than Conti."

"That would put her in her late thirties," Piper said, her interest piqued despite her initial frustration. "Is that about right?"

Scott rocked his hand. "Give or take. Italians age well, you know. Something to do with all the olive oil in their diet. She's very stylish, so I'd guess she's from Rome, or maybe Milan."

"Did you see them together?" Emma asked. "How did they behave?"

"I saw her arrive. I was just passing through that big-windowed lobby when the team was gathering to leave for practice. All heads turned when she climbed out of her taxi. Conti looked floored. He clearly wasn't expecting her."

"Happy floored or not so happy?" Piper asked.

"Not so, I'd say. But he recovered fast and put on a big show of welcome. There was the expected kiss-kiss, hug-hug, but it was fairly stiff, you know? Like what you see on TV talk shows. All for the audience."

"Aha!" Emma cried. "So all was not well between them! We might have a suspect! Someone better than Gerald. Piper," she said, "you should look into this."

"Me!"

"Well, you did so well with our last murder. Our bag-piper."

Right, and almost got myself killed.

"Bagpiper?" Scott asked.

"It's a long story, Scott."

"I'd be very interested," he said. "Especially the part about you doing so well with, what, a murder investigation?"

"I simply—"

At that moment, and to Piper's relief, Amy poked her head out from the back room. "I set the pectin to simmer and— Oh, sorry!"

"That's okay," Piper said. "Need some help back there?"

"No, I . . ." Amy began before catching the look Piper shot her. "Actually, yes, I'm having a little trouble."

"I'll be right there. Excuse me, Scott, Emma."

"Wait," Scott called, but Piper kept moving, muttering to Amy as she slipped on by, "Take over out there?"

Amy nodded. "Got it."

Piper closed the door firmly behind her and leaned against it, hearing Emma, Scott, and Amy all talking at once. Eventually things quieted down, and she heard Emma, then Scott leave, evidently worn down by Amy's nonanswers.

Piper sighed. She could only hope she'd gotten through to Scott about the need to stop dogging her every move under the guise of friendship. Her aim was to keep him at a distance, but now Emma seemed eager to pull him into her growing circle of Cloverdale crime solvers—and to have Piper lead them!

Never mind that stepping into a group project that included Scott would only get him started all over again. What Piper had done after the murder of Alan Rosemont, the bagpiper, was a totally unique, onetime effort. When it ended, Piper was more than happy to return to quietly running her business.

At that thought, she went over to check out Amy's pot of simmering, chopped Granny Smith apples—peels, cores, seeds, and all—which, once cooked and strained, would make a great stock for future jellies and jams. Picturing those delicacies coaxed up a smile, just as gently stirring the mixture gradually soothed Piper's agitation. This was what she had settled in Cloverdale to do, she reminded herself, and this was what she intended to stick with—as she also preferred to let Sheriff Carlyle do his own job.

"Piper, Sheriff Carlyle isn't doing his job!" Miranda Standley cried, having burst into Piper's Picklings, her usually perfect, long blond hair flying about in disarray.

It was late afternoon. Amy was on the verge of leaving for A La Carte, and Gil Williams had just popped in to report on the success of Piper's raspberry-lavender jam as a hostess gift. The green apple pectin stock had been strained, reduced, and parceled out into freezer and refrigerator containers in between dealing with an endless stream of chatty visitors to the shop, and Piper had just congratulated herself on getting through most of the day relatively unscathed.

Miranda suddenly noticed Amy's presence. "Sorry," she said. "I know he's your dad and all, but it's true."

"Why do you say that?" Piper asked, though she had an uneasy idea of what the answer would be.

"Because he's not making it absolutely clear that my father had nothing to do with Raffaele Conti's murder! He took Daddy in for questioning—something the entire town apparently watched—and now he's left the whole thing up in the air! No statement like 'Gerald Standley has been cleared of all involvement' or anything."

"Believe me," Amy said, "I know how you feel. When Nate was under suspicion, it was infuriating."

"The law needs to work very carefully," Gil Williams put in. "Gathering evidence takes time."

"But in the meantime, everyone's looking at my dad like he's a murderer." Miranda burst into tears. "It's not right!"

Amy went over and put her arms around Miranda. "Everyone's *not* thinking your dad's a murderer," she insisted. "We know your dad too well for that."

"Maybe *you* don't think he could be guilty," Miranda conceded, swiping at her eyes, "but there's still plenty who do. People are driving up to our farm and taking photos and posting them on Twitter and Facebook with stupid captions, like *What did the farmer do in the dill?* And my mom got a call from the head of the Cloverdale Women's Club suggesting she drop out."

"What!" Amy cried.

Miranda nodded. "It's true. Mrs. Pennington put it as though she was only concerned about Mom and how overwhelmed she must be. But she was really thinking of that club she's ruled with an iron hand for years. Like my mom would contaminate it or something."

"Leona Pennington is a consummate snob," Gil Williams said. "I wouldn't worry too much about her opinion."

"Mom knows that. But she's still upset. She did tons of work for that group, which she always thought did a lot of good despite Mrs. Pennington. So far she's not gotten support from anyone else in the club. And that's just two examples," Miranda said. "I know it's going to get worse until Dad's one hundred percent cleared of this murder."

"Maybe we can help," Amy said. She glanced at Piper as she said it, and Piper winced.

"That's why I came here," Miranda said. "I know what you did for Nate, Piper. Everyone still talks about it."

"Miranda, that was just—"

"Daddy really needs a few people to believe in him."

"We certainly believe in him," Gil said. He turned to Piper. "I don't think Miranda expects you to neglect your business or get involved in anything risky. But you and I both see plenty of people in our shops. We could do our best to turn people's opinions around, for one thing. But we can also ask questions and maybe ferret out bits of information that nobody thought to pass on to Sheriff Carlyle."

Piper nodded. Gil was right. She didn't have to—and really couldn't—promise Miranda an answer to who killed Raffaele Conti. But keeping an eye out for anything that might help her father was the least a friend could do. And she did consider Gerald Standley a friend, despite their interactions being limited to the times he dropped off her dill orders. And what would she do without his excellent dill? At the very least, she owed the Cloverdale picklers and pickle consumers guaranteed continued cultivation and supply of Gerald Standley's one-of-a-kind dill.

"I'll do what I can, Miranda," she said. When Miranda

and Amy both whooped she cautioned, "But please don't expect more than what Gil just said. I'll keep my ears open and see what I can pry out of people. But that's all I can promise."

"Thank you." Miranda ran over to give Piper a gasp-inducing hug. "And my dad and mom will be very grateful, too. I'm sure they'll be glad to talk to you whenever you want."

"That would probably be a good thing," Gil said after regaining his breath from an enthusiastic hug of his own. "And," he added, "it might be a good idea to keep this among ourselves—and your parents, of course, Miranda—for the time being."

Miranda nodded, but said, "I already told Frederico I was going to ask you. I hope that's all right?"

"Frederico?" Gil asked.

"A soccer player on the Bianconeri team," Amy explained. "Miranda's been seeing him."

Miranda flushed a bit, then said, "Daddy wasn't real happy when he found out about that. But only because he doesn't know Frederico! I mean, just because the one man from Italy that Daddy knew turned out to be awful doesn't mean they all are." She looked around for confirmation, which Amy quickly provided. Amy, after all, understood something of that.

Piper nodded, though she'd reserve judgment of Frederico until she met him herself. But Miranda's comment told her that the girl was aware of at least some of the history between Raffaele Conti and her father.

Thinking of that history—and the wounds that had

remained raw, judging from what she saw pass between the two men—Piper could definitely understand Sheriff Carlyle's reluctance to rule out Gerald Standley as a suspect. And the fact that Conti's body was found in Standley's field certainly didn't help. There must be another explanation for what happened, though. Now that she'd promised Miranda to keep her eyes open, Piper hoped that explanation would quickly present itself.

10

"I can't believe Leona Pennington actually did that!" Aunt
Judy sputtered when Piper called to tell her about the
women's club president's recent actions. Miranda's comment
that no other members of the club had contacted Denise
Standley about the situation told Piper that her aunt, at least,
was unaware of Mrs. Pennington's high-handedness.

"I'll spread the word among the others in the club. After
that I'll head over to the Standleys' place and see if I
can talk to Denise in person. Leona shouldn't get away with
this."

"Um, while you're there," Piper said, "you might mention
to Denise that I promised to do what I can to help clear
Gerald and would like to come by and talk with them sometime, too."

"Oh? You promised who?"

"Miranda. She was pretty upset, and with good reason. I agreed to keep my eyes and ears open to help her dad. I doubt it will make much difference, but—"

"Tall towers start with a single brick," Aunt Judy said. "Or is it long journeys and single steps? Well, never mind. You know what I mean. Every little bit helps, is what I'm trying to say. Would you like to go with me to the Standleys? Maybe come here for dinner after you close up, and we could run over afterward?"

Piper didn't need to ask if popping in for dinner on such short notice was convenient. Aunt Judy always seemed prepared for last-minute guests. And her house was always company-ready. Cleaning and cooking appeared to get done as naturally and continually by her aunt as breathing, and if asked how she managed it, she would probably say with surprise, "I just *do*." Piper often wished she possessed the knack, particularly when glancing around her own, much less tidy living quarters.

They arranged a time, Aunt Judy agreeing to let Piper bring along a jar of blueberry jam to spread on the homemade pound cake that she, of course, had on hand for dessert, and Piper finished the remainder of her workday thinking about what to ask Gerald and Denise Standley.

As Uncle Frank waved them off from the farm, he said, "Tell Gerald I'd be glad to pitch in if he needs help on that broccoli field of his." Piper had forgotten that Gerald Standley grew other crops, dill being the one she was most concerned with. But if Gerald had gotten behind on his work because of the murder as well as the tournament, she was sure he'd appreciate Uncle Frank's offer of help.

During dinner, Aunt Judy had reported on her flurry of phone calls to other members of the Cloverdale Women's Club. Many were as horrified as she'd been to learn of Leona Pennington's call to Denise Standley. Some, however, were disappointingly taking a wait-and-see stance.

"The trouble with wait and see," Aunt Judy complained, "is that by the time everyone *sees*, the damage has been done. Who knows how long it will take Sherriff Carlyle to catch the person who committed that awful crime? Should Gerald and Denise be expected to live under a cloud and in isolation all that time?"

Another reason to try to speed the process along, Piper thought. She drove toward the Standley farm, realizing for the first time that she'd never been inside their house. During the childhood summers Piper had spent with Aunt Judy and Uncle Frank there'd been no particular reason, such as playmates her age, for her to go there. Miranda had only appeared on the scene by the time Piper was ten or so and therefore was of little interest to Piper's childish self. It was too bad that it took a tragedy like this to draw her closer to the family.

"I called Denise to let her know we were coming," Aunt Judy said. "They're still getting so many nosey parkers coming by that Gerald has had to block their driveway. She said he'll watch for us."

"A shame they've had to go to such lengths." Piper slowed as they approached the far edge of the dill field, the one she'd driven by with such pleasure in the past, and looked for the entrance, which sadly was no longer marked with an identifying sign or mailbox.

"There," Aunt Judy said, "right after the pine tree."

Piper turned in and drove up the graveled driveway, coming before long to a barricade of sawhorses. A hand-lettered sign proclaiming "Private!" hung from the center one. Gerald Standley was trotting toward them from the other side, and he waved, then lifted the sawhorses out of the way.

"Will you ride up with us, Gerald?" Aunt Judy called as Piper pulled even with him.

"No, go on ahead. My truck is just around the bend. I'll set these back up and be right behind you."

Aunt Judy tsked quietly to herself as she raised her window, and Piper nodded silent agreement. How miserable to have to screen visitors to one's home that way.

They spotted Denise on the front porch as they drew near the house, and she waved toward an area on the right where Piper could park her car. As she and Aunt Judy climbed out, they saw Gerald's truck pull into a spot closer to a large barn, a few yards away. Denise stepped off the porch and met them halfway as they made their way to the house.

"Thank you so much for coming," she said.

Piper knew Denise was the same age as Gerald, in her late forties, but she could easily have passed for late thirties—on a good day. This, unfortunately, wasn't one of those. Denise's usually attractively curled, light brown hair was pulled back severely into a ponytail from which straggly wisps escaped. She hugged a bulky gray sweater around her, concealing an otherwise trim figure, and dark shadows beneath her eyes hinted at stress and sleepless nights. She'd added a swipe of color to her lips, but it did little to lighten the overall effect of gloom.

"I wish we'd been able to come before this," Aunt Judy said after giving Denise a fervent hug. "Frank and I just couldn't get through for the longest time, either to call or to come by."

Denise sighed. "I know. It's been a hassle for all of us." She turned to Piper. "Miranda told me about talking to you today. I think she's imposing, but why don't we talk about it inside. I have coffee ready."

Piper and Aunt Judy followed Denise to the old but well-kept two-story house, crossing a wide veranda with a white-painted railing and a welcoming porch swing. Once inside, Denise waved them toward the living room while she fetched the coffee from the kitchen. Piper followed Aunt Judy to a flower-printed sofa, glancing around at a cheery, light-filled room that felt out of sync with the recent happenings. Photos of a smiling Miranda—from childhood to high school prom to graduation—sprinkled the tables and walls, and a silver-framed photo of Denise and Gerald on their wedding day held a central spot on the bookcase.

"Here we are," Denise said as she rejoined them, carrying a tray with steaming mugs. She handed them out, offering cream and sugar, then sank into a chair with a mug of her own. They heard steps on the porch, and Gerald stepped in and joined them. He took a chair near Denise after picking up the final coffee.

"Glad you stopped by," he said, taking a tentative sip. "Denise hasn't had too many friends come to call."

"That's what we wanted to talk to you about," Aunt Judy said, setting down her mug on the low table before her. "At least, it's one of the things. I just learned today—from Piper—what Leona Pennington said to you, Denise, and I want you to know that she absolutely doesn't speak for all of us, even though she is club president. I, for one—and I know you'll hear from more ladies—want you to stay active in the club."

Denise's eyes filled for a moment before she blinked them clear. "Thank you, Judy. Leona has a point, though, hurtful as it seems. My showing up for club activities might be too disruptive right now."

"Poppycock! If the ladies of the Cloverdale Women's Club can't stand by one of their own at a time like this, then what use are we? We don't exist simply to plant flowers around memorials. Our motto, for heaven's sake, is 'To make Cloverdale a better place to live.' What better way to do that than by showing support to each other when it's warranted?"

"I'm afraid not everyone agrees that it's warranted." Gerald said it flatly but with a tightness around his lips. Denise reached out to gently squeeze his arm.

"Well, anyone who knows you as well as we do won't have an ounce of suspicion," Aunt Judy insisted.

"Thank you, Judy," Denise said. "And thank you, too, Piper. I appreciate your coming along with your aunt to add encouragement. But please don't feel you need to do anything more than that"—she smiled weakly—"despite my daughter's pleas."

"I only promised Miranda to keep my eyes and ears open for whatever might come up." Piper noticed Gerald frown at her mention of Miranda and wondered if it was because of their clash over Frederico. "Do you mind me asking a few questions? It could help me piece together any other bits of information I might learn."

"Go ahead," Gerald said.

"Who actually discovered Conti's body?"

"I did," he said. "I was up earlier than usual, and once it was light enough I decided to check on the latest dill crop. I do continual plantings of dill, every two or three weeks as long as the weather holds out."

Piper nodded, remembering that Gerald had once explained that cycle to her.

"I spotted something a few yards in," Gerald went on. "Thought it was a dog at first and went over to see. It was a shock, I'll tell you, when I realized it was a man. Then I got closer and saw it was *him*." Gerald shook his head.

"Conti's car was at the edge of the road. How far was he from his car?"

"Probably fifty yards or so. Coming from Judy and Frank's place, you wouldn't pass the part of the field where it happened. If you turn the other way on your way out, you'll see the area that's all trampled from the crime scene people."

Piper winced at the image of Gerald's lovely dill being tramped down, but Gerald shrugged. Losing part of his dill crop was clearly the least of his worries.

"You said you were up early. Did you hear anything during the night?"

Gerald uncrossed his legs and shifted in his chair. Denise stared down at her coffee. "Actually," Gerald said, "I didn't sleep much that night at all. Had a lot of things on my mind that I couldn't seem to shake. When that happens I usually go outside and walk around so I won't wake Denise or Miranda. It was dark, so I stayed close to the house. But I did hear a shot. This is farm country, though. We hear shots now and then. I didn't think much of it."

"What time was that?"

"I'm guessing around one thirty, maybe one forty-five. That's what I told the sheriff. He also asked if I went to investigate, which I didn't. First of all, sound travels funny sometimes. You can't always pinpoint the direction it comes from. Second of all, if someone's out there shooting at a deer or something, I sure as heck don't want to get in his way. I stayed where I was and went inside pretty soon."

"You didn't hear voices?"

"Nope."

Piper turned to Denise. "Did *you* hear anything?"

Denise shook her head. "I'm a pretty sound sleeper. And as Gerald says, shots are so unremarkable around here that if one went off I probably wouldn't stir."

"I'm sure the sheriff asked about any guns you might own," Piper said, and both Gerald and Denise nodded.

"They took the one rifle I have to compare it with the bullet in Conti. It didn't match." Gerald shifted uneasily again. "The problem is . . ."

"Yes?"

When Gerald didn't answer right away, Denise explained for him. "We owned another gun, a .44 Special handed down from Gerald's father. When the sheriff asked us to turn over all our firearms, we couldn't find that one. It's been years since we did anything with it, and we'd almost forgotten about it. We kept it in the house, originally. Then when Miranda was a toddler, I asked Gerald to put it somewhere safe in the barn, a place she couldn't get to."

"And I did," Gerald said. "But over the years I moved it around as needed until I eventually forgot all about it. I told the sheriff it probably was so rusted and dirty by now that it wouldn't work anyway. But he didn't like the idea that I couldn't locate it. I don't, either, come to that. I shouldn't have been so careless about it, and I don't like not knowing what happened to the thing."

Neither would Sheriff Carlyle, obviously, Piper thought. Which must be the reason he was unwilling to let Gerald off the hook. Looking at the faces of the others—including Aunt Judy—Piper could tell they were all thinking the same thing.

"Would the bullets from your old gun have been the same caliber as the bullet that killed Raffaele Conti?"

Denise and Gerald glanced at each other, the misery on both faces foretelling the answer. Then Gerald nodded.

"Oh dear," Aunt Judy said in a small voice, understating the large problem that created for Gerald Standley.

It, however, was something Sheriff Carlyle would have to deal with. Piper's problem at the moment was how to learn the source of Gerald's lingering fury toward Conti. She'd just drawn a breath to ease her way into the subject, when light steps sounded outside on the veranda.

The front door opened and Miranda flew in.

"I was hoping that was your car. Great!" she said excitedly to Piper, looking convinced that now all would be well.

Piper managed to smile but inwardly felt as though a fifty-pound weight had just been loaded on her back.

11

"Well," Gerald said, rising from his chair, "I've got a few things to do in the barn. If there's anything more you want to know, Piper, I'm sure Denise or Miranda can fill you in."

Piper nodded. That worked for her, since what she wanted to hear about—that past history with Raffaele Conti—might be easier to get from Denise without Gerald around. Piper hoped Gerald wasn't leaving because of Miranda's arrival, though. At a time like this, their small family needed to pull together, not get hung up on lesser disagreements.

"So," Miranda said, taking her father's chair. "Did Daddy explain how he found Mr. Conti?"

"He did. Did you hear the shot?"

"No, I sure didn't. Daddy said it was around one thirty. I was dead to the world then. Oops!" Miranda grimaced and rolled her eyes. "Bad choice of words, I guess. But that's what I was. Cheerleading, plus being out most of the afternoon with Frederico . . ." She glanced at her mother at that, but Denise simply nodded. "Anyway, nothing woke me until I heard the sheriff's car radio squawking. And he'd been here for a while by then." She turned to Denise. "I still don't understand why you didn't wake me right away."

"There was no need," Denise said. She paused. "And we didn't want you to see . . ."

"Mother! I'm not a child."

"Oh, Miranda," Aunt Judy soothed. "No matter how grown-up a person is, you wouldn't want a sight like that getting stuck in your head, believe me."

Miranda shrugged, disagreeing, but smiled politely at Aunt Judy. A soft trill sounded, and she reached into her pocket to check her phone. "Excuse me, I should take this." She got up, and Piper heard Miranda's voice fade as she made her way to the kitchen.

"Denise," Piper said, "would you mind explaining to me why Gerald held such hard feelings toward Raffaele for so long?"

Denise drew in a deep breath, looking reluctant.

"It's important, or I wouldn't ask."

"No, I understand. It's just that I feel so stupid for what happened. My only excuse is that I was young."

"All of us have needed that excuse at one time or another," Aunt Judy said. "Some longer than others."

Denise smiled. "If it will help Gerald, I can deal with it. By the time Raffaele Conti came to Cloverdale, Gerald and I had been dating for over a year. I was wearing his class ring, and though we both knew we were too young, we'd talked about marriage someday. Gerald, I knew, was head over heels for me, and I didn't have eyes for any other boy—until Raffaele arrived."

Denise shifted in her chair and clutched at her gray cardigan, pulling it together more tightly. "Raffaele just plain dazzled me. He had movie star good looks, and that accent! Add to that a nearly irresistible charm—the kind we didn't find in any local boys—and he had most of the girls falling at his feet. I did my best to keep my distance, but because he and Gerald both were on the soccer team it was just about impossible."

She cleared her throat. "It all started about the time that Gerald and most of the other players were furious because of Raffaele's behavior on the team. Looking back, I really think Raffaele came after me as just another way to get to Gerald. Gerald had been pleading with Coach Anderson to be more fair and not let Raffaele take over the team like he was, and Raffaele seemed to glory in the fact that Gerald got nowhere with that. Stealing me away from Gerald was just one more way to rub his nose in the dirt."

Aunt Judy tsked. "Not a very nice boy."

"No," Denise agreed. "Unfortunately I didn't see it then. I broke up with Gerald, I'm ashamed to say, and started seeing Raffaele. I knew I'd hurt Gerald terribly, but that mattered less to me at the time than being the 'chosen one' of the boy all the females at the school were gushing over. Gerald, though, had pretty much figured out Raffaele's true nature, and he tried desperately to get me to see it, too. When I wouldn't, Gerald took to watching out for me."

Denise smiled ruefully. "Some might have called it stalking, but, if so, it was for all the right reasons. Gerald was genuinely worried about me. Luckily, as it turned out."

"What happened?" Piper asked.

Denise sighed deeply. She looked toward the kitchen and, hearing the murmur of her daughter's voice on her cell phone, went on.

"It was the night of the prom. I went with Raffaele, and Gerald showed up with a couple of guy friends. He looked absolutely miserable—this was supposed to have been our big night, but I had ruined it for him. He could have stayed home, and nobody would have blamed him. But he donned a suit and put himself through the misery, all for my sake.

"Of course, I was oblivious—or tried to be. I saw Gerald but was so taken up with my own floating-on-air feelings that I brushed any negative thoughts away. Raffaele and I were the center of admiring attention—Cinderella and Prince Charming—at least I thought so. Who knew that Prince Charming had sneaked in a flask of vodka and had been adding it to the cups of punch he kept bringing me so gallantly?"

Denise shook her head. "Naïve, stupid me. I thought I was having a wonderful time. Every little joke became the funniest thing I'd ever heard! I'd never danced so well or had such a wonderful time! Of course, as the dance ended I'd never felt woozier, but I put it all down to the excitement of the evening.

"Raffaele didn't drive me straight home, but I didn't even notice until he pulled into that dark, empty spot next to Warren's Pond. That was the first I began to sense that all was not right. But I still convinced myself I could trust him, this Prince Charming who had taken me to the ball. He'd changed from that person, though. Even in the semidarkness I could see the expression on his face. I suddenly felt like a mouse cornered by a huge, feral cat.

"No wasting of time to seduce me. He attacked. I screamed and fought, but I could tell, especially in my state, that it would be useless. I'd never felt such fear in my life. Then, out of the blue, headlights blazed behind us. A car door slammed and in an instant Raffaele's door was yanked open and he was dragged off of me. It was Gerald!

"Gerald had kept up his vigilance, painful though it must have been, and followed us, knowing full well that if he was spotted he'd be ridiculed. He was concerned so much more for me than for himself. It didn't take long to deal with Raffaele. He was a coward at heart and didn't put up much of a fight. I quickly jumped into Gerald's car and we drove off, me sobbing and Gerald fuming while at the same time trying to comfort me."

Denise paused to smile weakly. "I don't know what my parents thought when I came home with Gerald instead of Raffaele. And it was past my curfew. But I needed time to calm down and patch up the damage. Plus apologize to Gerald, over and over. He, of course, blamed himself for not convincing me of what a rat Raffaele really was."

"You picked a good man," Aunt Judy said.

"I did, finally, and I'm so grateful he stood by me during my foolishness."

"You were seventeen," Piper pointed out.

"And so was he," Denise said, smiling. "Thank goodness one of us had developed some maturity and sense by then."

"I suppose that's why he's worried about Miranda," Piper said.

Denise nodded. "I've tried to point out that Miranda is much smarter than I was, besides being a couple of years older. I haven't gotten very far, though."

"Conti showing up unexpectedly after all these years must have been quite a jolt," Piper said.

"It was. If Raffaele had shown the least bit of remorse, it might have made a difference. But he didn't. Gerald said he could see that same arrogance the moment Raffaele stepped out of the bus."

"Both men had to be at Friday and Saturday's soccer games," Piper said. "And as far as I saw, kept their distance from one another. Did they ever come in close contact during those two days?"

Denise hesitated. "The sheriff asked that, too. Gerald said they didn't." She looked steadily at Piper. "And I believe him."

12

~~~~~~~

"Piper, go! Scoot!"

Standing in the center of the pickling shop's back room, Amy made sweeping motions, urging Piper to leave for her lunch date with Will and sounding eerily like Aunt Judy.

"There's still time for me to—" Piper argued, but Amy would have none of it.

"Go. Whatever it is, I'll do it. You look very nice, by the way."

"Thanks!" Piper had changed from her usual shop uniform of tee, khakis, and green apron to a pretty blouse, cotton blazer, and slacks. Lunch at the Cloverton called for a higher level of dress.

"And don't rush back," Amy ordered.

"Yes, ma'am," Piper said, smiling. "Any thoughts on what I should order?"

"I trust you to choose well. Now go! Will is waiting."

Piper and Will had agreed to meet at the hotel, since he planned to head to the bank after lunch to discuss a loan for new equipment for the Christmas tree farm—one reason he said he didn't mind slipping on a sports jacket for their lunch. Two birds with one jacket, so to speak. Though Amy had referred to their meeting all morning as a date, strictly speaking it would be a working lunch since Piper knew she would spend much of the time updating Will on Raffaele Conti's murder—not your usual date conversation. In addition, Piper hoped to talk to the Cloverton's desk manager, Don Tucker, about Conti's wife. Emma Leahy may have spoken to the man by then, but Piper wanted to ask her own questions instead of hearing things second- or thirdhand.

Piper gave Amy a quick wave good-bye and headed out back to hop into her Chevy hatchback. It was a great day— bright sun and air that was crisp and sharp with the scents of autumn, the kind of day she would have loved to savor with a walk. Time, however, was a luxury Piper didn't have with a business to get back to, so she drove carefully but quickly, winding her way through the several turns that would bring her to the Cloverton.

Built in the 1920s, the Cloverton had been renovated several years ago, evidenced by the large windows that Scott had mentioned, which added a modern look to the entrance of the building. Piper had been told the rooms on the upper floors were laid out in a maze of corridors and had been decorated individually in various styles, charming visitors who were accustomed to the bland, cookie-cutter décor of chain hotels.

Piper found a nearby spot to park on the street—an achievement that still managed to surprise and delight her after years of living in crowded Albany. As she climbed out of the car, she spotted Will waiting outside the hotel entryway.

"Am I late?" she called out.

Will made a show of studying his watch. "Approximately one minute and twenty-three seconds, but who's counting?" His deadpan expression morphed into a grin. As Piper walked up he said, "I got here early and reserved a table. It was just too nice to wait inside."

"Isn't it?" Piper agreed. "Too bad they don't have patio dining."

"From what I hear, the food will make up for it." He held the door for Piper and followed her inside.

"So you've never dined here?" Piper asked, knowing Will had lived in the Cloverdale area less than two years.

"Nope. Meeting you has opened up a whole new world for me."

Piper laughed. "You look very nice, by the way," she said, referring to his "business attire," which was quite different from his usual work duds of jeans and a flannel shirt.

Will acknowledged the compliment with a dip of his head. "I was about to say the same to you." They crossed the lobby to reach the restaurant entrance, and the hostess picked up two menus and led them to their table.

Will folded his hands on the white tablecloth. "So," he said, "what's the latest on the Conti murder?"

Piper waited, having noticed their waitress approaching.

As the young woman filled their water glasses and recited the day's specials, Piper and Will made their choices, each passing on the suggested cocktail or wine. Will may have been concerned with keeping a clear head for his upcoming bank negotiation, but Piper knew how embarrassingly likely she was to nod off by late afternoon if she had anything stronger than iced tea with her lunch.

Their food arrived quickly, and between bites of her delicious quiche and salad and to the accompaniment of soft background music, Piper described the Standleys' situation to Will as it now stood, including Gerald's reason for hating Conti, though, for Denise's sake, she kept that explanation to a minimum.

"Miranda is frustrated that Sheriff Carlyle hasn't cleared her father completely from his suspect list," she said, "but I can understand why he hasn't."

Will sliced a piece off his filet mignon. "That missing gun is a big red flag. How does a person lose track of something like that?"

Piper shrugged. "It had been Gerald's father's gun. I didn't get the impression they'd ever used it themselves, so it may have been simply forgotten about. With luck the gun will still turn up, otherwise . . ."

Will met Piper's eyes, both aware how dire that could be for Gerald on top of the strong motive he had for killing Raffaele Conti.

"The sheriff may have his suspicions, but I just don't see Gerald turning that violent," Piper said. "Murder would be too out of character."

"I'd like to know what Conti was doing at the Standley

farm in the middle of the night," Will said. "His car had a flat tire, sure, but why head into a dill field in the middle of the night if you need help? A field he must have known belonged to the Standleys?"

Piper nodded, having pondered the same things. She crunched on a tasty crouton from her salad as a familiar tune from the piped-in music caught her attention. She was working on identifying it—something from *The Pirates of Penzance*?—when a couple entered the restaurant. The man looked familiar, but it took her a moment to place him without his identifying team jacket: the coach of Bianconeri. And the woman with him was dark haired, stylishly dressed, and quite attractive, just as Scott had described.

Piper leaned toward Will. "I think that must be Raffaele Conti's wife!"

Will glanced over, his face doing a silent *Wow!* before he cleared his throat and said, "You might be right." He sneaked a second look. "That red dress doesn't exactly say 'grieving widow,' though."

"I imagine when she packed, she wasn't expecting to need widow's weeds, although from what Scott said, she and Conti didn't appear to be a devoted couple. Which is why I'd like to—"

"From what Scott said?" Will asked.

Piper made a no-big-deal shrug. "Scott—as well as half of Cloverdale—dropped into the shop yesterday to dissect Conti's murder. Emma Leahy got him started on what he witnessed in the hotel lobby."

Will swiveled to check the tables behind him as though suddenly fearing to find Scott sitting at one and quietly watching them. A rippling laugh carried their way from the red-dressed, dark-haired woman.

"No," Piper agreed. "Not exactly grieving." She thought for a moment. "I'm going over there."

Will's eyebrows flew up. "And do what?"

"I don't know. Offer condolences? I just want to get a sense of what she's like."

"What if she doesn't speak English?"

"Then I'll get a close-up look at that fabulous dress." Piper put down her napkin. "Wish me luck."

Piper pushed back her chair and stood. *What was the coach's name? She'd heard it mentioned. Tortorelli? That was it. Something Tortorelli.* She drew a deep breath and headed for the table.

"Excuse me. Signore Tortorelli?" Tortorelli turned and he looked up. "I just wanted to offer my condolences on the loss of your team manager, Raffaele Conti."

"Ah yes, thank you. Thank you very much. And you are?"

"Piper Lamb. I was at both soccer matches and was quite impressed with your team. This must be very stressful for you all."

Tortorelli tilted his head in acknowledgment, his features blunt and rugged but radiating intensity and intelligence. He gestured toward his table companion. "Miss Lamb, may I introduce Francesca Conti, Raffaele's wife."

Piper affected surprise, as though the idea that this woman could be Conti's wife had never occurred to her. "Signora Conti! Forgive me for intruding. I'm so sorry about your husband."

Francesca Conti studied Piper with a cool eye for several moments, and Piper wondered if she perhaps didn't understand English. But then she nodded and said, "*Grazie*, thank you." Close-up she was even more stunning than she'd appeared from a distance, with dark—Scott might have said "smoldering"—eyes, and full, red-glossed lips. Those lips curled slightly with what appeared to be private amusement, making Piper curious about what she might be finding humorous.

"I'm sorry that your visit to Cloverdale took such a terrible turn," Piper said. "Will you be staying with us much longer?"

At that, Francesca Conti actually laughed. "I hadn't planned to, but it seems I have little choice now." She glanced at Tortorelli with merriment.

"The sheriff?" Piper ventured.

"Mmm, yes," Francesca said, nodding. "Your sheriff. He obviously thinks I am a, how you say, a 'person of interest.' I am, of course," she said, smiling at Tortorelli. "I am very interesting, no? But not the way he thinks it, eh, Enzo?"

"No, of course not, Francesca." He added something in Italian which made Signora Conti laugh even more, though Tortorelli looked quite serious.

"*Scusa,*" Francesca said to Piper. "We are being very rude, and you are very kind. It's just a"—she paused, thinking—"a very *odd* situation."

Tortorelli said something more in Italian and glanced at Piper impatiently. She got the message and took her leave, heading back to her own table and a waiting Will.

"What did you get from that?" Will asked as she slipped back onto her chair.

Piper mulled it over. "Well, first, she *is* Conti's wife, and she speaks English very well—though the coach appeared to feel she spoke it a little more than she should. Beyond that, I found her red dress to be even more gorgeous close-up."

Piper paused. "And I'd say the color is most appropriate for the way Signora Conti seems to be feeling right now."

13

~~~~

I t was time for Will to head to his bank meeting. Piper
walked with him as far as the hotel lobby, where she lingered, hoping for a chance to talk to Don Tucker. She'd never
met Tucker, but Aunt Judy had described him to her, and
the man standing at the front desk—late sixties, gray haired,
medium height, slim build—fit the bill.

"Don took the job at the Cloverton after he retired from
the hospital over in Bellingham, where he worked in the
pharmacy," Aunt Judy had told Piper. "His wife had died,
and their daughter had moved away. I think Don needed to
get out of the house more than he needed the money. He
was the chief pharmacist, so I'm sure he was pretty well-set,
financially.

The couple who'd been checking out finally left, leaving
Tucker alone, so Piper went over.

"Mr. Tucker?"

"Yes? Can I help you?" Tucker looked up from the papers he'd been examining with a smiling, well-lined face. His navy blue hotel blazer framed an impeccable white shirt and perfectly knotted striped tie.

Piper introduced herself and mentioned Emma Leahy. "She may already have talked to you about—"

"About Mrs. Conti?" When Piper nodded, he said, "Emma was here this morning. And Phil Laseter came a little later. I seem to have become a *source*." He smiled when he said it, leading Piper to believe he didn't much mind, which was good news, since Piper hoped to pump him a bit more.

"I got the impression that his wife's arrival was a surprise to Conti," Piper said. "Is that right?"

"All I can say is that Mr. Conti's room was booked in his name only, not for the two of them. Since she arrived two days after he did, though, that wasn't too unusual."

"Would you say he was pleased to see her?"

"Well, from my vantage point, all appearances pointed to that," Tucker said. "But then, you see, her arrival was a rather public situation." He lowered his voice and leaned toward Piper.

"I happened to see them at a much quieter time. It was before the Saturday evening match. They walked in together, possibly from an early dinner together, and headed over to the elevator. The expressions on both faces were extremely stiff. They looked like they'd been arguing but had clammed up while others were around. When the elevator doors opened, she stalked in but he hesitated, as though he'd rather not have to join her, but he finally did. As the elevator doors closed, they were standing about as far apart as they could get."

"Mmm. No love lost there, apparently."

Tucker shook his head. "And she's such a beautiful woman. You asked if she'd surprised him by her arrival, and my guess would be she did. Before then, Conti was having a grand old time flirting with every woman in sight. A real Casanova, that man was. But his wife? She didn't strike me as the long-suffering type. I don't know how long they were married, but if he were still alive I doubt they would have stayed together much longer."

The desk phone rang, and Tucker reached for it, leaving Piper to think about what he'd just implied—that the Contis' marriage was unlikely to last. Conti himself, of course, didn't last more than a few additional hours that day. Could that have had anything to do with his wife? Tucker said she wasn't the long-suffering type, and Piper, from their brief meeting, would agree. Was Francesca, though, also the impatient type, eager to end her marriage in a swifter manner than divorce?

With Tucker still occupied, Piper wandered over to the restaurant entrance. From there she could see Coach Tortorelli and Francesca Conti sitting at their table. Francesca pulled out a cigarette and was preparing to light it when a waitress scurried up, probably to inform her that she couldn't do that. Words were exchanged, and though Piper was too far away to catch them, the angry tone and gestures told her enough—that Francesca Conti did not like to be crossed.

Piper hurried back to the pickling shop, even though Amy had urged her to take her time. She thoroughly trusted Amy's ability to handle things, but as far as her little shop was concerned she still felt like a mom with a new baby:

uneasy when she was away too long and certain that it was safest only in her own care. Besides, with the Conti situation still agitating the town, Piper hated to think of poor Amy having to deal with the influx of "news spreaders" that had been so active the day before.

She was relieved, therefore, to walk in and find things quiet, with only Nate keeping Amy company as she polished the glass front of a display case.

"Hi," Piper greeted them. "Everything under control?"

Amy set down her spray bottle. "Fine! No problems. Although," she admitted, "it did get a little busy at one point. But luckily Nate came by around then, and he gave me a hand."

"I've spent so much time here that I know where most everything is," Nate said, grinning.

Piper laughed. "Maybe we should make it official and I'll add you to the payroll."

"Uh-uh. Pickling's not my thing. Music is."

They chatted awhile about Nate's progress on the music demo he was working on, Amy looking proudly on until she suddenly glanced at the clock. "Time to get going," she said. "A La Carte awaits." She was pulling off her apron when the shop door opened, and two people walked in.

"Miranda!" Amy cried.

Piper didn't actually know the young man with Miranda, never having seen him close-up, but she wasn't at all surprised when Amy added, "Frederico. Good to see you!"

The handsome, dark-haired, athletic young man, now dressed in jeans and a tee instead of his Bianconeri uniform, smiled broadly at Amy. "Ciao, Amy!" He spotted Nate and greeted him as well.

"Frederico," Miranda said, "this is Piper Lamb, who I was telling you about."

"*Buongiorno*, Signorina Lamb." He took her hand and pumped it enthusiastically.

"Just Piper, please," Piper said, thinking she liked this very friendly soccer player with a decidedly open face, at least on first impressions. She reclaimed her hand after a moment or two. "I'm very glad to meet you, Frederico."

"Miranda, we have to take off," Amy called. "See you later!" She grabbed her purse and Nate's hand and headed for the door.

Miranda waved, then turned back to Piper. "I was telling Frederico how you've volunteered to help my dad out, and he was eager to meet you."

Not exactly "volunteered," Piper thought, though she wasn't regretting it—yet.

"Yes," Frederico said. "I tell Miranda, this must be a *fantastica* woman who goes to such trouble for her friends."

Indeed, Piper found her appreciation of the man increasing by the minute, though she insisted, "I'm not the only one who wants to help. And what I can actually accomplish might be very limited. I did, by the way, have a brief chat with Signora Conti and your coach, Signore Tortorelli, just a little while ago."

"See?" Miranda said, turning to Frederico, as though to say, *Didn't I say she'd take care of everything?*

"*Very* brief," Piper emphasized. "But it told me a few things. What is your impression of Signora Conti, Frederico? Other than that she's beautiful, of course."

Frederico nodded. "*Sì, sì*, she is *bella donna*!" He turned to Miranda. "But you are *bella ragazza*, a beautiful girl. Signora Conti, though," he paused, frowning, "she is not always the *bella persona*."

"Not a nice person?" Piper asked. "How so?"

Frederico shifted his weight uncomfortably. "I don't like to say. Is not very, um, *diplomatico*. Besides, with Raffaele dead, she now owns the team. Bianconeri."

"Really? Raffaele owned the team? I thought he was simply the manager."

"No, no, he owned. At least majority owned."

"And he ran it with an iron hand," Miranda said, "Didn't he?"

"*Sì*, he did. He was not a very, how you say, popular man."

"I've been getting that impression."

"Tell her about your awful contract," Miranda urged. When Frederico hesitated she jumped in. "It's terrible. It tied Freddy up for years! He thought he was signing on for only a year, but there are clauses that give Conti the right to keep him with Bianconeri as long as he likes. Freddy has had much better offers once everyone saw how good he is, but he couldn't accept any of them because of his horrible contract. Isn't that right, Freddy?"

Frederico looked uncomfortable, but he nodded. Miranda had volunteered that information to illustrate how despicable Raffaele Conti was, which it did. But she had also just presented an excellent motive for her Italian boyfriend to get rid of Conti. Piper was sure Miranda didn't realize that, but judging from Frederico's apparent uneasiness, he might.

But could a young man with such a friendly, open air be capable of murder? Piper wondered. Some weeks ago, she might have said no. But her belief that nice people didn't do bad things had since been thoroughly shaken. She was sorry to do so, but she might have to add Frederico to her suspect list.

"Frederico," she said, "has the sheriff been questioning the team members since the murder?"

"*Sì, sì*, very much."

"And I suppose he asked where each of you was at the time of the murder?"

Frederico nodded. "That was easy to answer. It was late, and we're all in training. Most of us were in bed, fast asleep."

"Including you?"

"Of course."

"And," Piper said, "I suppose you all share rooms and could verify each other's whereabouts."

Frederico shook his head. "How can you do that when you were sound asleep? My roommate, for instance, Marco, he sleeps—how you say—like the rock! Nothing wakes him, not even the alarm. Sometimes I throw water in his face to get him up!"

At that, Frederico grinned, looking for all the world like he didn't know he had just put himself in a very bad spot. Piper sighed. First Gerald Standley, now this likable young Italian. She was going to have to come up with something incriminating on much more clearly despicable people, though at this point they either hadn't surfaced, or they were hiding their darker sides very well.

14

After Miranda and Frederico left, Piper sank onto a tall stool and leaned onto the counter, resting her chin in both hands. She felt as if her head had begun to spin from all the random and widely varying pieces of information concerning Raffaele Conti that had been thrown into it. As she worked to sort it out, Emma Leahy came into the shop.

· "Too much wine during your lunch at the Cloverton today?" Emma asked. She looked once again like she'd come straight from her garden, with her cropped denims dotted with old stains and an oversize shirt, though her hands and face appeared freshly scrubbed. Piper wondered if the woman actually spent that much time with her plants (and if so her garden must be the most weed-free in the county) or if she simply chose comfort over fashion at all times. If they ever attended a wedding together, Piper supposed she'd have her answer.

"I didn't have *any* wine," Piper replied, straightening up. "And how did you know about my lunch?"

"Amy told me when I stopped in earlier. I wanted to share what I learned from Don Tucker, but I assume you talked to him yourself while you were there?"

Piper nodded. "He gave me the impression that Francesca Conti's sudden appearance in Cloverdale didn't exactly light up her husband's day."

"That's what I took from it as well," Emma said. "I hung around a little, hoping she'd show up, but I never got to see her."

"I did. She's just as Scott described her—very attractive and sophisticated, plus not particularly broken up over her husband's death. I also just learned that she most likely inherits controlling ownership of Bianconeri."

"Aha! A motive!" Emma cried.

"Well, perhaps, but if so you might claim every widow who takes over her husband's business has a motive for murder. There needs to be more. How lucrative was the team's income and how much else does Francesca inherit? Would she have lost it all through a divorce, perhaps because of a prenup? Or was money not the issue at all? Maybe, if she killed him, it was in a moment of passion?"

"Yes!" Emma's face lit up. "They argued over his endless affairs, she pulled out a gun, and he ran into the dill field in a panic!"

"Whatever the motive," Piper said, "we need to know

where Francesca was around one thirty that night. Or, rather, morning."

"I'm sure Sheriff Carlyle has asked her that." Emma's mouth twisted wryly. "And she probably claimed to be fast asleep."

Like Frederico, Piper thought. And most likely 99.9 percent of Cloverdale. So far, the only person she knew of who'd admitted to being awake as well as in the murder vicinity was Gerald Standley. That status needed to change.

"Oh, Piper," Emma said, "I'm so glad you've jumped into this. With your young man—the lawyer—staying at the Cloverton where he can keep an eye on the Italians for us, we should—"

"Hold on! Scott Littleton is not my young man. And I only promised Miranda to keep my eyes and ears open . . ." As she said it, however, Piper realized she'd been doing much more than that. It was impossible not to, after talking with Gerald and Denise. Was she, though, setting herself up for major trouble such as she'd run into the last time?

"You're such a clever young woman—obviously," Emma said, indicating Piper's so-far-surviving pickling shop with a wave. "And we're *delighted* to have you working with us. Phil Laseter has been busy as well, and we've recruited Joan Tilley. We're all going to meet tonight at my place. Would you let Scott know? Come around seven."

Let Scott know? "That's not going to work for me, Emma—"

"Seven thirty, then?"

"No, the time's not the problem. It's just . . ." Piper thought a bit. How to phrase it without sounding totally insane? "I . . . I just work better alone, Emma. I've never been a committee person. Not ever." Seeing Emma's puzzled eye blinks, Piper rushed on. "But I'm so glad you and Phil and Mrs. Tilley are working together on Gerald Standley's behalf. And Scott, too! And I hope you'll keep me informed as you did today. That's great! That's really great! So, um, I'll do whatever I can, and you three, no, four, can do what you do and we'll all just keep in touch with each other. Okay? How does that sound?"

"Well," Emma said, "I guess that would work. You're sure—?"

"I'm sure." Piper nodded vigorously. "Really sure. That will be perfect."

At that point, Piper spotted a far-too-familiar figure heading toward Piper's Picklings, and she pointed out the window. "There's Scott now. You can catch him right away and tell him about the meeting."

"Oh! How lucky!" Emma hurried out, intercepting Scott as Piper watched from the safety of her shop. She smiled as Emma turned Scott around, pointing and gesturing as she most likely gave detailed directions to her place for that night's meeting. Then something else apparently occurred to Emma that seemed to need Scott's immediate participation, and the two headed off in the other direction, Scott not exactly dragged but casting over-the-shoulder glances back toward Piper's place.

Welcome to Cloverdale, Scott, Piper mouthed silently, then smiled cheerily as she greeted her next customer.

As it neared six o'clock and things were quiet, Piper had begun to consider closing up shop, when Gil Williams walked in.

"Oh, excuse me," he said, pulling up short with mock surprise. "I must be in the wrong shop. I've obviously walked into a ladies' high-end boutique by mistake."

Piper laughed. "I didn't get a chance to change after my lunch at the Cloverton. And if my outfit is an example of high style in Cloverdale, I'm afraid the town is in major fashion trouble."

"Lunch at the Cloverton," Gil said with a soft whistle. "I hope the owners invited you to discuss adding your tasty pickles to their menu."

"I wish. But now that you mention it, that's probably something I should pursue. Later. After Gerald Standley is cleared and Conti's real murderer is behind bars. Which was my reason for dining out in the middle of a workday—with Will, I might add."

"Ah. And did you find said murderer? Perhaps lurking behind the palm fronds in the hotel lobby?"

"Wearing a T-shirt with a skull and crossbones on it and the words, 'Catch Me If You Can'? Unfortunately, no. But I did pick up a few interesting things." Piper related the details of her brief meeting with Francesca Conti as well as her talk with Don Tucker.

"Tucker's an astute man," Gil said. "All those years running the pharmacy over at the regional hospital, he'd have to be. I'd take his assessment of the tension between Francesca and Raffaele as accurate." Gil glanced at the clock. "Am I holding you up? I closed up a bit early, but you're possibly on the brink."

"No problem. I'm more than glad to chat." Piper, in fact, welcomed a visit from Gil, whose calm logic had helped her immensely on more than one occasion. "Aunt Judy told me that Don Tucker took the desk job at the Cloverton to fill his time after retiring from the hospital."

"Yes, I think he and Lois had plans to travel, but then she unexpectedly passed away. I half expected him to move closer to their only daughter after that—she's living in Baltimore, I believe—but he stayed put in Cloverdale. I'm glad he found a way to stay busy." Gil smiled. "I, on the other hand, have no plans whatsoever to retire from the work that's occupied me for most of my years—simply because it's never been work to me. Having a steady influx of books into my shop, both new and old, which bring me joy that I can in turn share with discriminating customers, is something I'm in no hurry to give up."

"I'm very glad to hear that," Piper said, meaning it.

"Which reminds me of why I stopped in." Gil slipped onto a stool next to Piper's collection of pickling cookbooks and reached for one, though Piper was sure Gil had no plans to put up any fall fruits or vegetables. "I had a customer in my shop earlier," he said. "He was looking for a copy of *The Maltese Falcon*, which is neither here nor there. But as we chatted, he happened to mention Carl Ehlers."

"Owner of Carlo's Pizzeria?"

"The very one." Gil, who'd begun flipping pages of the pickling book, paused and looked up from a recipe for pickled beets. "Seems this customer had heard Raffaele Conti's radio interview in which he'd pretty much trashed Mr. Ehlers's establishment. He said he shook his head at the time, thinking to himself that some things never change."

"What did he mean?"

"I'm afraid I don't know. He changed the subject after that, and another customer walked in, so I never had the chance to find out."

As Piper grimaced, Gil quickly added, "But, I thought you might want to ask him yourself."

"Who is it?"

"Martin McDow. He does accounting for some of the local businesses, prepares taxes, that sort of thing. His office is just a couple of blocks away from here."

"I suppose he keeps usual office hours—nine to five?" Piper said, glancing at her clock, which was closing in on six.

"Unfortunately, yes. But I happen to know that he plays the bodhran in a band, and—"

"Bodhran?" Piper cut in.

"It's a small, handheld drum, about the size of a tambourine. The band Mr. McDow performs with is an Irish group. They play mostly for their own enjoyment—and I'd imagine an accountant particularly needs some kind of outlet—but occasionally they're invited to perform at O'Hara's."

"I know O'Hara's. A bunch of us went there after the first soccer match."

"Then you'll know it draws a good crowd, particularly when a band is there. Which, coincidentally, they will be tonight. I checked O'Hara's website."

"Do you think I could manage to talk to Martin McDow if I went to O'Hara's?"

"I'd say so. Bands do take breaks. Perhaps you'd like to ask Will to accompany you?"

Piper frowned. "I think Will's going to be busy studying

whatever loan information the bank gave him today." She looked at Gil. "How about you go with me?"

Gil leaned back in surprise. "Me?"

"You're the one who encouraged me to get into all this in the first place, you know. Which I'm glad you did, but just saying." Piper grinned. "Besides that, you could introduce me to Martin McDow, which would make getting him to talk a lot easier."

"You're quite right—on both counts. Well," Gil said, "if you don't mind being seen with an old codger, the band is scheduled to play at eight. Shall I come for you a few minutes before that?"

"That would be delightful, Mr. Williams," Piper said, executing a curtsy. "I shall look forward to it."

"As will I, Miss Lamb," Gil said. He rose to take his leave, a glint of amusement in his eyes. "I can't promise a carriage. But my aging Buick should get us there safely enough."

15

At seven forty-five, Piper's front doorbell rang, and she trotted down the steps from her apartment over the shop to answer it. She'd changed from her Cloverton lunch outfit to what she decided was more O'Hara's-suitable: dark jeans topped with a cream-colored sweater. She'd added a bright silk scarf at the last minute on the off chance that she might be underdressed. As she opened the door, Piper saw that while Gil still wore his usual dark flannel slacks, he'd exchanged his bookseller's brown, elbow-patched cardigan for a green pullover.

"How appropriate," Piper said with a grin.

"I realize we're a long way from Saint Patrick's Day, but I don't get a chance to wear this very often. It was a gift from someone who thought I needed a bit more color in my life."

"It suits you," Piper said, wondering who Gil's "someone"

was but not dreaming of pressing for more information. Though she knew very little about her shop neighbor's personal life, that simply seemed the proper course of things— like never having known what her elementary school teachers did on their days off. It just felt highly inappropriate to inquire.

"Ready for an evening of intense but subtle detective work?" Gil asked, holding out his arm.

"Quite ready," Piper said as she slipped her own arm through his and stepped lightly out her door.

O'Hara's was crowded, even more so than it had been after the soccer match. As they entered, Piper could see the band setting up on the dais at one end of the room. Gil found them a small table at the opposite end, explaining, "You won't want to be too close to those amplifiers, unless you happen to have brought earplugs."

Piper, who'd attended her share of rock concerts, understood. The size of the room did not seem to justify the size of the amplifiers she saw, though in her experience it rarely did. She could only hope for Gil's sake that the crowd would soak up much of the sound.

A waitress came up to take their order. "Guinness, definitely," Piper said.

Gil agreed. "Make that two, and perhaps one of your appetizer platters?" he added, shooting an inquiring look at Piper, who thought that was a fine idea.

"You got it," the cheerful young woman said, taking off.

"Which one is Martin McDow?" Piper asked, looking toward the four men working busily at their equipment across the room, all dressed in jeans, black tees, and matching tweed caps.

"Hard to tell with most of their backs turned," Gil said. He craned his neck, peering between crowded tables. "We can eliminate the one with the long hair, and the large fellow holding a guitar. Ah! There he is. Martin's just pulled his bodhran out of its case."

Piper spotted him. McDow was testing his instrument with a small, bone-shaped beater, holding the round, hollow-backed drum up to his ear with his other hand. He was sandy haired and of medium build, with only a pair of round, wire-framed glasses hinting at his day job. In his current surroundings and getup, Piper thought he could have passed for a professional musician. Of course, the band hadn't yet begun to play.

Piper and Gil's order arrived just as one of the guitar players stepped up to the microphone and greeted the crowd. He introduced the band and its members and named their first song—something about a lass named Bridget—and after a count of "one-two-three-four" the group took off: two guitars, a whistle player, and Martin McDow, whose steady beats on the bodhran helped hold it all together. Many in the crowd were apparently regulars, and they began singing along during the chorus and clapping their hands in time to the music, something that the band's lead singer encouraged.

Piper quickly found her toes tapping and saw Gil's fingers bouncing on the table.

"They're not bad," Piper said, having to lean close to Gil's ear in order to be heard. He agreed with a smile and a nod.

Several more songs followed, some telling sad tales of

young lads dying, but more causing laughter and cheers. The musicians weren't always together, and the chords occasionally jangled off-key, but Piper couldn't fault their enthusiasm.

Finally, the band's leader, wiping sweat from his brow, announced a short break. Gil was instantly on his feet.

"I'll try to catch Martin before anyone else does."

Piper watched the bookseller slip between tables and tray-toting waiters, impressed with his agility. Years spent winding among shelves and climbing library ladders had apparently served him well. In a few moments, Gil was heading back, leading a glowing-faced Martin McDow. Gil intercepted a passing waiter, gave an order after a quick consultation with McDow, then continued on to where Piper sat waiting. Introductions were made, a third chair was scrambled up, and soon McDow was enjoying a frosty brew along with compliments on the band's performance from both Piper and Gil.

"Thanks!" he said with a grin. "I know we're not top level, but we have a lot of fun."

"Gil says you run an accounting business," Piper said. "How do you find time to fit in practice and performances?"

McDow shrugged. "It's something I *make* time for. Just as my wife, who's a nurse, makes time for her reading, which she finds relaxing." He turned to Gil. "Did you happen to locate that hardcover copy of *The Maltese Falcon* yet?"

"I'm still looking, but getting closer."

"Kate's a bit of a collector," McDow explained to Piper. "She loves Dashiell Hammett."

"She's not alone in that," Gil said. "Speaking of mysteries, you made an interesting comment at my shop this afternoon."

McDow's brow rose questioningly as he reached for his beer and took a swallow.

"We were talking about Raffaele Conti's radio interview," Gil explained. "He had dropped a few negative comments about Carlo's Pizzeria, and you said, 'Some things never change.' That piqued my curiosity. Would you mind expanding on what you meant?"

"Oh, that. All the news about Conti, lately, took me back to my high school days."

"Were you in his class?" Piper asked.

"A couple of years behind. Didn't matter, though. Everyone knew who he was." At Gil's invitation, McDow helped himself to a bacon-and-cheese-topped potato skin from a fresh appetizer platter the waitress had just plunked down. "What made me drop that comment was remembering the bullying side of Conti. Back then, people put up with it a lot more than they do today. If anyone behaved like that now toward one of my kids . . ." McDow's eyes blazed briefly at the thought. "But back then most people looked the other way and were just glad it wasn't them."

"Who was Conti bullying?" Gil asked.

McDow looked surprised, as though he thought he'd already said. "The pizzeria guy, Carl Ehlers." McDow shook his head. "Carl's changed since, of course, but in high school he was a skinny kid with a bit of a stammer. In other words, the kind who's ripe for bullying." He glanced from Gil to Piper. "You know, I never understood Conti's need to act that way. I mean, there he was, star of the soccer team with all the girls falling at his feet. You would have thought he had it all. Why would he need to put anyone down?"

Piper shook her head. "Fear?" she said, then added, "Fear that he might lose it all? Or that others might find out what a small person he really was?"

McDow nodded. "I suppose that could be it. Anyway, he'd do things to tease poor Carl all the time. Stuff like pushing him off the end of the lunch table bench and pretending it was an accident, then imitating his stammer when Carl got upset. The worst, though, was one day after school."

"What happened?" Piper asked.

"Carl had a job at Schenkel's. Remember that place?" he asked Gil, who nodded.

"It was an ice cream and burgers joint," he told Piper, "back before some of the chains moved in. A lot of the kids used to hang out there. Carl got a job bussing tables. I think he really needed that job, too. His folks weren't so well-off. Anyway, I was there with a couple of friends, and Raffaele Conti walked in with his usual entourage, kids who hung on his every word and laughed at every joke. No soccer teammates, though.

"Anyway, they grabbed a big table and made a lot of noise, making sure everyone in the place knew they were there. Since they also ordered plenty of food, management didn't bother them about toning it down. Then Conti spotted Carl clearing tables and started giving him a hard time. I remember feeling embarrassed for Carl but at the same time pretty helpless. Looking back, I wish I'd stood up for him, but at fifteen I didn't have the courage.

"Carl tried to ignore Conti and just do his job, but he

couldn't stay out of reach forever. At one point he had to clear a table that was right next to Conti's crowd. When he was carrying his loaded tray past them, Carl suddenly took a spill. Dirty dishes went flying all over the place, half-eaten food and leftover sodas making a big mess as well as dishes breaking. Nobody could say for sure, but the likelihood was he was tripped by either Conti or one of his lackeys.

"Poor Carl just lay there for a minute, the whole place shocked into silence. Then, when he pulled himself up, I saw his fists were balled. Apparently he'd had enough. Carl lit into Conti with both hands, pummeling away and yelling. Conti, of course, didn't just sit there and take it but was on his feet in a flash, as were most of his goons. Tables were overturned and people ran out screaming as three or four of them jumped on Carl."

"That's terrible," Piper said.

"What was worse," McDow continued, "was Carl got fired. All the manager saw was Carl lighting into Conti—a good customer—not any of what brought it on. Though I'm not sure that would have made a difference," he added, grimacing.

"Poor Carl. Was he badly hurt?" Piper asked.

"Black eyes and bruises, as far as I remember. Probably not as bad as—" McDow turned as one of his band members tapped him on the shoulder.

"Drink up, Marty," the musician said. "Break time's over."

McDow reached for his beer and quickly downed it. "Gotta go," he said, adding with a grin, "My fans await." He pushed back his chair, thanking Gil for the beer.

As they watched him head back to the band, Piper finished

McDow's interrupted sentence. "Carl's bruises were probably not as bad as the emotional scars he must have been left with."

"The list of people who may have had reason to knock off Raffaele Conti is growing," Gil said.

After listening to a few more numbers, Piper told Gil she was ready to leave. They'd accomplished what they'd come for, and her eardrums—and most probably Gil's—were on sensory overload. They were stepping out of O'Hara's when she spotted Scott in the parking lot, closing the door of his rented red Volvo. As he turned to head their way, his eyes were cast down, and Piper knew she could probably move off unseen, if she chose. But something about Scott's manner made her wait.

When he looked up, Scott cried, "Piper!" His eyes then shifted to Gil, and his surprise increased, followed by puzzlement as he looked back and forth between the two.

"Hello, Scott," Piper said. "Have you met Gil?"

The two men shook hands as Piper added last names but no explanation of Gil's and her presence there together. She found herself mischievously enjoying Scott's perplexity, and Gil, who must have picked up on that, simply said, "The band's pretty good tonight. As is the Guinness."

"I could hear the music from the road," Scott said, after more glances between the two. "It's why I stopped. I just spent the last two hours at Emma Leahy's house."

"Ah," Piper said. "So you've joined her group?"

Scott heaved a sigh. "There didn't seem to be much choice. Plus, I was under the impression that you . . . well, never mind." He rolled his eyes. "For two hours we drank tea and ate cookies as Mrs. Tilley took notes on the very few points that came up regarding the Conti murder. Mostly, though, Phil Laseter and Don Tucker reminisced about the first cars they'd ever owned and how little they paid for them, while Emma and Mrs. Tilley debated about the best places to find a good rib roast or get hair perms. It only ended because it was getting late. Apparently all four turn in no later than nine thirty."

Piper fought a smile. "So Don Tucker was there, too? I thought he'd already shared all he'd witnessed at the Cloverton."

Scott nodded glumly. "He rehashed the details a couple of times. Before moving on to the subject of cars, that is."

"Will you be meeting again?"

Another sigh. "We've all been given missions to report back on. Mine is to establish the whereabouts of the Bianconeri team members at the time of the murder. I could tell them what the answer will be right now: sound asleep in bed."

"Well, that should save you a lot of time," Gil said. He made a show of looking at his watch. "Whoo! Almost ten! Way past *my* bedtime. Nice meeting you, Mr. Littleton."

Piper bid Scott a good night and took Gil's arm to walk off toward his car, feeling Scott's eyes on her back. Her ex-fiancé had had a tedious evening that may have turned even more disconcerting after running into her. She grinned.

After all the grief Scott had given her? He deserved it!

16

~~~~~~

"Wow, poor Mr. Ehlers," Amy said. She slit the tape on a newly arrived box of pickling spices that she'd set onto one of the shop stools. "I'd never guess in a million years that he'd ever been picked on. But then, I've only known him as the employer of some of my friends—in other words, as the in-charge person."

"Everyone went through a growing-up period," Piper said. She stood at the shelf where the new spices would be set and shifted some of the jars. "Some had it rougher than others. Those tough times affect who they came to be, for better or worse."

"I know what you mean," Amy agreed, pulling out a jar of peppercorns and checking the label. "Like, this girl I knew whose little brother was in a really bad accident? She had to drop out of drama club and all her after-school stuff to help her mom take care of him. I know it was really hard for her at the time. But she came through it with an interest in health care she never had before, and now she's in college majoring in premed!"

"Good for her. That experience could have so easily gone another way, like getting angry over how her life was messed up and maybe acting out in retaliation." Piper took the jars that Amy handed her and set them in place.

"Mr. Ehlers came out of his bad experience okay, wouldn't you say?" Amy asked. She passed over two more spice jars.

"By all appearances. But you said his restaurant was already struggling when Conti made those cruel remarks on the radio. Anyone would be furious at that alone. But Carl Ehlers also had his history with Conti, which surely ratcheted up his reaction."

"Enough to make him grab a gun and go out looking to kill Conti?"

"Well, he certainly didn't do it right away," Piper said, "if he did it at all. There was a lapse of almost a whole day between the radio interview and the murder."

Amy pulled out two more spice jars and held them out. "Time to plan? Get hold of a gun and watch for an opportunity?"

"Maybe." Piper took the next jars from her assistant but held on to them a moment, thinking. "But that doesn't sound like him, does it? Martin McDow said that the seventeen-year-old Carl lit into Conti when he'd finally had enough, doing it in front of everybody, which got him fired. He didn't wait and try to catch Conti alone and unawares."

"He's older now," Amy pointed out. "And smarter."

"True," Piper acknowledged. "At least I hope the smarter part is true, because if he's smarter than his teenage self, he will also have learned how to handle his emotions and not run off and murder Conti."

"But you're trying to prove it wasn't Mr. Standley, so it has to be *somebody* else."

"I know, I know." Piper sighed. "But I don't want it to be anyone who's been pretty decent up until now, and whose life, and that of everyone around him, would be ruined."

"I think what you really want is for it not to be a Cloverdalian," Amy said.

"You're right, I don't," Piper admitted, then said wistfully, "I *like* this town, and I like thinking that its residents, quirks and all, are good people."

"I do, too," Amy said, then grinned. "So, why don't we focus only on nonresidents? Conti's widow, for one?"

Piper smiled. "That would be less distressing, for sure. But Frederico fits into that category, too, remember."

"Frederico! But he's way too nice."

"As nice as our locals?" Piper asked.

Amy laughed. "Okay, so our murderer will be whoever it will be, and we'll just have to deal with it. But first we have to identify him or her."

"And the sooner the better, for Gerald Standley's sake," Piper said. She set the jars she'd been holding onto the shelf. "Hand me two more mustard seeds. The rest of those can stay in the back for now."

Amy pulled out the two jars for Piper, then folded up the box lids. As she was hefting the box up, Erin Healy entered the shop. "Hey, Erin!" Amy greeted her friend. "Off duty from the doctor's office?"

"Uh-huh," Erin said. "Half day on Wednesdays." She plopped herself down on a nearby stool, looking dejected. "You know I love my job, normally. Dr. Dickerson's a great boss. But lately I can hardly wait to leave."

"Why? What's wrong?" Amy asked. She set her spice carton on the counter next to Erin. "Lots of sick people, coughing and hacking?"

Erin shook her head. "No more than usual. It's the chatter going on in the waiting room that I hear. It's all about the murder, and most everyone is convinced that the police believe Mr. Standley did it and that it's just a matter of time before he's charged."

"Uh-oh."

"And I have to pretend I'm not hearing any of it while I'm setting up new appointments or hanging on the phone waiting for test results. I'm sure Dr. Dickerson wouldn't like me getting into arguments with his patients, anyway."

Piper couldn't imagine mild-mannered Erin getting into an argument with anybody. But she could guess at the turmoil going on inside the girl as she was forced to listen to opinions she strongly disagreed with.

"I did pick up something that might be useful," Erin said after a moment.

"Oh?" Piper and Amy said together, both instantly alert.

Erin drew a breath. "Apparently Mrs. Conti—*Signora* Conti?—and the Bianconeri coach—what is his name?"

"Tortorelli," Piper supplied.

Erin nodded, taking that in. "Well, they've been seen together a lot."

"That seems normal," Amy said. "Doesn't it? After all, who else does she know here besides the coach and team?"

"Yes," Erin agreed, "but the implication was that they seemed to be on much closer terms than you'd expect." Erin shrugged, looking distressed. "I don't know. I'm just passing it on. And I wouldn't do that if I weren't so worried for Mr. Standley and his family."

Piper reached out to squeeze her arm. "We know you wouldn't. But this could be very helpful, if it's true. Did you catch *where* they've been seen?"

Erin nodded. "Walking through Sullivan Park, for one. Then at that Mexican restaurant over in Bellingham. The suggestion was that they went out of town to avoid being seen together so much."

"The Mariachi?" Amy asked. When Erin nodded she added, "Caitlyn Weber waits tables there."

"That's right, she does," Erin agreed.

"We should check with her. Maybe she's seen them or even waited on them."

"It can't hurt," Piper said. "Though the odds of that surely can't be great."

"One way to find out." Amy had her cell phone out in a flash and began pulling up Caitlyn's number. As Piper and Erin watched, Amy made the connection, listened for a moment, then made a face. "Voice mail." She waited another second, then said into the phone, "Hey, Caitlyn, it's Amy. Give me a call, or come on by if you're in the neighborhood.

I'm at the pickling shop right now. Thanks!" She disconnected and put her phone away. "She'll get back to me," she assured Piper. "She's a good kid."

Amy turned to Erin. "Remember her in that play? *Once Upon a Mattress*?"

"I do! She grew her hair for a year just so she'd look the part. Blond hair down to her waist!" Erin said to Piper, her brown eyes wide, having just painted a dramatic picture for Piper.

That image of Caitlyn stayed with Piper, which is why, when a young woman with intricately braided black hair walked into her shop an hour or so later, Piper made no connection whatsoever to the person they'd discussed, even when the girl asked for Amy.

"Amy's left for the day," Piper said. "You might be able to catch her at A La Carte, though she'll probably be pretty busy cooking up today's entrées."

"Darn! I knew I should have called. But her message said she was here. Course," she added with a good-natured wince, "that was at least an hour ago."

"Caitlyn Weber?" Piper ventured tentatively.

"That's me." The girl grinned, scarlet-glossed lips parting to reveal perfect white teeth.

"I guess I'm just a little surprised," Piper admitted. "I expected someone with blond hair."

Caitlyn laughed. "Oh, that was for another part. Dark hair goes much better with the peasant blouse and flowered skirt I wear at the Mariachi."

Well, the girl certainly took her work seriously, Piper thought, though she hadn't gone as far as covering her blue eyes with brown contacts—yet. Piper also wasn't sure how authentically Mexican the theater masks tattoo was that she'd spotted peeking out below Caitlyn's orange crop pants.

"Amy wanted to talk to you because of your job at the Mariachi," Piper said. "We hoped you might be able to help us out. Would you mind if I asked you a couple of questions?"

"Not at all. Shoot!" Caitlyn swung her large shoulder bag onto Piper's counter with a clunk and climbed onto the stool. "Somebody looking for a job there?"

"Not exactly." Piper explained about the murder situation.

"Oh yeah, I heard about that soccer guy getting shot. Weird, huh?"

"It is weird," Piper agreed. "Especially since nobody can say yet who shot him, and the one person I'm convinced is innocent is having fingers pointed at him. We just learned that the victim's widow has been showing up at the Mariachi with a man. Perhaps you've seen them? She's very attractive, dark haired, and they're most likely conversing in Italian."

"Oh, those two! Yeah, I know who you mean. Wow, I didn't know she was the murdered guy's widow! Or any guy's widow, for that matter. At least not so recent."

"Why do you say that?"

"Well, her and the man she's with? There's sparks flying. I mean, they got the hots for each other, no joke."

Piper hadn't picked up any hint of that at the Cloverton. "Have you seen them there a lot?"

"Last night and the night before—Monday and Tuesday.

And they like to sit in the back where it's real cozy." Caitlyn wiggled her eyebrows knowingly. "I'll bet a week's tips they show up tonight, too. If you want, I could save the table nearby for you. You could see for yourself."

Piper didn't jump at the idea of such a voyeuristic venture, but it occurred to her that confirming Caitlyn's possibly overly dramatic interpretation of the two might be a good idea. Taking along someone who understood Italian was an even better idea. Could she scramble one up? There must be *someone* around.

"Yes, save me the table," she said. "When are they likely to be there?"

"The last two nights, Romeo and Juliet—that's what I called them to myself, though they're a bit old for that—walked in at eight."

"Okay, eight it is!"

"See you then." Caitlyn grabbed her bag and swung her legs off the stool. As she headed toward the door, her large bag bumping into endcap displays of funnels, tongs, and canning jars along the way, Piper raced through a mental list of everyone she knew, searching for someone, *anyone*, who knew Italian. Then her eyes lit up.

Of course!

17

"**B**ut Coach Tortorelli would recognize me!" Miranda protested when Piper phoned and laid out her idea.

"How much and for how long did he actually see you?" Piper asked.

The line went silent as Miranda pondered that. "Not that much," she finally said. "And it was never one-on-one. I was with all the other cheerleaders when he was around."

"So you were one of several girls of similar age, many of them blond, and all dressed alike," Piper said. "I doubt he'd remember you from that, don't you? Did he ever run into you when you were with Frederico?"

"Oh no."

"Then I think you're safe. I, on the other hand, did speak face-to-face with Tortorelli just yesterday, but I'll figure out some way to be less recognizable."

Miranda giggled. "Dark glasses with a fake nose?"

"All out of them at the moment," Piper said, smiling. "But I'll come up with something. Are you okay with doing this, Miranda? It might make a huge difference, but it might also be a big nothing, or worse, turn into an embarrassment."

"I'm a hundred percent okay with it, Piper. If it helps my dad in any way whatsoever, it'll be worth it, whatever happens. I can't guarantee I'll pick up everything they say in Italian, though," Miranda said. "I didn't exactly get fluent in school. I've practiced a bit with Frederico, but we mostly stick to English."

"Just do what you can do," Piper said. "See you soon."

As she hung up, Piper thought about Miranda's disguise suggestion. Piper did have glasses, the emergency backups to the contacts she generally wore. Was the pair currently tucked into her end table drawer enough to significantly change her appearance? Her inclination was that they weren't. Then she thought of something and smiled. Did Aunt Judy still have that pair Piper had worn back in middle school? She'd find out.

"Uncle Frank teases me about all the odd things I hang on to," Aunt Judy said. "But isn't it lucky, now, that I do?" She held out the pair of oversize, cat's-eye-framed glasses speckled in a hideous orange and lime green that twelve-year-old Piper had thought were the coolest things ever. "I remember when you left them behind, that summer. I told your folks I'd send them on, but your mother begged me not to."

Piper grinned. "Looking at them now, I can understand why." She slipped the garish things on. "Think I'll be recognizable in them?"

"*I'd* know you with your face all bandaged up, of course," Aunt Judy said, patting Piper's hand. "But someone who met you just once?" She paused, tilting her head speculatively. "I'd say not."

"Good!" Piper said. She whipped the glasses off. "Trying them on over my contacts, though, is making me seasick."

"Are you sure what you're doing is safe?" Aunt Judy asked, a pucker of worry appearing on her brow.

"Absolutely," Piper assured her. "Miranda and I will stick together, plus we'll make sure Tortorelli and Signora Conti won't be the least bit aware of us. It's probably going to be a waste of time anyway," she added to lessen her aunt's concern. "But I want to cover all the bases."

"Well, you be careful," Aunt Judy said.

Piper promised and gave her aunt a quick kiss. Then she was off, holding at least part of her disguise and aware that, routine as she'd tried to make it sound, eavesdropping on two people who might turn out to be murderers wasn't exactly the safest thing to do. But as Miranda had stated, if it had at least a 1 percent chance of helping her father, it 100 percent needed to be done.

"I t's eight eleven," Miranda said, checking her watch. "When are they coming?" She'd slicked her blond hair back and twisted it into a French braid, a hairdo she'd never worn in Tortorelli's presence, and donned a long skirt and loose blouse, which was about as far as she could get from her short, formfitting cheerleader's outfit.

Piper had done her best as well to change her appearance. Besides the huge glasses, she'd tucked her brown hair into a velveteen beret she'd discovered under a jumble of things on a closet shelf, and topped dark slacks with a black sweater. She shrugged. "Caitlyn said they had reservations for eight. I'm sure she'll let us know if they cancel."

Miranda nodded, then started giggling. "I'm sorry. Those glasses are so awful."

"Hey!" Piper protested. "At least they pick up the green in my necklace!"

"Yes, they do," Miranda agreed, still grinning.

Piper had needed Miranda's help earlier in reading the menu, explaining, "My prescription has obviously changed since I was twelve. Go figure."

"I'm glad I drove us tonight," Miranda teased.

"All of Cloverdale and Bellingham should be grateful."

Caitlyn suddenly appeared at their table, her colorful Mariachi skirt swishing. "They're coming," she whispered, leaning in.

Piper snatched up her menu and held it in front of her face. Miranda did the same, leaving only her eyes visible as she peered beyond Piper's shoulder. "I see them."

Piper nodded, keeping her face covered until the couple passed by, trailing a cloud of Francesca's spicy perfume.

Piper and Miranda's table, angled as it was to Francesca and Tortorelli's banquette-style table, gave them a side view of the couple once they'd slid into their seats, and Miranda had taken the closer chair to better pick up conversation. A scattering of nearby tables were filled as well, so that Piper felt they weren't too noticeable.

"She's gorgeous," Miranda leaned forward to say.

Piper, who'd sneaked a peek as the two settled in, saw that Francesca had donned a black dress that evening, perhaps in an effort to appear more widowlike as she left the hotel. With its extremely low-cut neckline and snug fit that followed Francesca's generous curves, that dress was highly unlikely to have shown up at any funeral. She'd added a turquoise necklace and bracelet, while large hoop earrings peeked out through her long, dark hair. Tortorelli wore a tweedy sports jacket over an open-necked shirt and dark pants and looked more than pleased to be with his beautiful companion.

Caitlyn filled the couple's water glasses and recited the day's specials, which gave Piper another opportunity to check out the two as they focused on their waitress.

"Can you hear okay?" Piper asked in a low voice, leaning toward Miranda.

"I can hear Caitlyn just fine," Miranda answered just as quietly. "But then her voice carries to the back rows of the Cloverdale Playhouse without any problem." She lifted her palm when Tortorelli spoke, and listened. "The coach just asked for two margaritas. In English."

"And you heard it," Piper said. "Good."

Another server brought Piper's and Miranda's food, something Piper barely remembered ordering but which had plenty of lettuce and guacamole and beans. She poked at it with her fork, her focus remaining on the neighboring table. Caitlyn had whisked off to the bar with the drinks order, and Francesca and Tortorelli began conversing in Italian. Piper looked to Miranda, who was leaning back in her chair.

"Something about the weather, I think," Miranda said. "Yes, *la pioggia*. That means rain. They're worried it might rain tomorrow."

"Why?" Piper asked. "What do they want to do?"

Miranda listened. "She wants to go shopping. But she doesn't want to get wet. He said he'll get an umbrella."

"Wow, this is great," Piper said dryly. She found a chicken chunk amid her lettuce. "With luck, we'll get the next day's forecast, too."

Caitlyn delivered drinks to the couple and on her way back stopped at Piper and Miranda's table. "Everything okay here?" she asked brightly.

"Delicious," Miranda said, "but boring." She rolled her eyes in the direction of Francesca's table.

"Just wait," Caitlyn said, lowering her voice. "I told Jason to give their drinks some extra zip."

"Not enough to put them to sleep, I hope. They're putting me to sleep, already."

Caitlyn winked and moved on.

Francesca spoke, and Miranda translated the string of words, which were generally unflattering comments on the town. "She wants to go to Syracuse or Rochester for her shopping. He said something about *la polizia*, the police."

Piper perked up. "What about the police?"

Miranda shook her head. "I couldn't catch all of it, but I

think it was something about the police wanting them to stay, or it looks better to the police if they stay in town."

"Hmmm. A bit suspicious?"

"But now she's saying she doesn't care what the *polizia* think, and he's saying . . . Darn, I didn't catch it!"

"Don't worry," Piper said. "His body language just spoke volumes." Piper had noted through casually spread fingers held to her face that Tortorelli had slipped his arm around Francesca's shoulders and leaned closer to nuzzle her cheek. "Don't look," she warned as Miranda's head started to turn.

"No fair," Miranda complained. "You have the better view."

"I'd happily switch if I could translate Italian into English." Piper had taken care to shield her face as much as possible since the couple's arrival, either with a hand, napkin, or drinking glass, but her heart still skipped a beat anytime either the coach or Francesca glanced around. The frequency of that happening, however, was lessening as the margarita glasses were drained.

Caitlyn brought the couple's food, and things quieted down at the table. Piper was pleased to see that wineglasses had replaced the empty cocktail glasses and that a bottle remained at the table for refills. Some mutterings could be heard, but Miranda reported them to be comments on the food. From what Piper could see, the pair were enjoying their dinners immensely, tasting each other's dishes and following bites with generous swallows of wine.

How did Francesca keep that fabulous figure with an appetite like that? Piper wondered. Was the choice to dine at the Mariachi because of the cuisine rather than a search for privacy? But then, as their plates began to empty—along with the wine bottle—the couple turned their attention back to each other.

Caitlyn, Piper could see, hadn't exaggerated. Arm rubs, cuddles, and the occasional discreet kiss convinced her that Francesca and Tortorelli were definitely enamored of each other. The question was, had this flared up only since Conti's death? Or had the relationship been kept under wraps for a long time?

"They've just ordered coffee and dessert," Miranda reported. "That is, he's getting coffee, and she's getting dessert. Fried ice cream."

Piper sighed. Learning the couple's food preferences might have been more useful if Conti had been poisoned, not shot. How *did* Francesca manage all those calories?

It was while consuming some of those yummy calories, however, that Francesca finally dropped something interesting. Miranda's eyes widened as she listened.

"What?" Piper urged. "What did she say?"

"Um," Miranda said, pausing to gulp, "she just said she'd been waiting a long time to be rid of Raffaele."

Piper suppressed a yelp but couldn't stop her eyes from darting toward the couple. Unfortunately, Tortorelli glanced her way at the same time, and he was scowling furiously. Piper quickly raised a napkin to her lips and turned away. Had she been too late? Was Tortorelli scowling because he'd recognized Piper? Or was he angry over what Francesca had said?

"He just told her to be quiet," Miranda reported.

Piper wished she could see Francesca's reaction, but she didn't dare look.

"He said she needed to be more careful," Miranda said, her voice fairly squeaking by then.

Francesca's dismissive laugh carried easily to their ears. Piper heard the word *"stupido."* "Is she calling him stupid?"

Miranda's eyes blinked furiously as she processed what she'd just heard. "Not him," she said at last. Miranda looked squarely at Piper. "Francesca called Sheriff Carlyle stupid."

18

Tortorelli signaled for the check, and Piper leaned over to Miranda. "Let's go."

Miranda nodded and put down her napkin, whispering, "What about the bill?"

"We'll catch Caitlyn on our way out." Piper didn't know if Tortorelli had recognized her or not, but if he had and wondered why Piper had turned up at this out-of-the-way restaurant and at the very next table, she didn't want to be around for him to inquire.

Piper and Miranda slipped away from their table as casually as possible and headed toward the front of the restaurant, grateful for the clutch of late arrivals who passed by and quickly blocked Tortorelli's line of vision. Piper hailed Caitlyn with a silent wave and pulled a few bills from her purse. That taken care of, she turned toward the exit, when a voice nearby suddenly cried, "Piper!"

Piper froze.

"Piper, what are you doing here?" It was Ben Schaeffer, Erin's boyfriend and Sheriff Carlyle's intrepid volunteer auxiliary policeman. Piper wasn't sure which of them was the more surprised, particularly as Erin wasn't the pretty young woman who was sitting beside him. Instead, she was a stranger, who seemed to be about Erin's age but with red hair instead of brown.

Ben stood, effectively halting Piper's plan to hurry out the door, and began introducing her to his table companion. As he did, Miranda whispered in her ear, "They're coming this way!"

Piper turned her back toward the path Tortorelli and Francesca would take, while still managing to face Ben.

". . . Leila will be starting work at my office tomorrow," Ben was saying as Leila smiled broadly at Piper through pink-glossed lips. "My insurance business has picked up lately. I realized I needed help."

Piper caught a whiff of spicy perfume, and she tugged at her beret as she ducked her head. Miranda sank onto an empty chair at Ben's table and covered her face with her hands. Muttered words in Italian could be heard as the couple passed by, and—to Piper's relief—continued on. She took a deep breath and smiled at Leila.

"So, are you new to Cloverdale?" she asked.

"I am! I just moved there from Pennsylvania. I can't believe my luck in finding such a great job right away." She beamed at Ben.

"Leila's still settling in," Ben said. "I thought a dinner out . . . you know . . . to welcome her to the office and all . . ."

"I just love Mexican food!" Leila said, jumping in.

So of course, Piper thought dryly, taking his new employee to a restaurant out of town, where they wouldn't run into Ben's girlfriend, made perfect sense. In his defense, Ben *had* hailed Piper and, despite his verbal stumbling, didn't seem to find the situation embarrassing.

"Well, Leila," Piper said. "I hope you enjoy Cloverdale and your new job."

As they headed to the door, Miranda muttered, "Isn't Ben seeing Erin?"

"He is. And as far as I can tell this seems to be strictly him being a good boss. That's new to him, you know, being a boss. He's learning the ropes."

"Hmmph."

They headed for Miranda's car, Piper musing that it was interesting that Leila, with her red hair, had a strong resemblance to Amy, who had once been a major infatuation of Ben's. Was that only a coincidence? Piper certainly hoped so, for Erin's sake.

As they buckled into Miranda's car, Miranda asked, "Well, I think Francesca Conti has incriminated herself, don't you?"

Piper shook her head. "It sounded that way at first, but she hasn't actually gone that far."

"But she said she was glad she got rid of her husband!"

"What you translated to me was that she'd been waiting a long time to be rid of him, right? It's not quite the same thing."

"But it *could* be."

"Agreed. I think they both came off as suspicious, particularly with their obviously amorous relationship. But I don't think we have enough to take to the sheriff yet, who, despite what Francesca thinks, is very intelligent."

Miranda frowned. "That remark alone tells me she's guilty. She thinks she's getting away with something."

"Maybe she is. But is it murder, or is it simply Raffaele Conti's money, which she now gets free and clear without the trouble of a divorce?"

As Miranda mulled that over, Piper's mind ran down the list of others who might have wanted Conti dead. That included Frederico, unfortunately, which Miranda would not be pleased to hear. The fact remained that Frederico, by his own admission, had a good reason to want Conti dead. Conti had tricked him into signing a contract that tied him to Bianconeri much longer than he'd realized and kept him from accepting offers from much better teams. For a young man at the peak of his athletic ability, that must have been extremely frustrating. Piper didn't know if Conti's death changed Frederico's contract or not. Maybe with Conti out of the picture there were higher hopes of a negotiation? Or maybe his motive would simply be anger over Conti's deviousness?

It was hard to imagine anything murderous in the likable soccer player Piper had met and who Miranda clearly had feelings for. But neither of them knew him well. Frederico had motive, and if he'd been able to slip out of his hotel room unnoticed he also had opportunity. But what about the weapon? There was no way Frederico would have been able to bring a gun with him when the team flew into the country. Buying a gun once he'd arrived would be just as difficult. Yet Conti had been shot.

"Miranda," Piper said, having had a sudden disturbing thought she hoped the girl would be able to banish. "Frederico never visited your folks' farm, did he?"

"The farm?" Miranda glanced over at Piper, then looked quickly back at the road. "Why do you ask?"

That hint of evasiveness gave Piper a sinking feeling but she continued on. "I just wondered. I thought I remembered Frederico saying something about the beautiful farm . . ." He hadn't, but hopefully Miranda wouldn't catch that. "But I know your dad wasn't too happy about your seeing each other."

"That's putting it mildly," Miranda said. "Dad raised the roof when he first heard I was spending time with Frederico. But this was when he was simmering over Raffaele Conti showing up with the team. Who knew there was some kind of history between them?"

Miranda glanced into her rearview mirror. "That's weird."

"What?"

"Oh, nothing. I thought that car behind us wanted to pass, the way it came up so fast. But now it's just keeping pace."

Piper turned to look back but saw only bright headlights. "It doesn't look like a police car. You're not over the speed limit, are you?"

Miranda glanced at her speedometer. "Uh-uh. Well, anyway, there was no way to convince Dad that Frederico was not a bad person just because he was associated with Dad's old nemesis, and not by choice, I'll remind you! But Frederico really wanted to see the farm. He grew up on one, did you know that?"

Piper shook her head, not pointing out that there wasn't much she did know about Frederico.

"His folks have one in Tuscany, but not for growing crops. They raise sheep for cheese. Pecorino cheese. It's a pretty famous type made from ewe's milk. Have you ever had any?"

Piper admitted she had but didn't want to get sidetracked onto a discussion of Italian cheeses. "So you took Frederico to see your farm?"

Miranda nodded. "When Dad was out and Frederico had a couple of free hours from the team. Mom said it was okay. She didn't much like keeping it from Dad, but she wanted to meet Frederico."

"I see. What did Frederico think of the farm?"

"Oh, he thought it was great! He loved the dill field, of course. And he was very impressed with Dad's barn."

"He was? Why?"

"It's huge compared to what they have in Tuscany. Dad did a lot of work on it himself, too, and that impressed Frederico. I think the two of them would really get along if Dad would only give Freddy half a chance."

"I guess Frederico checked out the barn pretty thoroughly, huh? If he was so impressed with it, I mean."

"He really did! He climbed up to the loft and examined just about every inch. It's pretty dusty up there, though, and when he came down he was sneezing and coughing."

"I suppose you got him something to drink."

"Right. I ran into the house to get a couple of glasses of Mom's lemonade."

"Did Freddy come with you?"

"Hmm?" Miranda's attention had shifted to negotiating a sharp curve. When she'd done so, she gave the answer that Piper half expected but was hoping not to hear. "No, Freddy stayed in the barn."

Though Piper made no further comment, she groaned inwardly. Gerald Standley's missing gun had been stored somewhere in the barn. It was conceivable that Frederico had stumbled on it and contrived a coughing fit in order to secretly move it elsewhere. Possibly to a backpack left in Miranda's car?

Miranda brought the discussion back to Francesca and Tortorelli, rehashing all she'd overheard them say at the restaurant. Piper listened with half an ear, worrying over what she'd just learned. What Miranda had stated about the visit was, of course, fact. It was the rest that was simply conjecture at this point. So what was Piper going to do with it?

"Someone else from Cloverdale must have been at the Mariachi tonight," Miranda said. "I mean, someone besides us and Ben Schaeffer."

"Hmm?"

"That car behind us." Miranda was looking in her rearview mirror. "It's the same one I noticed from way back. I wonder who it is."

Piper looked back, and, as Miranda pulled into town, where streetlights shed more light, she could see a bit more of the car, though only that it was dark colored and a late-model sedan.

Piper looked again, but the dark car had dropped back. When Miranda drove through a stoplight that was turning yellow, Piper saw the car behind them slow, then stop as the light turned red. "Guess we'll never know."

As they drew close to the pickling shop, she thanked Miranda for acting as translator as well as providing the transportation. When Piper tried to chip in for the gas, though, Miranda wouldn't hear of it. "You're doing all this on behalf of my dad, which I really, really appreciate."

Would Miranda appreciate it if Piper ended up getting Frederico charged for the murder? She climbed out when Miranda pulled to a stop in front of the shop, holding those thoughts to herself and keeping her tone hopeful regarding Gerald Standley.

Piper had waved good-bye and was unlocking the street door to her apartment when she noticed movement farther down in the darkened street. About half a block away, a dark car moved forward slowly. Piper paused, watching as it gradually passed by. When it drove under the streetlight, Piper could see it was a black sedan, but exactly what make or model she couldn't say. Nor could Piper see who was driving or if there were any passengers—since all the windows were tinted.

19

Piper struggled with sleep that night as events of the previous evening looped through her brain. Visions of Francesca and Tortorelli, highly pleased with Raffaele Conti's demise as well as each other, mixed with images of Frederico discovering Gerald Standley's gun in its long-forgotten hiding place. That last came from Piper's imagination only, but during dead-of-the-night darkness, conjecture became disturbingly real and only increased her wakefulness as she worked to reason it away.

By the time she opened up shop the next morning, Piper felt in desperate need of refreshment, both physically and mentally. Fortunately, that existed in her workroom in the form of a pot of strong coffee and a bushel of green tomatoes. Uncle Frank had loaded the tomatoes into her hatchback when she'd collected her old pair of glasses from Aunt Judy. Green tomato relish was the plan, to add to the jars she'd put up a few days ago, and after a bracing mug of coffee she got started on it.

Chopping at tomatoes, sweet peppers, and onions worked its magic, and by the time Piper loaded batches into her food processor she was relaxed and humming. The tune she hummed to the rhythm of the processor's pulsing—"I Am the Very Model of a Modern Major-General"—reminded her of the time Will had caught her in midsong on his very first visit to the pickling shop, an embarrassment that had moved Piper to attach a warning bell to her shop door.

At that moment, something did jingle, but it wasn't the doorbell. Piper stopped working and picked up her phone.

"Piper's Picklings!"

"Good morning," Will said, and Piper burst into a laugh.

"Do you have ESP? I was just thinking of you!"

"That's good," Will said. "If they were positive thoughts, that is."

"Nothing but. How's the loan application coming?"

"It's a bear. That's what's kept me holed up and incommunicado the last two days. I'm sorry about that."

"Oh, that's okay. I managed to keep myself busy. Had a lovely dinner with a friend last night in Bellingham, for one thing," she said, teasing.

"Oh?"

Piper heard the concern and relented. "The friend was Miranda Standley. We were working undercover, eavesdropping on Francesca Conti and Coach Tortorelli as they dined at the Mariachi."

"Ah!" Will said, the uneasiness gone for a moment before quickly resurfacing. "Wasn't that risky?"

"Not at all," Piper said, choosing not to mention Tortorelli's angry glare in her direction when he may or may not have recognized her, or the car with its tinted windows that may or may not have been following them. She did share Francesca's suspicious comments as well as news of the couple's obviously passionate relationship.

"Sounds like they both had a reason to bump Conti off."

"It does, but so did a few other people." Piper told Will about her theory that Frederico could have found Gerald Standley's gun.

"That's certainly possible. Proving it is another thing."

"I know. If only they would find the murder weapon, *wherever* it originated from, ideally with the murderer's fingerprints on it."

"Wishful thinking," Will said. "My guess is it's sitting at the bottom of some lake. Have you thought about how Frederico would have made it to the dill field to shoot Conti, assuming he did? He doesn't have access to a car, does he?"

"I did think about that, during my mostly sleepless night last night. The best I came up with is that perhaps he was with Conti when Conti's tire went flat."

"Why would he be with him? Do you know where Conti had been that night?"

"I don't. And I don't know if the sheriff knows. Maybe I can find out." Piper's first thought was to check with Erin, who had heard the helpful information about Francesca at the doctor's office and who sometimes picked up police-related things from Ben, unofficial auxiliary police person though he was. That, however, reminded her of running into Ben with his new office assistant, Leila. Pretty, Amy-like

Leila. Would Leila affect Erin and Ben's relationship? She'd already taken up an evening that Ben might otherwise have spent with Erin.

Piper's shop door jingled. "Gotta go," she told Will. "I have a customer."

"Okay. I'll check with you later."

Piper headed out to the front of her shop, expecting to come upon one of her usual pickling ladies. Instead, a gray-haired, sixty-something man stood there, glancing around with interest. Dressed in denims and a windbreaker instead of the Cloverton navy blue blazer, Piper at first didn't place him. But when he turned toward her and the lines of his face crinkled in a smile, recognition dawned. "Mr. Tucker! How nice to see you. A day off from the hotel?"

"Oh, I work all sorts of odd hours," Tucker said. "I like the variety. Much better than spending every night alone in front of the television or every morning trekking to the diner for breakfast."

Piper remembered that Tucker's retirement, on top of being recently widowed, had left him with time weighing heavily on his hands. She gave him credit for finding a solution and one that added to his income. "Don't tell me you're thinking of adding pickling and preserving to your activities."

He chortled, shaking his head. "Lois handled all the kitchen chores, which is why I now get most of my meals out. Working at the hotel makes that mighty convenient. No, I stopped by because Emma mentioned you were working on Gerald Standley's behalf and that she'd hoped you would join up with our team. I wanted to add my vote to that. It could make a difference as far as Gerald Standley is concerned if we all put our heads together. We're pretty much a group of old fogies just muddling around, so it'd be a great addition to have a young person such as you to give a fresh take on things. We do have that new fellow, the lawyer, but so far he's the only one of us under sixty. I expect he'd be more than glad to have you in the group."

Piper was sure he would but shook her head firmly. "I'm afraid I can't." When Tucker pursed his lips, she added, "But that doesn't mean we can't still combine efforts."

"We should do that," Tucker agreed. "Even then I fear we have a big job ahead of us. Because of when and where it happened, there's no chance of witnesses unless you count a stray groundhog or two. And I'm guessing there wasn't much evidence found at the crime scene, either, things like footprints and such, or we'd be hearing about more people being pulled in for questioning, wouldn't you say?"

Piper nodded. "We haven't had rain in over two weeks, so the ground was surely too dry for footprints. Nothing helpful like the murder weapon or anything else has been found as far as I'm aware."

"Exactly. So without witnesses or physical evidence, does someone get away with murder? That would be terrible."

"It would. Plus it might leave Gerald Standley's reputation in lasting doubt if the case is never closed."

"I'd hate to see that," Tucker said, and Piper could see the sincerity in his face. She was glad that Miranda's father had another supporter and another person to brainstorm on his behalf.

"Mr. Tucker, I've been trying to get a better picture of the time leading up to the murder. I've never heard where

Raffaele Conti had been that night, before he was driving back so late. Did you hear anything about that, perhaps while working at the hotel desk?"

"No, nothing, though I can guess."

"Oh?"

"As I've said before, the man was a regular Casanova. I'll bet my last dollar he was with one of the women who were hanging around him—someone who never got over her teenage crush on him but who's married now and doesn't want to come forward and admit what she was doing."

Piper could see that was a possibility. "Do you know their names?"

"I do. I knew them as school friends of my daughter, Robin, though if I'd known at the time how silly they were I might have had a word or two with her about them."

"Would you write the names down for me?" she asked, grabbing a pen and paper. As Tucker worked on that, Piper thought that his theory of Conti's whereabouts that night was useful as far as Frederico was concerned, since it could let him off the hook. Frederico certainly wouldn't have gone along for the ride that night if Conti were heading to a tryst. If he had no other way of getting to the dill field then his alibi for the night was good. Did Frederico have another means of transportation, though?

When Tucker handed her his list of names, Piper asked, "Do you happen to know if there were cars available for the Bianconeri team members to use?"

"The players, you mean?" He shook his head. "The coach and Conti had their rental cars. That's all. The players traveled to the games on the bus. The hotel is in the center of town, so during their off time they could walk to just about any-where they wanted."

"But not get out to Gerald Standley's dill field, which is several miles out of town."

"Right. That would be difficult. Unless one of them bor-rowed the coach's car."

"Oh! Did that ever happen?"

"Seems to me it did." Tucker rubbed his chin. "I remem-ber seeing the coach handing his keys to one of the young fellows and asking him to run some kind of errand."

"Which player?"

Tucker looked at Piper sadly. "They all look the same to me. Young, fit, most of them dark haired. Ah! But I do remember the coach telling this young man to just leave the keys in the usual place."

"The usual place? Where would that be?"

Tucker shrugged. "Darned if I know. But I got the impres-sion it was a well-known, fairly accessible place. Like, any of them could help themselves to his keys if they had a mind to."

Well, that put Frederico firmly back in the suspect col-umn, Piper thought regretfully. But as Don Tucker had pointed out, there was a scarcity of real evidence to either convict or clear anyone on that list so far.

Piper was starting to feel as though the trail she was fol-lowing were made of cucumber vines that forever branched off but were producing nothing. Was she missing a crucial signpost that pointed in the right direction? She must be. She'd have to look harder—and quickly, before signs faded and those vines withered away into dust.

20

Don Tucker had been gone from the shop only a minute or so when Aunt Judy walked in. "I got your text last night that you were safely home from the Mariachi, but I just felt like checking in on you anyway. I know I'm being silly, but—"

"Not at all. You're just acting like my stand-in mom again, something I always appreciated, especially when my mom and dad were halfway across the world and out of reach."

"It was Uncle Frank's and my privilege to step in for your folks when needed. Have you heard from them lately?"

"Got a postcard from Bulgaria where they've been managing a dig on a Thracian site. I had to look that up. Thracians were ancient Greeks. Mom's promised to do a Skype chat as soon as they get back to Sofia and find reliable Internet."

"Won't that be nice! Be sure and give them my love."

"I will. Mind continuing this in the back?" Piper asked, waving her aunt toward the workroom. "I was chopping up Uncle Frank's green tomatoes for relish when Don Tucker interrupted me."

"Can I help?" Aunt Judy asked, following Piper.

Piper shook her head. "I just have one more batch to do before I mix in the salt and let it stand for a few hours." She filled the food processor with the last of her tomatoes and peppers, then pulsed the machine several times, skipping her previous hummed accompaniment.

As Piper emptied the finely chopped vegetables into a large preserving pan with the rest of the lot, Aunt Judy asked, "What was Don Tucker doing here?" She reached for the salt and handed it to Piper.

"He's part of Emma Leahy's crime-solving team, and he'd hoped I would join them." Piper measured out the salt and stirred it into her tomatoes. "We did a little brainstorming about Raffaele Conti while Don was here, and he gave me the names of the women who'd been hanging around Conti. I'm doubly glad you stopped in. I'd like to go over the list with you."

"Certainly. But how will this help Gerald Standley?"

"I think the more information we have on where Conti had been before driving back to the hotel that night the better." She covered the preserving pan and, ignoring the cleanup for the moment, pulled the list of names out of her pocket. "Help me figure out who Conti might have been visiting who wouldn't want that fact known," she said, handing over the sheet of paper.

"Oh dear," Aunt Judy said, taking the paper somewhat reluctantly and studying it. "Well, you can cross Julia Widner off right away," she said. "I happen to know she was at her mother's all night. Poor Marjorie took a tumble off her back porch steps Saturday afternoon trying to scoop up that big old cat of hers and ended up spraining an ankle. She was lucky she didn't break anything. Anyway, when I heard about it and called to see if there was anything I could do, Marjorie said Julia had been staying with her after bringing her home from the emergency room." Aunt Judy winced. "I'm not sure how that's been going. Those two will argue about what time the sun came up that morning."

Piper smiled. "So Julia Widner is out. Anyone else?"

"Well, I don't know what Debra Babcock may or may not have been doing that night, but I do know her house is in the wrong direction. Raffaele Conti wouldn't be driving anywhere near the Standley farm if he was coming back from her place."

Aunt Judy shook her head over the next name. "Tammy Quimby can be a silly bubblehead sometimes, but her husband adores her and treats her like a queen. I think she at least has the sense not to jeopardize that. I'd say if Tammy were hanging around Raffaele Conti, it was simply because of all the excitement and publicity surrounding him. Or maybe to pretend she was sixteen again. But nothing more."

Aunt Judy grew somber as she pondered the last two names. "Wendy Prizer," she said.

"Yes?"

"Her house is the right direction beyond Gerald Standley's farm. So is Lisa Brinkman's, but Lisa has a full house with her family, which would make it highly difficult, I'd imagine, to arrange anything of this sort. Wendy, though, lives alone since she and Roger separated."

"Would you pick Wendy, then, as the most likely person on this list for Conti to have been visiting?"

Aunt Judy grimaced. "Since it's just between you and me, and because it's to help Gerald, then I'd have to say yes, there's a good chance it's Wendy."

"You said she's separated. Is her husband in the area?"

"No, and that was probably part of their problem. Roger was always away, working on oil rigs. He was in Alaska at one point for several months, which must have put a strain on their marriage. I believe he's down in Louisiana right now," Aunt Judy said. "But there's another problem." Aunt Judy's brow furrowed about as deeply as Piper had ever seen it.

"What's that?"

"Well, from what I've heard, after the separation Wendy started seeing Carl."

"Carl Ehlers?"

Aunt Judy nodded. "You know I don't spread gossip, Piper, but I can't always avoid hearing it. Apparently, Wendy and Carl had once been an item. I mean years ago." Aunt Judy sighed. "But Wendy ended up choosing Roger over Carl, which reportedly broke Carl's heart. He never married, you know. He may have been pining for Wendy all this time and felt this was his second chance."

"Until Raffaele Conti showed up and threw a wrench in the works."

Aunt Judy looked at Piper unhappily. "Possibly so."

Piper was pondering what to do with what Aunt Judy had told her, when Gil Williams came into the pickling shop, holding a small, white envelope.

"This was delivered to me by mistake," he said, handing it to Piper.

She glanced at it. "Looks like a bill. Sure you don't want to keep it?"

Gil smiled. "I have plenty of my own, but thanks."

"If you have a few minutes, I've got plenty to update you on," Piper said, slipping the envelope unopened into her "bills" drawer.

"Go right ahead," Gil said. He settled onto a stool. "I left my shop open, but I can keep an eye on it through your windows. What's been happening?"

Piper took a deep breath before launching into a description of her trip to the Mariachi with Miranda, along with her thoughts on Frederico and the missing gun. She finished up with her theory that Raffaele Conti had been returning that night from a visit to a certain woman, but kept Wendy Prizer's name to herself for the time being. "This woman," she said, "also has—or had until Conti came along—a romantic connection to Carl Ehlers."

"Hmm. So the motive for Mr. Ehlers to commit murder grows stronger."

"Theoretically, yes, but that's the problem," Piper said. "All I have so far are theories and motives, which might be all the sheriff has as well, and I'm finding that extremely frustrating." She bounced a tightly curled fist on the counter. "How will anyone be able to come up with concrete evidence, something that will clear Gerald Standley from suspicion and remove a murderer from our midst?"

Gil reached over to pat her hand. "Give it time . . ." he began, but turned his head as the bell on Piper's door jingled.

"Hey, guess what!" Scott called out as he whirled in, his face bright until he spotted Gil. "Oh!" His gaze then shifted to Gil's hand, which covered Piper's. "Er . . . hi, there," Scott said. "You're, um, ah . . ." He fumbled for a name.

"Gil Williams," Gil supplied smilingly as he swiveled to face Scott more squarely. "And you're Scott Littleton, aren't you? We met the other night outside of O'Hara's."

"Right!" Scott's eyes moved back and forth between Gil and Piper, much as they had the other night in the O'Hara's parking lot. Piper watched, amused at her ex-fiancé's misplaced consternation.

"Did you enjoy the band?" Gil asked.

"Band? Oh, that Irish group. Yes, they were fine. I didn't stay long, though." Scott cleared his throat. "I just wanted to tell you, Piper, that I've moved into my new office down the street."

Gil stood, having noticed a customer heading into his bookshop. "I'll be going," he said. "Nice to see you again, Mr. Littleton."

"Scott," Scott said automatically as Gil headed for the

door. "Oh, and if you happen to need a lawyer . . ." He pulled out a card to hand to Gil. "I just had these printed up."

Gil gave the card a quick glance before slipping it into a sweater pocket. "Let's hope any legal need that comes up will be of a routine nature," he said with a smile.

"Anything. Anything at all."

As Gil took off, Piper said, "Things have moved fast for you, Scott."

"It's going great. You have to see the new digs. Come on over."

Piper shook her head. "Sorry, I can't."

Scott glanced back at the door Gil had just closed behind himself but seemed surprisingly unable to articulate what was probably going through his head. This was a first for Scott, which made Piper struggle not to laugh. She was about to dispel Scott's off-base assumptions when Amy rushed through the door.

"Sorry I'm late," she cried, pulling off a cream-colored cardigan as she spoke, her red curls flying.

"Are you? Late, I mean." Piper glanced at the clock. She'd lost track of time but realized over two hours had flown by since she'd opened her shop. "Wow, all of ten minutes," she said. "Horrendous!"

As Amy scuttled into the back room, Scott said, "Great! There's someone here to watch the shop, so you can come see my office now. I want your opinion on which of my travel photos I should hang on the waiting room wall. We could grab a nice lunch after. Or come after closing, and we'll head out for dinner afterward."

Piper looked at Scott with disbelief. What happened to their agreement to give her space? Was the man's memory that short? Or had he simply decided to disregard it? Highly annoyed, she firmly said, "No, Scott," and quickly switched the subject. "Don Tucker stopped in earlier. He sounds as determined as Emma Leahy to track down Raffaele Conti's murderer."

Scott blinked at the sudden change of direction, but said, "Does he? I'm surprised. I got the impression all he was interested in was ancient cars. That, and Emma Leahy's homemade cookies." He puffed his cheeks and blew out. "They're having another meeting tonight. I've got to get out of it somehow."

"Oh, I wouldn't do that if I were you," Piper said, still aggravated and feeling Scott had earned a penance.

"Huh?"

"Emma, Don, Phil Laseter, and Joan Tilley are pillars of the community. You don't want to offend them just as you're establishing your law practice." Piper didn't know if any of that foursome would be described as a pillar or not, but they were certainly respected townspersons, she justified.

"But—" Scott protested.

"No, really, I wouldn't advise it." Piper heard the soft clatter of Amy cleaning up the mess from the green tomato relish project.

"Well, if you think so . . ."

"I do, Scott."

"Then I guess I'll show up," he grumbled. "Emma assigned me the task of doing an Internet search on all the Bianconeri team members and reporting on it. Huge waste of time."

"I'd get busy on it if I were you," Piper said solemnly.

Scott heaved a tremendous sigh. "Like I don't have enough to do." With drooped shoulders, he turned to leave while Piper watched, keeping a sympathetic but encouraging expression on her face.

Once he was out the door, a small grin replaced the look of sympathy, and Piper went back to lend a hand in Amy's cleanup efforts.

21

~~~~~~

"She's his new office assistant?" Amy stared openmouthed. Piper had just explained who the mystery woman was, the woman who'd been seen dining the other night with Ben at the Mariachi. The Cloverdale gossip mill had, of course, clued in Amy and brought about her worry.

"Her name's Leila Something-or-other," Piper added. "I was a bit distracted when Ben was making the introduction and didn't catch everything." Piper and Amy were tidying up the shelves at the front of the shop after a flurry of customers had swept through.

"But why did he take her out to dinner? And in Bellingham? Why not here in Cloverdale?"

Piper shrugged. "All I know is she likes Mexican food."

"Something's weird there."

Piper didn't mention Leila's resemblance to Amy, which

to Piper was the weird part. "Does Erin know about her?" she asked.

Amy shook her head. "I don't know. Everyone's waiting to see."

"Well, this may be a big nothing as far as Erin and Ben's relationship is concerned. But if not, it should probably be left for the two of them to work out alone."

"I know," Amy said, straightening a row of spice jars. "We all just care about Erin a lot. Nobody wants to see her get hurt."

"And nobody can really prevent it, *if* it's going to happen. I don't think Ben is the cheating type, do you? He's simply hired an assistant who happens to be fairly attractive. Maybe she's a real wiz on the computer." And maybe Ben had never quite gotten over his unrequited, head-over-heels crush on pretty, red-haired, oblivious Amy, which might have influenced his assessment of Leila What's-her-name's office skills. But Piper was definitely going to keep that thought to herself.

"Amy," she asked, "do you know anything about Wendy Prizer?"

"Mrs. Prizer? You mean the tai chi teacher?"

"Is that what she does?"

"Uh-huh. Over at the community center. Are you interested in taking classes?"

"I might be." Piper stepped over to her laptop, which, during shop hours, she kept near the cash register for quick access. Sometimes customers asked pickling questions that she couldn't answer but might find the solution with a few clicks on the laptop. She woke up the device and ran a search for the community center's website. When she found it, she checked the schedule of classes. Wendy Prizer, it turned out, was presently conducting a tai chi class.

"Mind watching the store on your own for a bit?" Piper asked, clicking out of the site. She untied her apron as she headed over to grab her jacket.

"Sure," Amy said, agreeable as usual but surprised at the suddenness. "Have an urgent need for exercise?"

"Yes, but for my brain cells rather than my muscles. I'll tell you more when I get back."

The community center was a one-story redbrick building framed by tall trees dressed in their autumn finery. The flower gardens flanking the front door were tidy but looked ready to hunker down for the coming winter, their few remaining blooms pale and drooping. Piper pulled into a parking spot as memories of crafting classes taken during her childhood summers with Aunt Judy and Uncle Frank flooded her mind. Thanks to at least one of those classes, Aunt Judy now had enough yarn-wrapped or photo-decorated tin can pencil holders to last her a lifetime.

Piper walked into the center and spotted a spikey-haired teen sitting at a desk and sipping from a straw stuck into a huge frosty cup as she paged through a magazine.

"Hi," Piper said as she approached. "I'm looking for Mrs. Prizer's tai chi class."

The girl glanced up and waved her drink cup vaguely behind her. "Room C. It's already started, though."

"That's okay. I was hoping to talk to Mrs. Prizer when she has a minute."

The girl glanced at the clock. "She's got another ten minutes to go. You can wait outside the room."

The teen had already returned to her magazine by the time Piper said, "Thanks." She ambled toward Room C, following the sound of soft, Asian-sounding music. The door was open, so Piper stood to the side but close enough to see in without disturbing the group. About a dozen people—mostly women—of various ages were gracefully lifting arms and shifting weight in place, most sock-footed and all intensely focused as their teacher—Wendy Prizer, she presumed—led them through various moves.

Piper found herself fascinated, never having explored the intricacies of the exotic exercise. It looked both easy and difficult at the same time since none of the positions appeared strenuous, but the chain of steps, continually flowing as they did from one to another, clearly required concentration and memory. The expressions on the faces of the students ranged from otherworldly relaxed to a squinty-eyed, pinch-lipped look that hinted at inner struggles.

The class continued for several minutes in that strain until the music came to an end and the movements stopped. Wendy Prizer praised her students for their performances, made an announcement about the upcoming schedule, then wished them all a restful day. As the group gathered belongings and began to file out of the room, Piper slipped in.

Wendy stood near a table in the corner speaking with one class member, a middle-aged woman in gray sweats and a tee. Piper hung back, waiting, then moved forward when they'd finished.

"Mrs. Prizer?"

Wendy Prizer, slim, dressed in black yoga pants and a red tank, turned with a smile. "Yes?" Close-up, Piper saw that she looked near her probable age of late forties, though it was definitely a trim and healthy-looking late forties. Her long brown hair, which held a few strands of gray, was pulled back into a ponytail, and her makeup-free face, while not cover-girl beautiful, had a friendly prettiness that made it easy to understand the attention from such men as Carl Ehlers and Raffaele Conti.

Piper introduced herself and asked, "Do you have a couple of minutes?"

Wendy glanced at her watch and nodded. "I have at least ten. That's when my next class arrives." She took a sip from a water bottle. "Were you thinking of signing up?"

"No," Piper admitted. "Though tai chi does look intriguing."

"It can improve your muscle strength, flexibility, and balance, *and*," Wendy added with a smile, "lower blood pressure."

"I have no idea if my blood pressure needs lowering," Piper said, grinning, then grew serious. "Actually, I'm looking into Raffaele Conti's murder."

"Oh!" Wendy's cheeks flushed, and she took a deep breath. "That was such a shock." She turned away slightly and took a long swallow from her water bottle.

"I'm sorry. I know you were friends."

"We knew each other in high school."

"And you reconnected when the soccer team came to town?"

"We did." She bent down to the CD player that sat on the small table and popped out a disc, replacing it with a second one. "It was like all the years since we'd last seen each other simply melted away. It was quite overwhelming."

"I imagine it must have been. I've heard Raffaele was very charming."

"'Charming' isn't strong enough to describe him," Wendy said. She pulled a chair out from the table and waved for Piper to take the other. "'Hypnotizing' would be closer."

Piper could see Wendy had fallen hard. "He was at your place the night he was murdered, wasn't he?"

Wendy had raised her water bottle for another sip but stopped midway. She nodded silently.

"And you shared this with the sheriff?"

"I did. Once I got past the shock of it all, I realized he would need to know Raffaele's whereabouts before the . . . what happened. I had hoped that information wouldn't get out, though. My students tend to be pretty conservative."

"It won't go any farther from me, I promise. But you may have heard the rumors concerning Gerald Standley. They're flying about because of the long-standing bad blood between Raffaele and him as well as the fact that Raffaele was found in Gerald's dill field—among other things. Things are pretty tense for Gerald right now."

"I realized the family had pretty much hunkered down after Gerald blocked off his driveway. But I thought it was because of all the curiosity seekers showing up. I had no idea he was considered a suspect."

"Did Raffaele say anything to you about Gerald?"

Wendy thought a moment. "He made the odd comment here and there, but mostly having to do with the soccer team. He seemed fairly impressed with the Cloverdale players themselves but thought Vince Berner and Gerald Standley were, well, not up to his standards as coaches."

That didn't surprise Piper, who figured Wendy had likely softened Conti's actual words. "Did he mention having met with Gerald or any plans to meet?"

"No, nothing. But if he did intend to meet with him, I can't imagine it would have been in the middle of the night in the dill field, can you? When Raffaele left my place, I had every impression he was heading straight back to the hotel."

"Did anyone know he would be at your place?"

Wendy shook her head. "I made sure Raffaele understood it was important to me to be discreet. I've been separated for months, and although the final papers haven't gone through, I consider myself divorced and free to do as I wish. But besides the opinions of my students, or prospective students, there were someone else's feelings to consider. Someone I'd been seeing, although briefly."

Piper didn't ask who, certain that Wendy was referring to Carl Ehlers. "So Raffaele didn't let anyone from Bianconeri know where he'd be?"

"I'm sure he didn't. When I informed Sheriff Carlyle, he seemed surprised, and he'd already questioned that group."

Wendy paused and cleared her throat. "I'm also assuming

Raffaele's wife didn't know," she said. Two red spots appeared on her cheeks. "I say that because he was just as circumspect with me." She looked straight at Piper. "When we arranged for Raffaele to come over, believe me, I had no idea he was married."

22

As students from the next class began to arrive, Piper left Wendy, then sat in her car in the community center's parking lot, thinking. A stomach growl interrupted her thoughts, reminding her it was well past her lunchtime, which also decided her on her next move. With a little luck it might produce more than take-out food to share with Amy. She put her car in gear and turned it toward Carlo's Pizzeria.

The dozen or so plain wooden tables at Carlo's were empty, and the sole person at the front counter—a stocky woman of about forty whose pinned-up, frizzy blond hair had slipped in several places from its cap—looked bored. She brightened considerably at Piper's entrance. "Hi! Takeout or eat in?"

"Takeout," Piper said and glanced at the large overhead menu. "How about a thin crust medium pizza with the works?"

"You got it." The woman, whose name tag identified her as Crystal, sent the order to the kitchen, then took the credit card Piper held out. As she handed Piper a receipt to sign, she said, "It'll be a few minutes. Most people call ahead so it's ready when they come."

Piper had particularly not called on her cell phone, hoping for the chance to chat with someone like Crystal. "That's okay. I don't mind waiting." She glanced around. "Things are quiet today."

Crystal sighed and leaned down to rest her forearms on the counter. "We were busier earlier, but it hasn't been close to what it used to be. Ever since that soccer guy went on the radio."

"Oh, the one who said Carlo's wasn't authentically Italian, um, among other things."

"Yeah. It was the other things that hurt the worst. Business dropped like a rock. It's a damned shame, 'cause there's no truth to that dumb remark. Our kitchen has always passed inspection. But what can you do? Take out ads that say, 'We don't have bugs'? We really don't, by the way," she assured Piper.

"Carl must be pretty upset, huh?"

"Upset? He turned purple when he first heard about it! I thought he was going to run out and kill the man." Crystal covered her mouth. "Oops! I forgot. That's the guy who was shot in the dill field, isn't it?"

Piper nodded.

"Well, I didn't mean *really* murder him, of course. It's just what you say when you'd like to do that but you actually wouldn't, you know? Besides, Carl got over it. By Sunday he was more his old self. I suppose he's assumed people will forget all about it, especially with the man found dead, and all."

Yes, Piper thought, a murder in the area can definitely divert public attention. It was interesting that Carl apparently calmed down after Conti's murder, though there could be more than one way to interpret that. Was Carl's reaction simply relief that an old enemy was gone? Or was it satisfaction over having finally gotten revenge?

The door opened and Don Tucker walked in, dressed in his hotel uniform of navy blazer, tie, and gray slacks.

"Afternoon, ladies. Crystal, may I have a large Coke to go?"

"Sure thing, Don."

"You must be heading to work," Piper said.

"Right. My hours change all the time, which works for me. And since it's such a nice day, I'm walking. Seeing you turn in here made me think a cold drink would be good to take along."

"Here you are." Crystal handed him the plastic-lidded cup. "Your pizza," she said to Piper, "has just two minutes to go."

"Late lunch, huh?" Don said, reaching for his wallet. "On second thought, Crystal, give me a couple of those cheese sticks." He grinned. "Just smelling what's coming from the kitchen has made me hungry."

As Don was pulling out his cash, Piper asked Crystal, "How late are you open on Saturdays?"

"We close at twelve."

"I was here last Saturday after the soccer match, and Carl

was here, too. Closing up at twelve must make for a pretty late drive home for Carl, huh? I mean, because there's usually so much for the owner to do after closing up. I find that with my own shop."

Crystal had opened her mouth to answer when Carl Ehlers walked out from the kitchen area. "Afternoon, folks! Crystal, you can take your break. I'll take over for now."

"But—" Crystal began, looking surprised, but stepped back without further comment and disappeared through an "Employees Only" door.

"These cheese sticks yours?" Carl asked Don and began to ring the order up, saying, "Great weather we've been having, eh?"

As Don agreed that it was and added a comment about the forecast, Piper wondered how long Carl had been nearby and within earshot and if her question to Crystal was what had drawn him out of the kitchen.

A young man with a white cap and apron appeared with a flat, white, delicious-smelling box. "Medium with the works?"

"That's me," Piper said, holding up her receipt. "Crystal already rang it up."

"Good, good," Carl said, nodding and smiling, though his smile struck Piper as somewhat forced. "Enjoy, and have a good day, both of you." Was he a bit eager for them to go?

"See you, Carl," Don said as he held the door for Piper. She smiled her thanks as she walked out, then turned toward where she'd left her car. Don turned the same way, which surprised Piper since the Cloverton was in the opposite direction.

"What you mentioned back there jogged my memory," he said as he walked beside her.

They'd reached Piper's car, and she paused, keys in one hand and the pizza box balanced in the other. "What was that?"

"That thing about Carl probably driving home late on Saturdays. I'd almost forgotten that there were a few nights, or early mornings, actually, when I did see Carl locking up the pizzeria about one in the morning as I'd be heading home from the hotel. Once in a while I do the late shift, though it's not my favorite."

"Did you see him last Saturday?"

"'Fraid not. Didn't work that shift then. But I'm saying it's very possible Carl could have been driving home around the time Conti would have been stopped with his flat tire near the dill field. I say that reluctantly, 'cause I've always had a good opinion of Carl. He's worked hard to get to the point of owning his own business."

"Which was hurt badly by Conti's remarks on the radio."

Don Tucker nodded. "As I said, I'm sorry to say it. But we can't exactly pick and choose our suspects, can we? Well, your pizza's getting cold, and I have a job to get to." Don bid her good day and turned to head toward the hotel.

Piper set her pizza box on the passenger seat and slid behind the wheel, the aroma of pepperoni, oregano, and onion filling the small space by the time she'd buckled up and turned her ignition key. She was eager to get back to the pickling shop, but not only because her pizza was cooling. The trail toward finding Conti's murderer, she felt, had just grown warmer.

~~~~~~

"Mr. Ehlers?" Amy asked, chewing over the possibility of the pizza restaurant owner as killer while at the same time enjoying his pizza. "I don't know. I still can't picture him doing something as violent as that. He always seemed so, so . . ." She searched for the right word.

"So harmless?" Piper offered.

"Right."

"But Martin McDow described a Carl Ehlers who'd been pushed to the limits and went ballistic."

"As a teenager."

"True. But is it a stretch to believe that the adult Carl, having been pushed once again by an old nemesis, held his reaction in check for a while but snapped when he saw an opportunity—Raffaele Conti alone on a dark, empty road?"

Amy considered that a few moments. "Maybe not. But Conti was shot. Would Carl have had a gun with him?"

"I don't know, but I wouldn't be surprised if he kept one with him for protection, particularly if he were leaving his pizzeria late at night carrying the day's receipts."

Amy nodded, then took a bite of the dill pickle Piper had added to their lunch treat. It crunched crisply, having been, of course, perfectly prepared by the two of them.

Piper's shop bell jingled and Amy jumped up. "I'll get it," she said, wiping her hands on a paper napkin. As Amy dealt with the customer, Piper continued working at her own slice of pie, thinking that Carl really did make a very good pizza, no matter what Raffaele Conti thought of it. Conti, though, may have said what he had on the radio simply from meanness, which Piper had been gradually learning seemed an ingrained part of his character. What a shame, she thought, since the man had a lot going for him—athletic talent, charm, good looks, certainly enough intelligence to handle a sports team. Why did he feel the need to regularly hurt those around him?

He'd been an outstanding soccer player during his single year at Cloverdale High, but had alienated most of his fellow teammates. He had dozens of girls falling at his feet but went after the one who was in a steady relationship with a fellow soccer player—then nearly date-raped her. He'd married a beautiful woman but continued to chase after other women, and he'd gathered a team of young athletes eager to begin a professional career but tricked at least one into signing a bad contract. Maybe the real question was how the man managed to survive as long as he had instead of who finally shot him in the dill field.

Except, Gerald Standley needed to be cleared of all suspicion. With a crowd of people besides Gerald who would have loved to see Conti dead, the difficulty was narrowing it down to only one. Had Carl Ehlers just moved up a notch on the list?

Piper's cell phone signaled the arrival of a text. She wiped her hands on her napkin and pulled the phone from her pocket, wondering if the message might be from Will. He wasn't big on texting but had occasionally resorted to it. A glance at the display erased that thought, as she saw an unfamiliar number. Thinking it must be spam, Piper nonetheless opened the message out of simple curiosity. Instead of a pitch for worry-free banking or low insurance rates, though, she found:

"Keep your nose out of other people's business or you WILL regret it."

Piper blinked, unable to believe what she'd just read. After rereading the message for perhaps the fourth time it sank in. She'd been threatened!

The number that had sent the message offered no clue to its origin. A disposable cell phone? Most likely. Whoever had sent it, however, somehow knew Piper's cell number. He or she was also aware of what she'd been doing lately. Piper glanced around uneasily, having a sudden urge to pull her shades and lock her door.

Who, she wondered, was watching her?

23

~~~~

"You should tell my dad about that text message." Amy was wrapping up the last leftover slice of pizza to put away as Piper flattened the box for recycling. She'd shown Amy the threatening text after first dialing the number from the shop phone. Not surprisingly, no one picked up.

"I don't know what Sheriff Carlyle could do about it," Piper said, "but maybe you're right. I'm sure he'll second the warning to keep my nose out of the investigation."

"Are you going to?" Amy looked at Piper with genuine concern.

"Amy, do you remember how you felt when Nate was looked at with such suspicion for a crime he didn't commit?"

"I do, and it was awful!"

"Well, that's how Miranda is feeling right now about her father, as well as Denise Standley and Gerald himself. I promised all of them I'd do what I could. I'm not going back on that because of one anonymous text. And don't worry. I think I've learned something since Nate's situation about being careful."

Amy still looked concerned but stopped her protesting.

Piper's shop phone rang, and she hesitated. Despite her assurances to Amy, the text message had shaken her a bit. Was this call going to be a second threat? She shook herself and grabbed the receiver.

"Hi!" Will's cheerful voice came through the line like a refreshing breeze.

"Hi, yourself, hermit."

Will chuckled. "I've left my hut and climbed blinkingly into the sunlight. Finished the loan application and just dropped it off at the bank."

"Congratulations! Come on by and we'll crack open a jar of pickled radishes to celebrate." Piper heard a soft cough and grinned.

"Let's hold the celebration until the loan is approved. But I'm glad to stop by. In about five seconds, as a matter of fact."

Piper looked up and saw Will's green van had pulled up to the curb outside her window. She laughed and went to the door as he climbed out of the van, pocketing his cell phone.

"I can't stay long," Will said, giving her a quick hug. "Working on that application meant neglecting things at the tree farm that I have to catch up on."

"So you don't have time for a pickled radish?" Seeing Will's face at first pucker then quickly shift into polite neutral made Piper burst out laughing. "Never mind. I do have an extra slice of Carlo's pizza, though, which I could heat up in a second if you're interested."

Will's face lit up at that. "I did skip lunch."

"I'll warm it up," Amy volunteered, already heading to the back room.

"Thanks, Amy," Piper said. "And I'll update you about what's happened since we last talked."

"Which wasn't all that long ago."

"I've been busy." Piper told him about having learned where Raffaele Conti had been before ending up dead in the dill field, leaving out Wendy Prizer's name. She then explained about the added motive for Carl Ehlers to want to exact revenge on Conti.

"Carl had just restarted his relationship with this woman after possibly years of pining after her. Then Conti blows into town and proceeds to mess up Carl's life a second time."

Amy brought out the warmed-up pizza on a plate, and Will thanked her, taking a huge bite and chewing as he mulled over what Piper had just shared.

"There's lots of conjecture there," he said after a swallow. "But if you're right, Carl is looking pretty suspicious."

"Plus," Amy said, "he leaves his pizzeria late on Saturdays and could have been at the dill field when Raffaele Conti got stranded there."

"Don Tucker dropped that bit of information after we left Carlo's," Piper explained. "We'd been chatting with Crystal until Carl came out front and took over."

"Would Carl have overheard anything you wouldn't want him to?" Will asked, his brow creasing.

Piper shrugged. "Conti's radio interview came up, but I'm sure Carl's heard that talked about ad nauseam."

"It's just"—Will shifted on his seat—"you don't want to be tipping off the wrong people that you're checking up on them."

Piper thought about Coach Tortorelli's glare in her direction at the Mariachi, plus her questions to Miranda about Frederico's visit to the Standley barn, which Miranda might have innocently passed on to the soccer player. Then there was Carl Ehlers's tight smile and hurry to send them off. Amy looked like she wanted to bring up the anonymous text, but Piper shot her a look.

"Nothing to worry about," she assured Will.

At that point, the shop door opened.

"Erin!" Amy cried. "How are you?"

Piper thought Amy's tone sounded overly anxious, but then she knew what was behind it.

"I'm fine," Erin said, looking a bit puzzled. "I just got off work from Dr. Dickerson's and thought I could walk with you when you head over to A La Carte." She glanced at the clock. "You'll be going soon, right?"

"In about five minutes. That'd be great!"

Will stood up. "I'm heading back myself and could give you both a lift."

"No," Amy said. "A walk will give us time to catch up on things, right, Erin? We haven't chatted in ages."

"I was here yesterday."

"Right! But that was different. I mean girl talk."

Piper knew exactly what Amy had in mind and hoped it

went well. She liked Erin, too, and though she didn't totally understand Erin's feelings for Ben, they were *her* feelings, and Piper didn't like to see them cause her heartache.

Will, Amy, and Erin took off for their destinations, and Piper had a quiet moment—which lasted all of thirty seconds. That was when Emma Leahy walked in.

"Don Tucker told me you're suspicious of Carl Ehlers." Emma was in her usual supercasual gardening clothes, and Piper wondered if she'd been to the Cloverton in them until Emma added, "I just got off the phone with him."

"I'm suspicious of several people. Carl's just one more on the list." Piper decided not to mention her latest information about Carl, Wendy Prizer, and Conti for the moment.

"Well, Carl's likelihood of being out and about at the time Raffaele was shot is something we should all keep in mind," Emma said, moving around the shop and picking up the occasional item as she spoke. "He had a good reason to be furious with Raffaele after that radio interview." She grabbed a spice jar to examine, then put it back. "Plus, my daughter, Joanie, reminded me that Raffaele had picked on Carl during that high school year. Kids don't forget that when they grow up."

"They don't. And it sounded much worse than being picked on. Raffaele was a real bully." Piper told Emma about the incident in Schenkel's ice cream and sandwich shop. "Carl took quite a beating, from what I was told, and also lost his bussing job."

"I didn't know about that. I'll definitely share that with the group tonight. Don won't be there, though. He's working."

"Yes, I ran into him on his way to the Cloverton. It sounded like he didn't mind the changeable hours."

"Well, he lives alone, of course. I had hoped when Lois died that Robin, his daughter, might move back to Cloverdale."

"Where is she?"

"Somewhere in Maryland. Baltimore, I think. She apparently has a very good job of some kind, so giving it up was not an option, which I can understand with my own Joanie having to move to Pittsburgh. Cloverdale is a great place to live for a lot of reasons, but it can't offer the more specialized jobs that some of our young people are looking for."

Piper's first thought was regret that Scott's field of law made it possible for him to relocate so easily. There was always the chance he would change his mind about Cloverdale, though, if his one-man firm didn't draw enough clients. She wondered how he was getting along with his research assignment for Emma's little group and felt a twinge of guilt over her little prank, though it served him right for ignoring his promise to give her space. She wondered if she should stop in to see his new office to make up for it—unannounced and with a quick getaway plan—but then scrapped the idea.

"I'll take these cumin seeds and paprika," Emma said, breaking into Piper's thoughts. "Going to put up some pickled turnips. Have you ever done those?"

"Yes!" Piper said, happy to be back on familiar and very pleasant ground. "Aunt Judy and I did a bunch at the farm once or twice."

"That might be where I got the recipe," Emma said. "Or maybe I gave it to her. It's been so long, I can't remember. All I know is they're delicious and great with pork." She handed the jars to Piper, who rang the spices up and bagged them.

Emma left, and Piper sank down on a stool, hoping to have a longer quiet time than the previous half-minute break. A lot had been happening, and she needed to pull her thoughts together. Visions of Wendy Prizer's tai chi class came to her, along with the peace-filled expressions on many of the faces. What a great way that seemed to be to decompress. If customers gave her a hard time for having run out of Zanzibar cloves, she could head to the back and do a few minutes of the White Crane for patience. Or if—

Piper's phone rang, snapping her out of the virtual exercise. She reached for it with some reluctance.

"Miss Lamb?" the familiar voice on the other end asked. "Sheriff Carlyle here. I understand you have something to tell me?"

Piper tried not to sputter as she struggled for a response. "What, ah, what do you mean?"

"I ran into Amy a few minutes ago. She's worried about you. And don't blame her for spilling the beans. I know when my daughter's bothered by something, and I'm generally pretty good at getting information out of people. So tell me about this threat."

"It's nothing, really. Just someone texting me to stop poking into things."

"Things like our recent murder?"

"Well, yes, I suppose that's what was meant."

"And you don't know where it came from?"

"An unknown number."

"Hmm. I'd like to come by and see that, if you don't mind. You saved the text?"

"Yes, and you're welcome to check it out, Sheriff, but I don't know what you can learn from it."

"Let me figure that out."

Sheriff Carlyle held Piper's phone in his hand as he studied her worrying text. "Any thoughts as to who might have sent this?"

Piper shook her head. "I've been talking to plenty of people about Raffaele Conti's murder and asking questions, but I think I've been fairly discreet."

The sheriff exhaled loudly, and Piper pictured him doing a mental White Crane. "Who have you been talking to?"

Piper listed the names and watched as he wrote them down in his notebook. "I've just been trying to help the Standleys," she said. "They're going through a lot because too many think Gerald did it. You don't, do you, Sheriff?"

"It's an ongoing investigation, Piper, which *I*," he emphasized the last word, "am conducting. I'm not prepared to make statements as to who is or isn't under suspicion."

"But—"

"I'll need your permission to examine your cell phone records," the sheriff said. "Maybe we can trace that text."

"Do you think that's likely?"

"Likely? No. Possible, maybe."

"Good luck, then."

"Let me know if you get any more of these." When Piper nodded, he added, "And stick to your pickling, would you please?" His voice suddenly softened. "I don't want to hear about anything worse than a threatening text message in the future."

Sheriff Carlyle replaced his hat and strode out the door, not waiting for the assurance from Piper that he probably knew wasn't going to come.

"Piper, your dilly beans are done. Turn off the timer!" Emma Leahy was in Piper's shop kitchen, waving her hands frantically.

"I can't. It won't turn off!"

"But the beans will disintegrate if you don't stop that ringing. All two hundred gallons of them! The sheriff will take away your license. You have to turn it off now! Hurry! Hurry!"

"I'm trying, I'm—" Piper sat up in her bed, blinked, realized where she was, and groggily reached for the cell phone that had been chiming away on her nightstand.

"Piper?"

Piper recognized the voice, despite the distress that distorted it. "Miranda, what's wrong? Where are you?"

"I'm at the hospital. Frederico was brought here. He's hurt real bad." Miranda's voice choked. "Piper, someone tried to kill him."

24

"How's the boy doing?" Gil Williams had entered Piper's Picklings holding his mug of morning coffee. He looked grim.

Piper was sure her face didn't look much better after losing several hours of sleep from worry and phone calls. "Not so well. He's still unresponsive."

"Was he not wearing a bike helmet?"

"He was. But from what I heard, it practically split from the impact against the rock. A witness said Frederico flew off his bike. He probably would have been killed if it weren't for the helmet."

"Thank heavens at least for that." Gil pulled out one of Piper's stools and sat down, taking a sip from his mug. "What was he doing out on the highway so late, anyway?"

"Exercising." Piper took a seat on the stool beside the

cash register on her side of the counter. She'd already had copious amounts of coffee and contented herself with a sip from a water bottle. "Miranda said Frederico's an avid bike rider. With the soccer team so inactive, he borrowed a bike to keep in shape and work off excess energy."

"Was that the first time he did that?"

Piper knew what Gil was thinking. They both had wondered at one time how Frederico could have made it to Gerald Standley's farm if he'd been the one to shoot Raffaele Conti. Getting there by bicycle hadn't occurred to either of them, but they couldn't ignore the possibility now, though it wasn't something Piper particularly wanted to think about. Picturing the friendly and cheerful Italian soccer player struggling for life was more than enough to deal with for the moment.

"I don't know if Frederico's been on a bike around here before," she answered. "But he might have misjudged our relatively quiet roads as perfectly safe. The car that was involved didn't actually hit Frederico but somehow caused him to run off the road. The driver didn't stop."

Gil shook his head in disgust. "I suppose with no fender damage or paint scrapes there'll be no clue as to who it was."

Piper nodded. "Other than that the car was dark colored, from what I've heard."

"Probably covers three-quarters of the cars in the area." Gil paused. "Gerald Standley—"

"I know," Piper said, grimacing. "Gerald Standley has a dark gray Camry."

"Not that I think it actually was Gerald," Gil said. "But it's common knowledge he didn't like his daughter seeing the boy."

"He'd have to be crazy, though, to do something that extreme simply to break them up," Piper protested. "Gerald has more sense than that."

"Agreed. But some people might think if Gerald murdered Raffaele Conti he was just as likely to murder a second person he didn't want in his life."

"A big *if* in that reasoning. Hopefully the sheriff isn't thinking that way."

"I'm sure Sheriff Carlyle is looking for solid evidence. It's unfortunate for him, though possibly better for Frederico, that the car never touched the bike."

Piper exhaled deeply, still barely able to believe what had happened. "Who would have wanted to kill Frederico? What possible reason could there be?"

Gil drained his mug and stood. "That," he said, scraping the stool back into place, "is what we'll have to find out."

A customer walked into the shop, and Gil bid Piper a polite good morning and left to return to his shop. Piper managed a welcoming, though tired, smile for the woman and helped her find what she wanted and rang it up, grateful that her customer seemed unaware of the latest incident and therefore shared no thoughts on either Frederico or Gerald Standley. That, Piper knew, wouldn't last.

As the morning wore on, Piper fielded plenty of off-the-wall speculation on the hit-and-run from customers and others, so during a lull she was particularly pleased to see a familiar blue Equinox pull up outside Piper's Picklings.

"I've just come from the hospital," Aunt Judy said as she made her way into the shop.

"How is Frederico?" Piper asked, though from the expression on her aunt's face she expected the answer would not be good.

"They're seeing encouraging signs, but he's still in very bad shape." Aunt Judy sank onto a stool, looking wrung out. While always ready to jump in with aid and comfort to friends when needed, Aunt Judy's natural empathy sometimes took its toll.

"Broken bones?" Piper asked.

"His right shoulder and arm, which took part of the hit. His skull, thank goodness, remained intact, but the doctors don't know how much trauma his brain received. They say the next few hours will be critical."

Piper grimaced. "How is Miranda doing?"

"She's coping. Denise is with her."

"Not Gerald?"

"Not when I was there." Aunt Judy gave Piper a worried look. "He may have been, earlier. I don't know."

"I hope he was. It could be taken the wrong way if he wasn't."

"I'm not sure Gerald thinks that way—I mean, caring how things look to others. If he feels what he's doing is right, that's all there is to it. He may simply have thought coming to the hospital wasn't necessary. But as I said, I don't know for sure if he came or not." Aunt Judy looked around. "You wouldn't have a little coffee on hand, would you?"

"Oh, of course! I should have offered." Piper hurried to the back room, followed more slowly by her aunt. "All I've been able to think of this morning is Frederico." She picked up the half-filled carafe that was keeping warm on its burner and poured out a mugful.

"That's all any of us can think of," Aunt Judy said. "But eventually it catches up with us." She took the mug from Piper gratefully, stirred in a generous spoonful of sugar, and took a long swallow. She sank into a nearby chair with a sigh.

"Food?" Piper asked. "A sandwich? I can throw one together upstairs in a flash."

Aunt Judy waved the offer away. "This is all I need. I couldn't bring myself to try that vending machine coffee at the hospital."

"Gil was here earlier," Piper said as her aunt savored Piper's brew and rested. "We discussed how Sheriff Carlyle would have a hard time tracking down the car and its driver, which would make rumors of it having been Gerald Standley fly. I've already heard the beginnings of that this morning, though I tried my best to quell them."

"Gerald's been having a rough time since the murder," Aunt Judy said, setting her mug down for the moment. "Denise confided that many of his regular orders have been canceled. They're still getting gawkers coming to the dill field, with some actually tramping through it to take pictures! But the worst thing is that too many people they thought were friends have been avoiding them. Denise used the word 'shunned.'"

"That's terrible!"

Aunt Judy nodded. "And I'm afraid this latest incident will only escalate things."

"I told the Standleys I would help," Piper said, "but nothing I've done so far has made any difference."

Aunt Judy shook her head. "At least they know some of us are on their side."

Piper was silent for a bit. "What about the hit-and-run witness. I never got a name. Did you?"

Aunt Judy brightened. "Yes, I did. Miranda told me. The man who saw it was Josiah Borkman."

"Josiah Borkman?" The name didn't ring any bells for Piper. "Do you know him?"

"I've met him. He's"—Aunt Judy paused—"an unusual man. A wood-carver. His place is a few miles from where Frederico was hit." Reading the look on Piper's face she asked, "Were you thinking of going there?"

"I'd like to get a few more details from him."

"Get Uncle Frank to go with you, why don't you? I'd offer, but I'm bushed. And Frank would be better, anyway. He'd know how to approach him."

Piper was intrigued. "I'll give Uncle Frank a call. Maybe we can set a visit up for when Amy comes in."

"Josiah's studio is just up the road a piece. You'll see the dirt driveway," Uncle Frank said from Piper's passenger seat. She had picked him up at the farm after Amy arrived to take over at the shop.

"Studio?" When Aunt Judy mentioned wood carving, Piper had pictured Borkman sitting on his front porch whittling a stick of wood with his pocketknife.

"Josiah has his work in galleries. Maybe not museums—yet. But I wouldn't be surprised if it happens someday."

"Wow. Why haven't I heard of him?"

Uncle Frank hesitated, much as Aunt Judy had done. "Josiah keeps to himself." When Piper glanced over, her uncle shrugged. "He's an artist."

"There!" he suddenly said, pointing ahead. "That's the driveway on the right."

"I see it." Piper slowed and turned her hatchback onto the packed-dirt driveway, which led up a rise through dense, brightly colored trees. At the top of the rise she could see a barnlike structure in a clearing off to the left with several logs of varying thicknesses and lengths lined up beside it. "Is that it?" she asked, and when Uncle Frank grunted something affirmative-sounding, she drove toward it, picking up a buzzing sound as they drew near.

"What *is* that?" she asked as she parked a few feet from the barn and turned off her engine. The buzzing had grown quite loud and sounded close by.

"Chain saw," Uncle Frank said as he unbuckled his seat belt and opened his door, letting in a few more decibels.

Piper climbed out her side, but before she could move forward Uncle Frank signaled her to wait. They stood, Piper picking up the sweet scent of freshly cut wood as she listened to the chain saw whine, which she realized by then was coming from inside the barn. When it stopped, Uncle Frank reached for the barn door and pulled it open, shouting, "Josiah!" He repeated it a second time, louder.

Piper saw the need for the shouts as the tall, burly man

standing in the center of the barn and holding a chain saw turned, then reached up to move aside his thick ear protectors. A long white beard hung halfway down Borkman's red plaid flannel shirt, which was tucked into tan-suspendered canvas pants. The fierce scowl he threw in their direction, making him look like a highly irritated Santa Claus, clued Piper in that Josiah Borkman was unlikely to chuckle any *ho-ho-ho*s to rosy-cheeked children. His ferocious glare, in fact, made Piper want to backtrack out of the barn, though she conquered the impulse and managed what she hoped was a friendly-looking smile.

"Josiah," Uncle Frank said, stepping forward. "This is my niece, Piper Lamb. She'd like to talk to you."

"What about?" Borkman barked, clearly not pleased to have company. The thick, upright piece of wood the carver had been working on, however, was impressive. It appeared to be in the process of becoming a standing bear, the animal's head and paws just beginning to emerge from the wood. *How did he do that?* Piper wondered, then recalled a sculptor's explanation she'd once heard: *We just cut away everything that shouldn't be there*, which might make sense to sculptors but to few others.

"Mr. Borkman," Piper said, "I'm sorry to interrupt your work, which is beautiful, by the way." Carvings of eagles with outstretched wings, fish, and stylized human figures were placed about the studio in various stages of completion.

Borkman's glare softened a tenth of a degree but remained fearsome. "I don't sell from the premises. You have to go through the galleries." He shifted the weight of his chain saw as though ready to fire it up again, so Piper hurriedly said, "I wanted to ask you about the accident you witnessed."

"What about it?" He'd lowered his saw but continued to look impatient.

"Josiah," Uncle Frank said. "The details of what happened to that bike rider might be very important to Gerald Standley. We'd appreciate it if you could tell us exactly what you saw. "

Borkman appeared to consider that for several moments before setting his chain saw down on the dirt floor. He gestured to Piper and Uncle Frank to follow him out a back exit, which they did, passing a makeshift kitchen and small bathroom on the way. Since Piper hadn't seen a house nearby, those were clearly necessities for whatever amount of time Borkman spent working in the barn.

Outside they found a set of benches that almost certainly had been carved by Borkman. Piper hesitated to sit on what seemed more art than utility, but the bench Borkman dropped his heavy frame onto withstood the jarring, so Piper took a seat on the other, alongside Uncle Frank.

"I already told Sheriff Carlyle what I saw," Borkman said. "But he didn't mention anything about Standley. Where do you want me to start?"

Piper noticed that Borkman didn't ask how his tale might help Gerald Standley. Apparently the statement coming from Uncle Frank was enough for him, making her doubly glad her uncle was with her.

"How about when you first saw the dark car," Piper said. Borkman stroked his long beard, loosening a few stray wood chips, which dropped to his lap. "I'd just made a right turn onto 432 on my way home. I worked late, trying to get that damned bear to stop looking like my dog Roscoe and more like a bear. There wasn't much traffic—never is that time of night. This was around eleven or so. What the heck was that biker doing out so late, anyway?"

"Exercising," Piper said, which brought grunts from both Borkman and her uncle, two men who obviously got all the exercise they needed from their work and had no desire to go looking for it anywhere else.

"Anyway," Borkman said, "I heard this knock coming from my engine and pulled over to check it out. Cut my motor and headlights, so I probably was close to invisible out there on the dark road. I was reaching for the flashlight in my glove compartment when I saw this wobbly light coming from the other way. I remember staring at it, trying to figure out what I was seeing, when a car came up behind him, picking the biker up in its headlights. That's when I figured out the bouncing light was the bike's headlamp.

"Was the biker on the road?" Uncle Frank asked.

"Shoulder. And it's pretty wide on both sides, as you know, Frank. Wide enough for my Jeep with room to spare. There's no reason that biker should have been in any trouble." Borkman's thick eyebrows pulled together into an angry, V-shaped line.

"Why was he, then?" Piper asked.

"Because the car behind went right for him. I caught it all. The fellow on the bike looked back and saw it coming. All he could do was try to swerve out of the way. But he must have turned too fast, or maybe his wheel hit something,

I don't know. The next thing I saw was him flying through the air." Borkman carved a dramatic swoop with one hand that ended with a smack against the other. Piper winced as she pictured Frederico's head doing the same with a rock. "The driver surely saw it, too, but he never stopped. Floored it instead. Maybe he spotted me by then, who knows? He was out of there before I could do or see another thing."

"You didn't catch a license number or see who was driving?" Piper asked.

"Nope. Most I saw was bright headlights and the dark shape of some kind of midsize car." Borkman scratched at his chin. "Now that I think of it, though, I did *hear* something."

Borkman, at that point, started coughing and worked at clearing his throat while Piper waited on the edge of her seat. When he could speak again, Borkman said, "I heard this whining sound coming from the car when he straightened his wheels. Worn wheel bearings, I'd say."

Uncle Frank nodded, agreeing.

"That's good!" Piper said. "If Gerald Standley's Camry has good wheel bearings, that could eliminate him."

"Worn bearings aren't that rare," Uncle Frank warned.

"He's right," Josiah Borkman said. "Let's hope Gerald's kept up his car maintenance. I'd hate to be the one got him deeper in hot water. He's a good man. Showed up to clear the snow out of my driveway many a time with one of his tractors, among other things. Never would take anything for it. I never believed any of the stuff flying around about him."

"He'd be glad to know that, if you haven't already told him," Piper said. "Mr. Borkman, you've referred to the driver of the car as 'he.' Are you certain it was a he?"

Borkman scowled, his thick eyebrows bouncing as he considered that. He looked up after a moment and shook his head. "No, I'm not. I suppose I just assumed. For all I saw— or didn't see—the driver of that car could just as well have been a woman."

25

Piper and Uncle Frank were silent as they walked back to her car, along the way passing Josiah Borkman's stacked logs waiting for their inner beauty to be released. It wasn't until Piper had driven halfway out the long driveway that Uncle Frank voiced what was in Piper's thoughts. "A woman?"

"If it was a woman, there's Raffaele Conti's wife, Francesca."

"Does she have a car?"

"Raffaele Conti did. A rental. She may have held on to it."

"But why go after the boy?"

"Why would anyone? That's what we don't know. If Frederico would only come out of his coma and talk to us . . ." Piper didn't finish, thinking of Frederico's perilous condition. Being able to point a finger at his attacker was important. But the first order of business for Frederico was to survive.

She drove the rest of the way lost in thought until they reached the farmhouse. Jack instantly raced down from a sunny spot on the porch, his black-and-white fur flying as he barked happily.

"I'll see if I can get over to Standley's place," Uncle Frank said as he climbed out, reaching down to pat Jack, whose excited yips and bounces would have made one think Uncle Frank had been away for months instead of an hour. "Maybe I can find out if the wheel bearings on Gerald's Camry whine or not without asking straight-out. Not that I think it was his car, of course."

"Of course." Piper lowered her window to reach out to Jack, who had scurried over to the driver's side, and was rewarded with a sloppy tongue wash. "Keep me updated," she said, retrieving her hand and putting her car into reverse.

Uncle Frank whistled Jack away and waved Piper off. The somber look on his usually cheery face made Piper wish, as she had more than once, that Raffaele Conti had never chosen to come to Cloverdale as an exchange student all those years ago, thus setting into motion events whose negative effects seemed wide and unending.

A s her latest customer left the pickling shop, Amy turned to Piper. "I didn't get a chance to say I'm so sorry. I mean for blurting everything out about that creepy text message to my father. I know you didn't want to bring him into it."

"It's not a problem. Really." Piper had washed her hands

and was slipping a green apron over her head, ready to get back to work.

"It's just, I was worried for you, and Daddy has this way of practically reading my mind. It's scary how he does it. He gives me that laser-look and everything comes spilling out."

"Maybe he'll be able to track the sender down," Piper said, not really believing it but wanting to make Amy feel better.

"Oh, I hope so. I hope it was just a prank. Maybe Daddy will find that others got the same stupid message."

"Maybe. How did it go with Erin?" Piper asked, thinking of Amy's goal the day before of finding out how much Erin knew about Ben's new assistant.

Amy replaced a colander that her customer had been considering and turned toward Piper with a frown. "It was kind of odd," she said. "Erin did know about Leila, but she didn't seem at all bothered by her."

"Had she met Leila?"

Amy's eyes widened. "Maybe not! At least she didn't actually say so. Maybe Ben just mentioned his new employee over the phone."

"Where was Erin heading when you walked off with her on your way to A La Carte?"

Amy gulped. "Ben's office."

Well, that might have been interesting, Piper thought, knowing Erin couldn't fail to notice how much Ben's new employee resembled Amy. Piper suspected Erin had been aware of Ben's long-standing crush on Amy even if Amy wasn't. But Amy's eventual attachment to Nate put an end to it. Or seemed to.

If Erin thought that lingering feelings for Amy had led Ben to hire an Amy look-alike, how would she react? Calmly, Piper supposed, as was Erin's nature, at least outwardly. Whatever distress she might actually be feeling over the situation, Erin would tend to keep it to herself. Until a good friend could draw it out.

"Maybe you should give her a call," Piper said. "Is she working today at Dr. Dickerson's office?"

"I'm not sure. Her schedule changes a lot. Let me try her cell." Amy pulled up Erin's number on her own cell. In a moment, with the phone pressed to her ear, she shook her head. "Voice mail." She left a message for Erin to call her back.

Amy glanced at the clock. "I guess I'd better get going to A La Carte. Maybe Erin will get back to me on the way." She pocketed her phone and started gathering up her things.

"I hope so," Piper said. "Let me know how she is if you can."

Amy nodded, concern for her friend clouding her green eyes.

On her own at the shop and with no sign of approaching customers, Piper decided to make a call of her own to Don Tucker, hoping to catch him at the Cloverton. She was pleased when his familiar voice answered at the hotel's front desk.

"Mr. Tucker, it's Piper Lamb. Do you have a minute?"

"Absolutely, Piper. What can I do for you?"

"Can you tell me if Francesca Conti kept her husband's rental car?"

"Oh, that was picked up days ago. I suppose she had no need for it, since Mr. Tortorelli had his and drives her anywhere she wants."

"Do you know what kind of car Tortorelli has?"

"I sure do. Our valet service brought his car out front for them dozens of times. A blue Acura."

"Light or dark blue?"

"Dark."

"I don't suppose," Piper asked, "you've happened to be outside and nearby as they drove off in it, have you?"

"Afraid not. Why?"

Piper explained about the whine Josiah Borkman heard coming from the car that had caused Frederico's accident.

"And you think the coach and Mrs. Conti might have been driving that car?"

"It's a possibility. Do you know if they were out last night?"

There was a pause as Tucker apparently thought back. "They didn't go out to dinner. They ordered room service around seven. But I got off at nine and can't say if they left the hotel after that or not." Another long pause. "Tortorelli did leave around eight thirty this morning alone. He didn't tell me where he was going, of course, but he still hasn't returned. I know, because Francesca has been in and out of here, looking like she's at loose ends. I wonder if he may have driven somewhere out of town to get his car worked on? Or maybe to trade it in for another rental?"

"Uh-oh. I'd better share that with Sheriff Carlyle," Piper said. "If he hasn't already, the sheriff should check on that car before anything's done to it." She was about to end the call, when she remembered something. "That blue Acura," she said. "Did it have tinted windows?"

There was another pause, and Piper waited, assuming that Don Tucker was scouring his memory. She was picturing the dark car with tinted windows that had followed Miranda and her after they left the Mariachi.

"You know," Tucker said, "I think it did. Why? Did Josiah say the hit-and-run had tinted windows?"

"No, he didn't, it was just something I . . . well, never mind. The bad wheel bearings are what's important right now. Thank you, Mr. Tucker. You've been very helpful."

"Glad to hear it," he said cheerfully. "By the way, how is the young Italian doing?"

"Last I heard he was still in a coma. I intend to run over there tonight and can let you know more tomorrow."

"I'd appreciate that."

Piper hung up and connected to the sheriff's office, whose number was stored in her own memory as well as her phone's, having had too many occasions to call it since settling in Cloverdale. The sheriff was out, but Piper left her message with a deputy, stressing that it should be passed on quickly.

As she hung up, she found herself hoping that Tortorelli's car would be found to be the hit-and-run vehicle. Upsetting as it would be for his team, it would be a huge relief for the town to find that the murderer was not one of their own. Tortorelli certainly had a motive for wanting to kill Raffaele Conti. But why would he want to kill Frederico? If only Frederico would recover enough to tell them.

Piper was startled out of her thoughts when her shop bell

suddenly rang and two women walked in. One greeted Piper familiarly, which threw Piper for a loss for a moment. Then she mentally placed a Carlo's Pizzeria cap on the woman's frizzy blond hair and added a white apron to her stocky frame. "Hi, Crystal," Piper said, grateful that the woman's name came back to her as well. "Not working today?"

"It's the in-between time right now," Crystal said, then helpfully spelled out what she meant. "In between lunch and dinner. Business won't pick up until around four thirty, so we decided to check out some of the newer stores. My friend here, Vicky"—the slimmer, dark-haired woman with Crystal lifted her hand in a finger wave—"loves anything to do with food and cooking. So here we are!"

Piper welcomed Vicky and launched into a discussion of what Piper's Picklings offered and how that might fit with Vicky's interests. Quite well, it turned out, as Vicky had done some pickling and preserving in the past and was keen on getting back into it. So Piper helped her stock up on canning jars as well as choose a cookbook that specialized in fall fruits and vegetables.

Crystal browsed quietly during all that but brought up the hit-and-run as Piper was ringing up Vicky's purchases. "I heard that soccer player was out jogging in the middle of the night when it happened."

"No," Vicky corrected. "He was on his bike. Isn't that right?" She turned to Piper, who nodded.

"Around eleven P.M.," Piper added.

"Still late to be out, don't you think?" Crystal said.

"It is," Piper agreed, sliding a credit card slip toward Vicky for her signature. "All I can guess is that he was hoping for a traffic-free road in order to pedal away at top speed."

"Yeah. Maybe so. Those soccer guys must be desperate for any exercise. What a shame, though. Probably a drunk driver, huh?"

Piper saw genuine sympathy in Crystal's face and was relieved not to hear blame laid on Gerald Standley. As Vicky signed her slip, Piper asked, "Carlo's serves beer. Did you see anyone overindulge last night and maybe leave close to eleven?"

Crystal shook her head. "We hardly ever see anyone get drunk at Carlo's. People come mainly for the food, and all that cheese and stuff probably keeps them sober. Besides, we close at ten on weekdays. So whoever it was didn't come from our place."

Piper knew Crystal was thinking only of customers. But what about the owner? She was ready to ask what time Carl Ehlers had left, when Crystal added, "And I was out of there by ten after ten, thank goodness, and safe at home before this crazy drunk was out there on the road."

Piper had handed Vicky her bags and the two women were halfway to the door when Crystal suddenly turned back. She pulled a printed sheet from her purse. "Here, maybe you can use this. I picked it up at Mindy's knitting shop."

Piper took the flyer and read it. It offered a $2.00 discount on tickets for the Harvest Shindig, featuring food, beer, and music by the Scalawags. She recognized the band that she and Gil had gone to hear at O'Hara's, and whose bodhran player, Martin McDow, they'd spoken with.

"It's tonight," Crystal explained, "so I can't use it. I have to work."

"It's fun," Vicky added. "They hold it outdoors, with bonfires and all, in a field they rent at old Mr. Cavanaugh's farm. You know where that is?"

Piper did, having visited every farm in the area at one time or another with Aunt Judy and Uncle Frank. She handed the flyer back. "Thanks, but I can't use it, either," she said. "I'm going to the hospital tonight to see Frederico, the soccer player."

"That poor kid," Crystal said, tucking the flyer back in her purse. "Let him know we're all pulling for him."

Piper promised she would, saying a little prayer that Frederico would be conscious enough to hear that and, with further luck, be able to shed some light on who had run him down.

St. Ambrose was a regional hospital that served several small towns in the area, including Cloverdale, which was about ten miles away. As Piper drove there, she was reminded of the scary time, several summers ago, when Uncle Frank had been taken to St. Ambrose after a fall from his tractor. The hospital staff, besides giving him excellent care, had been extremely calming to an upset and worried Aunt Judy and Piper, assuring them that Uncle Frank's injuries were not major and that he would be fine soon.

The facility had expanded since that time, and Piper found herself disoriented as she stepped into the much larger main lobby. A kindly, pink-jacketed volunteer at the information desk pointed her in the right direction, and eventually Piper was heading down the hall leading to the critical care unit. Up ahead she could see Miranda Standley as well as a few young men milling around who Piper guessed were Frederico's Bianconeri teammates.

Miranda spotted Piper and came to meet her.

"How is he?" Piper asked after a long hug.

Miranda shook her head. "About the same." She led Piper to the window through which she could see Frederico. Piper barely recognized the young athlete with his head and right shoulder and arm swathed in bandages and dark bruises covering large areas of exposed skin. A multitude of tubes and wires connected him to drip bags and computerlike machines. Piper thought she'd prepared herself, but it was still a shock, and a soft groan escaped her.

Miranda, who'd held on to Piper's arm, rubbed at it. "It's hard to see, isn't it? I only get past it by telling myself it's all helping him get better."

The nurse inside the room, who'd been recording various readings and checking drip bags, typed her notes on a nearby keyboard then headed toward the door. "You can come in for five minutes," she told them. "Please use the hand sanitizer first." She directed them to the dispenser on the wall.

After carefully sanitizing, Piper and Miranda went in and stood at the bed, gazing down at the unconscious athlete. Miranda then took hold of the uninjured hand that lay on top of the sheet. "Frederico, it's Miranda. Can you hear me?"

Piper watched for any reaction and saw nothing beyond a draw of breath.

"Frederico, Piper is here," Miranda said. "You remember

Piper, don't you? We went to her pickling shop and talked about how she wants to help my father?"

Mention of Miranda's father made Piper wonder if Gerald had been to the hospital yet. She hadn't seen him or Denise when she'd arrived.

"Frederico," Miranda said softly. "Please get better. I really want you to. I care about you," she said, her voice catching.

Miranda's head suddenly jerked toward Piper. "I think I felt a squeeze! Frederico, did you do that? Did you hear me?"

Both Piper and Miranda waited for a sign, but Miranda shook her head.

"May I try?" Piper asked and changed places with Miranda, taking Frederico's free hand in her own.

"Frederico, it's Piper. We need to know who was driving that car. Did you see who it was?"

Piper waited for any movement—an eye flutter, a lip twitch. Nothing. Then she felt Frederico's index finger tremble slightly. "Did you just answer?" she asked.

The finger moved again, but oh so slightly. Was it voluntary or just a muscle spasm?

"Frederico, do you know who was in the car?"

Piper waited but nothing moved again. Frederico's breathing seemed to have deepened, as though whatever awareness he might have had had slipped away for the time being. She looked up at Miranda, who shook her head.

"I've tried a lot. It seems to come and go. I don't know if he's really hearing us or not."

"It might be too early."

"That's what the doctors say. That I should be patient.

It's hard, though." Piper patted Miranda's arm and gave her back her place beside Frederico until the nurse returned and asked them to go.

"How is he, Signorina Miranda?" one of Frederico's teammates asked as they came back into the hall. His dark hair curled loosely around a face filled with worry.

"I think he's a little better," Miranda said encouragingly, and the gloom on the athlete's face cleared a degree. He went to share that hopeful opinion with the others, and Piper and Miranda found seats in a nearby waiting room.

They ran through the details of the accident again, then Piper told about her visit to the only witness, Josiah Borkman. Miranda cheered a bit at the additional information Borkman had remembered regarding the noisy wheel bearings.

"That's good!" she said. "That might catch the awful person who did this to Frederico." She glanced in the direction of the injured man's room. "Though it won't undo the damage."

Seeing Miranda look so unhappy, Piper changed the subject, coming up with anything distracting she could think of. She was in the middle of telling Miranda about Nate's progress on his record demo when Denise Standley walked by. She caught sight of the two and joined them. Piper remembered how stressed and worn Denise had looked that day at the farm and thought she looked worse, despite having obviously taken pains to spruce up for the visit, with her hair curled around her face and makeup dabbed over the dark circles under her eyes.

"Honey, have you had anything to eat?" Denise asked Miranda.

When Miranda admitted she hadn't, Denise insisted she

come with her to the hospital cafeteria, including Piper in the invitation.

"Thanks, but I'd better get on home." Piper gathered her things and walked with the two to the nurses' station where they caught a down elevator. After a promise to check in with Miranda again, she got off at the main floor then headed toward the parking lot to find her car.

As she buckled in, Piper reran her brief time with Frederico. Had he actually been responding, or did his finger movements have nothing whatsoever to do with her questions? She wanted to believe he'd heard her, that he was improving and had something to tell her. But if so, it looked like she would have to wait awhile.

Piper put her car in gear and backed out of the parking space. Her thoughts continued to mill around Frederico and the multiple others affected by his injury as she wove her way out of the lot, reversing direction at one point to correct a wrong turn.

As she paused at the exit to the highway, she was vaguely aware of a dark-colored car that had left its space soon after she had and followed her identical route out of the lot.

That car had just pulled up behind her.

26

~~~~~~~~

Traffic thinned the farther Piper drove from St. Ambrose, and overhead lights disappeared as she left the populated area of the hospital to pass through long stretches of farmland. Soon, the only illumination came from her own headlights and those of the single vehicle behind her, which seemed to be steadily keeping pace—a not unusual thing, but it caught her attention.

Piper normally loved driving on the quiet roads surrounding Cloverdale, finding it relaxing, especially after the congestion she'd regularly dealt with in Albany. She wasn't feeling particularly relaxed, though, at the moment. In light of the recent happenings, what Piper experienced as she glanced at the headlights reflected in her rearview mirror was a growing tension, and she found herself pressing harder on the gas.

Her speed picked up, but the distance between her car and the one following didn't broaden. They could have been connected by a giant rod, so steadily did they stay together.

Piper began to breathe more rapidly. Was that car deliberately following her? What were the driver's intentions? She had several miles to go to get back to brightly lit and well-populated Cloverdale. Until then, could she believe this was just another tailgater who happened to be going her way?

She drove on, uneasy with her higher speed, especially on the sharp turns. Then the car behind suddenly closed the gap between them. The headlights filled her rearview mirror, temporarily blinding her, and she felt a jarring bump. He'd hit her!

The bump wasn't more than a tap, but it shouldn't have happened at all! Piper fought down panic as she picked up speed. She had to get away. The distance grew between them briefly but then began to shrink. He was racing to hit her again. Piper's tires squealed as she swung widely around the next turn, praying there were no oncoming cars. The demon car behind her dropped back. She doubted it would be for long.

What could she do? Her mind raced, picturing the road before her. An intersection, she remembered, lay ahead. Piper slowed, which gave the chase car alarming moments to catch up, then, as she came to the small intersection, she pulled widely to the right and made a skidding, heart-stopping U-turn. The car behind, caught by surprise, sped on.

Piper knew he would soon double back, and she scrambled to think of what to do next, how to keep from being slammed or forced into a crash as Frederico had been. Up ahead, off to the right through the trees, a flickering light caught her eye. Where was she? Then it came to her. The old Cavanaugh farm! The Harvest Shindig! It must be, mustn't it?

She heard the roar of the returning car and saw its headlights speeding toward her. Where was the turnoff for the farm? There must be a marker, a signal of some kind. Then she spotted it! A lantern hanging from a tree, with a hand-printed sign beneath. She'd breezed past it going the other way, so focused had she been on the menace behind her. She slowed just enough to make her turn, allowing the car behind to draw terrifyingly close, and swerved onto the dirt road, sending gravel and dust flying.

She kept on, her eyes flicking between the road ahead and the view behind her. She saw headlights rush by the road entrance and heard a screech of brakes. The headlights reappeared as the car backed up, and she held her breath. There was a pause, and she watched, every muscle tensed, until the car moved on. Piper gasped in relief.

She drove forward, seeing lights, then cars, and people. Blessed, beautiful people! Piper laughed with joy. She came to several rows of vehicles in a clearing and pulled into an end spot, then leaned her head against the steering wheel, taking deep breaths until her heart rate slowed to normal. She opened her door and climbed out, teetering slightly. She was safe here and not in any hurry to get back on that road. Music drifted from the field, and Piper followed the sound along the path to a man standing near a gate that was decorated with more lanterns. An orange vest and a white canvas bag hanging at his waist identified him as a ticket taker.

"Welcome to the Harvest Shindig!" he called as she approached. "Only twenty dollars for all the food you can eat and beer you can drink. A bargain at half the price!"

Piper smiled at his joke and dug into her purse.

"And for a pretty girl like you, two dollars off!" He held out a discount coupon similar to the one Crystal had offered her earlier.

"Thanks," Piper said, taking the coupon and handing him several bills.

"Just follow the yellow brick road," the man said, pressing a purple stamp onto the back of her hand. "Or the cow trail, to be honest." He chuckled. "But watch your step."

Still edgy, Piper walked toward bonfires and wandering people sipping from tall paper cups and holding paper-wrapped hamburgers, hot dogs, or popcorn boxes. Food seemed like a good idea to calm her, so Piper turned toward the first stand she came to. She asked the white-aproned, bearded attendant for a chili dog, which was quickly and cheerfully slapped into her hands, then she headed toward the bandstand, where most of the crowd had gathered. Safety lay in numbers, and she felt a strong need for that. Moving forward with her gaze locked on the scene ahead, Piper suddenly felt a hand grip her shoulder. She yelped and spun around.

"Piper! It *is* you!" Scott stared at Piper as though he had just discovered her leaving a tattoo and piercings parlor. Piper was nearly as astonished. An outdoor beer-and-burger fest was not where she'd expect to find her sushi-and-wine-loving former fiancé.

"What are you doing—" they both said at once, then laughed nervously.

"You first," Piper said.

"I came because I'm deathly sick of hanging around the hotel and was desperate for something—*anything*—different," Scott said. "Now you. Why are you here? And by yourself?"

Piper paused. Suddenly, the realization of what could have happened to her out there on the road overwhelmed her. "It was a sudden decision. I, I needed to get away. To hide. Someone was trying to kill me."

"What!"

Piper nodded, fighting back tears that sprang embarrassingly to her eyes.

Scott took her arm. "Over here," he said, leading her to a nearby bench of baled hay. "Tell me."

Piper did, feeling relief at putting the horrific experience into words, even though Scott wouldn't have been her first choice of listener. She poured out everything, from going to the hospital to see Frederico, to getting much too close to landing there herself in the same condition. Or worse.

"But why?" Scott asked. "You make pickles. Why would anyone want to kill you?"

Piper took a deep breath. "Well, I haven't exactly been minding only my business. Even though I didn't join up with Emma Leahy's group, I've been doing my own investigation of Raffaele Conti's murder. For Gerald Standley's sake. Along with Miranda and Gil Williams and whoever else could help. I guess the wrong person noticed."

"You . . ." Scott stopped, obviously processing that information. "Gil Williams? The old guy from the bookstore?"

Piper nodded.

"And that's why you two were at O'Hara's the other night?"

"Uh-huh."

Piper watched Scott's face as he carried that forward.

"So you're not . . ."

She shook her head, seeing the humor but not in much of a mood for laughing.

Scott gave a quick store-this-away-till-later nod then returned to the matter at hand. "So, I don't suppose you caught a license plate number?"

"Uh-uh. And I can't say what kind of car it was, either. All I saw were blinding headlights that came much too close." Piper stopped, thinking.

"What?" Scott prodded.

"I just realized something. I kept thinking of the driver as *he*, just as Josiah Borkman did. But I really have no idea if it was a man or a woman at the wheel."

"Josiah Borkman?"

"The witness to Frederico's hit-and-run. I went out to Mr. Borkman's studio to talk to him."

"Well, you *have* been busy. And all I've been doing is scouring the Internet for anything to do with the Bianconeri team members."

Piper shifted uneasily, aware that she'd urged Scott to continue with that time-consuming busywork to stay in good graces with Emma's group, the supposed "pillars of the town." "I'm sure it helped to at least eliminate several people," she said weakly.

"I did come across something interesting, as a matter of fact, though I didn't recognize it as such until now."

"What's that?"

"Besides running through the team, I also looked around the Internet for anything to do with Conti's wife."

"And?"

"And Francesca Conti, it seems, participated in sports car racing before her marriage to Raffaele. At an amateur level, but she was pretty good. I came across a couple of photos of her accepting trophies."

"Really!" Piper stared at Scott, who nodded. "Well, that puts an interesting wrinkle on things, doesn't it?"

"I'd say so," Scott agreed.

"So you're saying you think Mrs. Conti was trying to kill you as you were driving back from the hospital?" Sheriff Carlyle gazed at Piper from behind his desk, his chair tipped back on its spring. She had gone to his office early, before opening up Piper's Picklings that morning, and perched on the edge of a wooden chair on the opposite side of his desk.

"I'm saying it *could* have been Francesca Conti."

"But you couldn't see the driver, right?"

"Right, and I'm not making an accusation. I just wanted to report what happened to me last night and to let you know what Scott found about her background."

The sheriff considered her thoughtfully. "I got your message about the whine Josiah Borkman heard coming from the car involved in the bike injury."

"And?"

"And we're still checking into Coach Tortorelli's rental car, which he exchanged for a new one."

"Still checking . . . ?"

Sheriff Carlyle sighed. "The car he returned was rented out almost immediately to someone who has left the area."

"That's unfortunate."

"It's also more than I needed to tell you. But I appreciate your passing information directly to me instead of spreading it around town, as some might do."

"Oh, I would never—"

"Or acting on the information," he added, "which I fully expect you not to do."

"I'm only—"

"Sheriff?" A deputy leaned into the office after a quick knock. "That call you were waiting for . . . ?" He gestured toward Carlyle's phone. "Line two."

"Right." Sheriff Carlyle laid his hand on the phone and said to Piper, "Just consider where your 'only' actions got you last night. Then there's the matter of that threatening text message."

"Did you—?" Piper began, but Carlyle shook his head.

"No luck tracing it. But no reports that anyone else got anything similar, which tells me you need to take it seriously." He softened his tone. "I'm paid to protect the citizens of Cloverdale. Sometimes that protection takes the form of advice, which I've just given you. I sincerely hope you'll heed it and leave the investigating to me. Excuse me now."

"Of course." Piper popped up, just as glad to end the discussion. As she pulled the office door closed behind her, she heard the sheriff saying, "Carlyle here. What do you have for me?" and wondered if the call had anything to do with Tortorelli's rental car or Raffaele Conti's murder in general.

Sheriff Carlyle's advice was sensible, she knew. But she couldn't help thinking that the solution to Conti's murder was very near. The murderer must have been keenly worried about where Piper's investigation was taking her—a direction the sheriff's investigation had missed. If she was careful—and she fully intended to keep away from deserted highways at night—surely she should be able to come up with that deciding clue and make the sheriff's warnings unneeded.

Piper was driving down Beech Street, heading back to her shop, when she spotted Ben Schaeffer's new assistant, Leila, on a corner, looking lost. Piper pulled over and lowered her window.

"Hi! Need some help?"

Leila was dressed in a short black pencil skirt topped with a cropped gray tweed jacket. A green ruffled blouse softened the businesslike look. Leila leaned down to Piper's car window, holding back her long red hair as a sudden gust of wind grabbed it.

"You're Piper, aren't you? I met you at the Mariachi."

"That's right. How's the new job going?"

"It's been great! Really great!" Her lightly penciled brows pulled together in a tiny frown. "But I'm having a little problem right now."

"That's why I stopped. How can I help?"

"You can tell me where to find the Eggs-tra Special Café. I thought it was around here, but it's not."

"Half a block that way." Piper pointed down Fourth Street, and Leila turned to look.

"I see it! Thank goodness! I thought I was going to be late. Thank you so much."

"You're welcome. Catching a quick breakfast before work?" Piper assumed this was one of the alternate Saturdays that Ben's office was open.

"Yes, but maybe not so quick." Leila grinned. "Ben was shocked when I admitted I never had more than a glass of juice before coming in to work. He claims a hearty breakfast is the only way to start the day. So we're meeting at Eggs-tra, where he says he'll order something amazing for both of us." She giggled and patted her very flat stomach. "I may not have to eat the rest of the day!"

Piper managed to smile before Leila took off but found herself thinking *poor Erin*. She drove on, shaking her head but aware there was little to be done. If Ben's feelings were leading him, however unconsciously, in another direction, well, that was something Ben and Erin would simply need to work out.

27

Piper was setting up shop when her cell phone rang. Cautiously checking the number first, she quickly smiled. "Hi there!"

"Hi, yourself." Will's voice matched Piper's for liveliness but turned serious as he asked about Frederico.

Piper told him about the soccer player's grave condition and her attempts to communicate with him. "I think for a moment he was trying to tell me he knew who had tried to run him down." She paused, then said, "The same person may have followed me from the hospital."

"What! What happened?"

"Don't worry, I'm fine," Piper said, choosing to save the details for a later, face-to-face time. "It could have simply been a reckless tailgater. But after what happened to Frederico, I decided to play it safe and turned in to the Harvest Shindig to shake him."

"Whoever it was could have waited for you to come back out," Will said, sounding concerned.

"I stayed a good while. Then Scott followed me home," she said, immediately thinking *Oops!* as it slipped out.

"Scott?"

"I ran into him there. It was a relief to come across someone I knew."

"I wouldn't have minded if you'd called me," Will said.

"I know. And if your tree farm had been within reach, believe me, you would have found me pounding on your door. This was just how it worked out. In a way, it was lucky Scott was there. He learned something interesting about Francesca Conti that he might not have mentioned otherwise." Piper told Will about Francesca's past sports car racing activities, adding that she'd already passed that on to the sheriff.

"Hmm," Will said. "I'd be just as glad if it turned out to be the wife. Much better for the town."

"My thoughts exactly." She glanced up to see Emma Leahy heading toward her shop. "I have to go. Talk to you later." She disconnected as Emma pushed through the door, dressed, of course, in her usual gardening clothes.

"I just came from talking with your young lawyer," Emma said.

I don't have a young lawyer, Piper wanted to say but instead asked, "Scott Littleton?"

Emma threw her a look that said *of course*. "He told me

what happened last night. Wasn't it fortunate he was there to rescue you? Are you all right?"

"I'm fine, Emma. Actually, I was fine by the time I stumbled across Scott. Just a bit shaken up."

"I should think so! Someone definitely wants to keep you from looking into this murder, and we both know it isn't Gerald Standley. Did you report what happened to the sheriff?"

"I did, as well as the tidbit about Francesca Conti's race driving that Scott discovered."

"Yes, that was clever of him to discover that. We're so lucky Scott came to Cloverdale when he did, aren't we?" Piper mumbled a vague agreement, and Emma added, "I can't wait to tell the others."

"By 'others' I assume you mean your group," Piper said. "Would you see that they keep that information to themselves for now? And my incident on the road, too? I haven't told Aunt Judy about that yet, and I'd rather she hear about it from me."

"Absolutely," Emma said, patting Piper's hand. "What about Frederico? How is the young man doing?"

"Badly injured and unconscious, but Miranda claims to see signs of improvement. I did get to speak to him, very briefly, and while I can't say for sure, he may have actually responded when I asked if he could identify the driver."

"That would be excellent. I hope you're right and that he will provide the final proof to put our murderer"—Emma lowered her voice—"who you and I both know it must be— behind bars."

Piper nodded general agreement, though she was not as

ready as Emma to pronounce Francesca to be her husband's murderer, tempting though that was. There were still questions that remained to be answered. Piper hoped those answers would come soon.

"Ben's been taking Leila to breakfast?" Amy paused in the middle of tying on her green apron, her expression incredulous.

"Just the once that I know of," Piper clarified. "This morning."

"But what boss takes his employee to breakfast?"

"It happens," Piper said, playing devil's advocate. "When I worked in Albany, we sometimes had breakfast meetings."

"That's different." Amy shook her head firmly. "What Leila described wasn't a business meeting. Ben shouldn't be treating his assistant to meals right and left. Or worrying about her diet. First the Mariachi, now this. It's not a good sign."

"Have you talked to Erin yet?"

"No, and that's very odd. Usually she returns my calls the same day."

"Well, if you reach her, I'd suggest letting her take the lead, waiting to see what she wants to talk about."

"Don't you think she should know what Ben's doing behind her back?"

"I suspect she's heard about it, don't you? I mean, does anything of that sort go unnoticed in this town?" Piper was remembering her early dates with Will being commented on—many times—by people she wouldn't have expected to have noticed or cared, a phenomenon she never experienced in Albany.

Amy nodded. "You're right. Someone must have clued Erin in by now." She looked worried. "All the more reason to get in touch with her. I hope she isn't deliberately avoiding her friends. Erin should know we're here for her."

"I'm sure she does. Maybe she just needs a little time. She may be getting her own thoughts together."

Amy looked uncertain, but before she could say anything more, Gil Williams appeared at the shop door. Piper had asked him to stop over, wanting to tell him about her ordeal of the night before. As soon he came in, she sat him down, checked that no customers were heading their way, then disclosed to both Gil and Amy the details of her visit with Frederico and her harrowing drive afterward.

"Wow!" Amy said, her eyes round.

"Who do you suppose it was?" Gil asked.

"Francesca Conti is a strong possibility," Piper said. She told him what Scott had learned. "But I don't see how she would have known where I was."

"Who *did* know?" Gil asked.

Piper thought about that. Who had she mentioned her plans to visit Frederico to? "You, of course," she said with a hint of a smile before scouring her memory further. "I said something to Crystal." When Gil looked blank, she explained, "Crystal works at Carlo's Pizzeria. She was in here with a friend during her break time and is the reason I knew about the Harvest Shindig. I told her I couldn't use the discount coupon she offered me because I was going to the hospital."

"She could have told Carl Ehlers that!" Amy said.

"Could have," Gil agreed. "Would she, though? I mean, how likely is it that the subject would come up?"

"Crystal is very chatty," Piper said. "She could have talked about what she did during her time off. Or, if Carl were really interested in my whereabouts, he could have asked questions that brought the information out."

Gil nodded. "What about Mrs. Conti? Any reason she or the coach would know where you'd be?"

Piper slowly shook her head. "None that I can think of. She, or they, could simply have followed me to the hospital, though, and waited for an opportunity. Oh!" she said, remembering. "I did tell Don Tucker I was going to see Frederico when he asked about him. I'd called Don to ask about Coach Tortorelli's rental car."

"Would Mr. Tucker have let that slip somehow to the Italians?" Amy asked.

"I can't see that happening. Don is part of Emma Leahy's group, and he's as suspicious of Francesca and Tortorelli as we are."

"It looks like you need to be more cautious about what you say to whom," Gil said. "You can't always trust that anything, anything at all, that you say to one person won't be spread, however innocently, to others. It's advice we hear about posting things on the Internet and how easily it can be passed around. The same might be said for Cloverdale, which has its own information network in place."

Amy nodded agreement, possibly thinking about what they'd discussed that morning—that Erin was likely aware of Ben's activities.

Mary Ellen Hughes

"You're right," Piper said. "I'll watch my mouth more carefully from now on."

Amy had left for A La Carte, and traffic to the shop had slowed, so Piper went to the back to work on the small pumpkins Uncle Frank had given her. She'd come across a recipe for pumpkin chips, something she'd never tried, and thought the work would offer a double benefit—an opportunity to pull her thoughts together and an interesting new preserve.

She was busy cutting through the orange flesh and scraping out seeds, humming along with a soothing rendition of "Poor Wand'ring One" that she'd downloaded to her iPod, when she thought she heard someone come into the shop. Setting down her knife and wiping her hands on a towel, Piper popped out to check, but found no one there. Thinking it had been something in the music that she'd heard, she returned to her work, peeling and cutting her pumpkins into thin slices. When she'd layered her slices in a preserving pan along with the sugar, spices, and freshly squeezed lemon juice the recipe called for, she covered everything and set the pan in her refrigerator to let all the delicious flavors blend.

Piper turned to cleaning up her area, dumping peels and the stringy inner pumpkin mess into the garbage and scrubbing her cutting blocks clean. She then went out front to see what needed to be done before closing up. To her surprise, a fruit basket wrapped in cellophane and tied with a red bow sat on her counter.

There was a note underneath. Piper slipped it out to read:

Didn't want to disturb you and have to run. The cheer-leaders brought this for Frederico. Nice of them, but . . . Thought you'd like it? Many thanks for everything.

It was signed *Miranda*.

Piper admired the colorful pyramid of oranges, apples, and grapes crowned with a single, beautiful pear. That particular fruit had ripened to a perfect, blemish-free yellow with a touch of blush hinting at soft, juicy, sweet flesh. It practically purred *Taste me*.

Piper reached toward the bow.

28

~~~

Piper's shop phone rang, and she left the fruit basket to go answer it.

"Miss Lamb? This is Lorraine Jackson. I was wondering if you carried crushed fenugreek?"

"Fenugreek?" Piper thought for a moment. "I'm sure I carry it, but let me check if it's in stock." Piper set down the phone and hurried over to her spice shelves. She ran her finger along the alphabetically arranged jars and came to an empty space next to fennel.

"I'm so sorry, but I'm totally out," she reported. Hearing a sigh, she quickly added, "I can probably get it within two days. Would you like me to?"

"Oh, please do! I have this lovely recipe for Indian lemon pickle that I got from my friend's mother. I'm so eager to try it."

Piper took down Lorraine's contact information and

promised to let her know the instant the fenugreek arrived. She also hoped that when she came to pick it up the woman would be open to sharing her recipe.

That done, Piper returned to her fruit basket. Instead of untying the red bow at the top of the basket, she picked up the note that lay beside it. Piper didn't know Miranda's handwriting, but it wouldn't have mattered if she did. The few words on the note had been printed, scribbled really, as though in haste. That made sense, since Miranda certainly had much to catch up with during the minimal time she took away from Frederico's side.

Piper knew she could have been heard chopping busily in the back. So leaving the fruit basket with a note to save both women time and where Piper would quickly find it was reasonable.

She loosened the bow and pulled back the cellophane. The perfect pear caught the sun beaming through the window and fairly glowed. Instead of plucking off the luscious-looking fruit and biting into it, though, Piper pulled out her phone. She scrolled down the names and chose Miranda's number— and got voice mail. Piper disconnected and immediately called at the Standley house. Denise Standley answered.

"Denise, this is Piper. Is Miranda there?"

"No, she isn't. I'm sure she's at the hospital right now."

"She probably turns her phone off while she's there, right?" Piper asked.

"Yes, that's the rule. She does leave the area and check in with me once in a while. Would you like me to give her a message?"

"Ask her to call me, please. It's important."

Denise promised she would, and Piper sat down, staring at the pyramid of fruit perched on her counter.

She'd closed up shop by the time Miranda called, and Piper explained her concern.

"A fruit basket? No, I didn't leave you one. I've been here all day. Why would someone say it was from me?"

Why indeed? "I'll look into it," Piper said. "How is Frederico?"

"A little bit better," Miranda said without much conviction. Piper instead heard plenty of fatigue in her voice.

"Don't exhaust yourself," she cautioned. "Frederico is in safe hands. You'll want to save energy for when he wakes up."

"I will," Miranda promised, though the conviction once again was missing.

Piper disconnected and took a deep breath. Then she called the sheriff.

"This will have to go to the crime lab. We may not know anything for a few days." Sheriff Carlyle had carefully bagged the entire fruit basket, including the note supposedly written by Miranda.

"Any thoughts as to who actually left it here?" he asked.

Piper shook her head. "Whoever it was waited until I was alone and occupied in the back of the shop. They could have learned that with a quick peek through the windows in the back. They also managed to slip in the front of the shop without setting off my bell. How they managed that, I don't understand. I always hear the bell, even when I have music playing as I did."

The sheriff walked over to Piper's shop door. He stepped outside, pulled the door closed, then opened it a millimeter at a time. The wire Piper had attached to the door and strung across the ceiling didn't move the bell enough to make an alerting jingle.

"It needs a brisk motion," he said, "the kind your average customer makes when coming in. Your intruder apparently was prepared to deal with that."

Piper shivered at the word "intruder." She'd been alone in the shop. What if her intruder had decided on a more direct threat?

"I'll check with your neighbors. Maybe someone saw this person carrying a fruit basket."

"Maybe," Piper said, though she doubted they would be so lucky. Whoever had done this had obviously planned carefully.

After the sheriff left, Piper called Will. "Hi," she said when he picked up. "I'm in need of a strong shoulder to lean on at the moment. Got one to spare?"

Piper and Will walked into the front entrance of the Bellingham Mall, Will having overridden Piper's offer to fix dinner for the two of them at her place. "I think a few hours away from Cloverdale would be better for you," he'd said, and it didn't take much urging for Piper to agree.

They ended up at a chicken and ribs place located in a side alleyway of the mall after first passing up an Italian restaurant. Piper normally loved lasagna and Chianti, but that night anything Italian held little appeal for her.

Over their meal, Will was the calm, thoughtful listener she'd known he would be as she shared her thoughts on the latest developments. The last thing she had wanted was someone who would insist she stop what she'd been involved in and hide away at Aunt Judy and Uncle Frank's place until everything had blown over.

"I feel we're getting so close!" she'd said.

What she needed was someone to simply hear her out, possibly help her to see the clues more clearly, and reassure her of her ability to keep herself safe (possibly with his backup) as she worked to unmask the murderer who still walked free in Cloverdale.

Will did all this and more, and by the end of the meal Piper felt 100 percent better than she had a few hours before. They passed on the cakes and pies listed on the dessert menu and went in search of ice cream cones instead, which they found in the food court not that far away. With a scoop of chocolate almond fudge for Piper and blueberry swirl for Will, they continued their stroll through the mall, fingers laced cozily together.

They wandered past shoe shops, camera shops, and computer shops, saying little but just fine with that. At the sporting goods store, though, they paused. There, in the window, was a display of soccer shoes, jerseys, and black-and-white soccer balls. Piper gazed as though transfixed.

"Does it seem ages ago that we sat in the stands and cheered for the Cloverdale All-Stars?" she asked.

"It does," Will agreed. "And looking back it seems like a different world. The worst thing we had to deal with then was the Bianconeri player faking an injury near the end of the second game and taking the match. Now there's a man murdered, another in a coma, and someone very dangerous still on the loose."

Piper headed to an unoccupied bench across from the sporting goods store. "I'm beginning to have second thoughts that Francesca is our culprit," she said.

"Even after learning about her expert racing skills?" Will asked, taking a seat beside her.

"Even after that. I'd much prefer it to be her, or even Coach Tortorelli. I can totally picture either of them running down poor Frederico and terrorizing me. But what bothers me is the thing with the fruit basket. How would either of them have known to open the door to my shop so carefully that my bell wouldn't jingle? They've never been to Piper's Picklings."

"Hmm." Will polished off the rest of his cone and swiped the paper napkin over his mouth and hands. "Taking those two out of the mix, though, narrows it down to someone local." He tossed his crumpled napkin into a nearby trash basket.

"I know, and that's regrettable. But if it is, it is."

"So who knows your shop really well and also has the strongest motive to kill Conti?"

Piper dropped the last of her cone into the trash, having lost her appetite for the treat. "When it's put that way," she said, her voice pained, "the answer has to be Gerald Standley."

After Will brought her home, Piper paced her apartment. She wasn't the least bit happy with her statement about the most likely murder suspect. After all, she'd become involved in the first place because of her strong belief in Standley's innocence. But the fact remained that the dill farmer knew her shop well from all the deliveries he'd made to it. He had probably the strongest motive for wanting to kill Conti, as well as one for removing Frederico from his daughter's life.

Carl Ehlers also had a solid motive for murdering Conti. But she couldn't remember him ever having been in her shop. She also couldn't think of any reason he would want to harm Frederico.

She must be missing something. Gil had asked her to list the people who were aware that Piper would be on the road the night of her hospital visit, and she mentally ran down that list: Crystal, who was Carl Ehlers's employee and could have passed it on to him; Don Tucker, who Piper herself had told over the phone; and Miranda, of course, who could have easily shared it with her father, Gerald.

After that, there were the people who were aware she was looking into Raffaele Conti's murder: Emma Leahy and her group, which included Phil Laseter, Joan Tilley, and Don Tucker. They all seemed trustworthy. Tucker made both lists because of his job at the Cloverton Hotel as well as his involvement with Emma's group, but Piper didn't know of any link he would have had to Conti other than through Conti's stay at the hotel. Francesca Conti and Coach Tortorelli may have spotted Piper at the Mariachi. Could they also have learned about her investigative activities through Don Tucker, perhaps overhearing him on the phone? Then Piper thought about Wendy Prizer.

Wendy knew that Piper was looking into the murder. Had Piper overlooked her as a possible suspect? Conti had been to Wendy's home the night he was murdered. She'd claimed they'd left on good terms and that she'd been unaware he was married until after his death. But was she? What if she'd found out earlier and they'd argued? Piper shook her head. It didn't make sense. Assuming Wendy had such strong feelings for a man she had only recently reconnected with, why would she kill Conti in the Standley dill field?

That led Piper back to Gerald Standley, exactly where she hadn't wanted to be. Her phone rang. A glance told her the call was from Miranda.

"Great news," Miranda cried. "Frederico is awake!"

Piper lit up. "Wonderful! Were you able to talk with him?"

"No, he's still terribly groggy. But the doctors are very pleased because he was able to tell them his name! Piper, I'm so happy!"

Piper could hear that in her voice and pictured Miranda bouncing with excitement. "I'm delighted, too! Thanks so much for calling to tell me. Is there anything I can do?"

"Just say a little prayer and keep your fingers crossed that the progress continues. I've got to go. Got a lot more calls to make."

Miranda rang off, leaving Piper smiling into her phone. That was certainly great news. And if Frederico could tell them soon who had tried to kill him and why, it would be even better.

29

With the shop closed on Sunday, Piper took the opportunity to drive over to Aunt Judy and Uncle Frank's
farm. She hadn't yet told them about Friday night's bad experience on the road. She hated worrying them but hated worse
the thought of lying by omission to two of the most important
people in her life. After affectionate welcomes from her aunt
and uncle as well as from their dog, Jack, when she arrived
(Gracie simply opened one yellow cat eye at Piper's appearance
before lazily reclosing it) Piper bit the bullet and spilled all.

"Oh!" Aunt Judy cried, her hand pressed to her cheek.

Uncle Frank looked grim and shook his head.

They looked even more concerned when Piper told them
about the mysterious fruit basket.

"We don't know yet," Piper hurried to say, "if there was
anything malicious in the fruit. It's still being tested." One

of Uncle Frank's eyebrows shot up, but he glanced at Aunt Judy and said nothing.

"Please don't worry about me," Piper begged. "I won't be driving after dark for the time being, and I'm surrounded by people at the shop. Besides, I'm sure all this will be over with soon. Miranda called to say Frederico has come out of his coma."

"That's wonderful!" Aunt Judy said, a smile easing the worry on her face and Uncle Frank's as well.

"Someone obviously wanted to keep Frederico from sharing something important," Piper said. "As soon as he can communicate more, we'll know what that is."

"Oh, I so want this to be over," Aunt Judy said.

"It will be," Piper assured her.

She stayed awhile longer, doing her best to keep the conversation upbeat, then left before the light began to fade, taking with her the usual plastic containers of extra food that Aunt Judy always seemed to have on hand whenever Piper visited, these filled with homemade vegetable soup and slices of sweet potato pie.

Monday morning, Piper was glad to further share the news of Frederico's improvement with any and all who entered Piper's Picklings. Even the very few who hadn't been aware of the situation were pleased to hear of the upswing in a very serious condition.

"I'll take a loaf of my fresh-baked bread over to the young man," eighty-something Mrs. Teska said. "Along with your apple butter," she added, reaching for the jar with a bony, age-spotted hand. "As soon as I bake the bread, that is."

"That would be great, Mrs. Teska, but I wouldn't hurry," Piper said. "Frederico has more recovering to do before he can fully appreciate a treat like that."

Piper had called Gil with the news as soon as she saw his shop lights go on, and he stopped over during a quiet time, coffee mug in hand and a smile on his face.

"Any further updates?" he asked.

"Nothing yet. I gathered the progress will be very gradual."

"Progress is progress. We—and he—will just have to be patient."

Piper realized Gil didn't know about the fruit basket, and she told him then. His smile faded. "How soon before they know if there was anything dangerous in the fruit?"

"The sheriff said a few days."

"That's very worrying. I don't like the idea of you here by yourself. Whoever left that fruit—and I think we have to assume it was left with malicious intent—is bound to know by now that the attempt failed. What might they try next?"

"Sheriff Carlyle has promised to have his deputies keep an eye on my place."

"That's good, but we both know the limits of that."

"It'll be fine. We know this person is intent on remaining undiscovered. He—or she—won't try anything blatant. As long as I keep to the front of the shop where customers are always popping in, I'm certain nothing bad will happen. And all my doors have double locks for after hours."

Gil looked unconvinced but said, "I will check on you regularly. And I've just decided to spend the night at my shop."

"Don't do that," Piper cried, but Gil waved away the protest.

"I won't be sleeping on the shelves, you know. There's quite comfortable accommodations upstairs, which Nate once used, you'll remember. It will save me driving back and forth, and you can reach me anytime, if needed."

Gil had a determined, no-arguments look on his face, so Piper simply sighed. "If it makes you happier," she said. "I hope the bed up there is comfortable."

"It is. Hopefully, I won't need to use it very long."

Piper sincerely hoped so as well.

That afternoon, Piper got another call from Miranda. "They've moved Frederico out of critical care to the observation unit."

"That's good, right?"

"Very good. It means they think he's doing so much better that he doesn't need constant care."

"Great! Have you spoken with him yet?"

"Just a little. This location change happened with plenty of hustle and bustle and he's resting now. But he definitely knew me. He smiled, and he almost got my entire name out! With the therapy they'll be starting soon, I know he'll be so much better."

Piper was pleased to hear that and said so. She was also glad to hear that Miranda planned on heading home for a rest of her own. To Piper that was an even better sign of

Frederico's improvement—that Miranda was comfortable with leaving him for a while.

When Emma Leahy stopped in a little later, Piper shared that news.

"Excellent!" Emma cried. "I'll let the others in our group know." Then she grew serious. "Have they allowed that coach, Tortorelli, and Francesca Conti to visit?"

"I don't know. I saw several team members at the hospital when I was there, but I didn't see those two."

"I don't think either of them should be allowed within a hundred yards of the boy, do you?"

"I won't argue that it could be for the best, but I'm not sure the sheriff has grounds to do that." Piper didn't share her recent doubts of the Italian couple's guilt, and she definitely didn't mention her worries that without Francesca and Tortorelli in the mix, Gerald Standley moved up to first place. She might be very wrong on both counts, though she hoped to be wrong at least about Standley.

"Perhaps Carlyle can come up with something," Emma said. "The more I think about keeping those two away the stronger I feel. Especially now that you tell me Frederico will be much less watched."

"Perhaps the best thing would be to put a guard on Frederico's room?"

"Good idea. I'll go see Carlyle about that right now."

Emma turned and took off, a determined look on her face, though Piper wondered how much success she would have with her mission. As Gil had reminded her, the sheriff's department was limited and probably stretched thin. Then she thought of Ben Schaeffer.

~~~~~~~~

Ben jumped at the idea, as Piper had expected he would. "I'll run it by the sheriff," he said. "But I think he'll okay it."

"That'd be great, Ben," Piper said. She'd explained some of her reasoning as to why Frederico needed protection but was nonspecific about from whom, not having any confidence at that point about naming names. If Ben, however, simply kept everyone except hospital staff away, Frederico would be fine. Now Sheriff Carlyle had only to approve Ben's being there. Piper hoped that the pressure from Emma Leahy followed by Ben's timely willingness to step in would seal the deal, and she was right. By late afternoon, Ben called with confirmation.

"I'll be heading over to the hospital as soon as I change into my uniform," he said. "Luckily, I have Leila here to take care of a few things while I'm gone and then close up. She's been a fantastic help."

"Great," Piper said, though with mixed feelings. She could hear the enthusiasm in Ben's voice and hoped it was mainly due to his upcoming auxiliary officer duty.

Piper felt better, knowing that Frederico would have added security overnight. She wished she'd thought of suggesting that Ben take along a thermos of strong coffee, but if he didn't think of it himself, there were always the vending machines at the hospital.

She dealt with a few more customers before closing time, then locked the front and back doors and went around checking the windows. Satisfied, she trudged up the stairs to her apartment, more than ready to kick off her shoes and grab a little dinner. Her phone rang, and Piper pulled it out, expecting it to either be Will, Aunt Judy, or Gil Williams checking up on her. To her surprise, it was Emma Leahy.

"Piper," Emma said, her voice breathy.

"What's wrong?" Piper asked, having heard the stress in that one word.

"It's Don Tucker," Emma said. "He's been taken to the hospital."

30

Emma's words snapped Piper out of her end-of-day fatigue. "What happened?" she cried, imagining Don Tucker in the kind of road accident she herself had narrowly escaped. Emma's answer, however, shocked her more.

"He may have been poisoned."

"Poisoned! What do you mean? How could that happen?"

"He became terribly ill while working the desk at the Cloverton this afternoon. The people at the hotel who ran to help said Don pointed to the mug of coffee he always keeps nearby and indicated that he thought something terrible had been slipped into it. Don would surely recognize the symptoms, wouldn't he? I mean, he *is* a pharmacist."

"Yes, and thank goodness for that. Was anything left in the mug?"

"There was and it was given to the sheriff, who arrived

not long after the medics." Emma paused, then said with a less steady voice, "Don was perfectly fine just an hour before, when I called him."

"It sounds like he got the right help in a hurry. I'd say there's a good chance he'll be okay."

"I hope so," Emma said. "His daughter needs to know, and I don't know how to reach her. I've tried my daughter Joanie. She might have Robin's contact information. But Joanie's not picking up."

Piper knew Emma's daughter lived in Pittsburgh, and that she had been in school with Tucker's daughter. That, however, was many years ago, and who knew if they'd stayed in touch. "No one at the hotel has an emergency number for Robin?"

"That was one of the first things I asked. For some strange reason Don listed Phil Laseter as his emergency contact."

"Why on earth would he do that?"

"I know; it's odd. The only thing Phil and I could come up with was that Phil lives close by, unlike Robin, who's down in Baltimore. But then Don should have given Phil Robin's number, shouldn't he? But he didn't, so short of breaking into Don's house . . ."

"Let me call around before you try that, Emma. Surely someone in Cloverdale can produce Robin's number."

"Oh, would you do that? I feel so, so *discombobulated* that I just can't think straight. I wish Joanie would answer her darn phone!"

"Sit down and have a cup of tea, Emma. I'll get working on it."

Piper started immediately, calling Amy first. Although too young to have known Robin Tucker at school, Amy had floods of friends in Cloverdale, one of whom might be that golden someone-who-knew-someone.

Amy, though appalled at the news, quickly became all business—as Piper knew she would—saying, "I'll see what I can dig up."

Piper next called Aunt Judy, hating to distress her again after having so recently done so in sharing her own received threats. But her aunt was a second prime source of contact to Cloverdale residents, hers reaching generations beyond Amy's.

"How awful!" Aunt Judy cried after Piper told her about Tucker. She *was* distressed, but the immediate need to reach Tucker's daughter helped tamp it down. "I don't know how to reach Robin," she said. "Was she working at a hospital down in Baltimore? That comes to mind but I can't be sure. Let me look into it, Piper."

After that, Piper stared at the phone, wanting to do more. But what? An Internet search? Maybe, she thought, a simple white pages search for the Baltimore area would turn Robin Tucker up. Piper turned on her laptop and got to work but quickly hit a dead end. Robin, of course, might have an unlisted number or no landline at all. Piper then turned to social networking sites but again came up short. There were plenty of Robin Tuckers, but none that matched the one she was looking for.

Not having heard back from anyone yet and aware of growing hunger pains, Piper left the laptop to see what she could grab in a hurry. She spotted the vegetable soup Aunt

Judy had sent her home with the day before and popped it into her microwave, the familiar aroma soon bringing welcome and soothing memories of Aunt Judy's cozy kitchen. As she ate, Piper's thoughts remained on Don Tucker. Would he be okay? Would his early recognition of poisoning lead to successful treatment? Piper could only hope so.

Why did someone want him dead? What possible threat was he? As she sipped perfectly seasoned broth and savored home-grown diced vegetables, Piper ran over conversations she'd had with the man, trying to uncover a clue. Tucker had given her the names of the women Raffaele Conti had flirted with during his time in Cloverdale, which had led Piper to Wendy Prizer. Was there more that Don knew about Wendy than Piper had found out? Tucker had also clued Piper in to the fact of Carl Ehlers's Saturday late-night routine, which could easily have put Ehlers at the crime scene. Did Carl somehow learn about that?

Piper finished the last of her soup and had started washing up when her phone rang. It was Amy.

"I got it," she announced. "Sally Forester is on the high school reunion committee for Robin Tucker's class. She said the number is old but at least it's something." She read it off to Piper.

"Great," Piper said, scribbling it down. "We'll give it a try. Thanks, Amy!"

Piper immediately dialed Emma Leahy but got a busy signal. She waited five minutes and tried again but couldn't get through. Emma clearly hadn't taken Piper's advice to sit quietly with a cup of tea. Piper then remembered Phil Laseter. He'd been Don Tucker's emergency contact and had obviously been in the thick of all the recent goings-on with Emma.

Piper had to look up Phil's home phone and was relieved to find it listed. When he picked up on the second ring, she gave him Robin's number, explaining that she'd promised Emma to look for it but had been unable to get through on Emma's line.

"She's probably talking to everyone in town," he said. "I'll call Robin, then let Emma know."

"Any news on how Don is doing?"

"He's been checked in at the hospital—room 618 as a matter of fact—so I'm taking that as his being past the emergency phase and into the recovery stage."

"That sounds very encouraging."

"I'd say so. Luckily he recognized what had happened to him and was able to tell the paramedics." Laseter chuckled with what Piper took as relief for his friend. "I predict he'll be back to work at the Cloverton by the weekend. And not on that damned third shift that kept him from being in on our regular Saturday-night card games. He's been trying to get off that shift for weeks. This should do it."

"I hope he'll take his time recovering. From what I understand, Don doesn't really need the job, financially speaking."

"That's true. He mostly wanted to get out of the house. Said it was just too depressing to sit around twiddling his thumbs."

"Well, I hope that phone number for his daughter works. Keep me updated on things, will you?"

"I sure will."

Piper finished cleaning up in the kitchen, then fixed a

cup of calming herbal tea and carried it with her to the sofa. She kicked off her shoes and stretched her legs onto the hassock, heaving a sigh that things seemed to be fairly well in hand. For the moment.

The question still remained: Who had poisoned Don? Rerunning all her previous thoughts got her nowhere, so when she'd finished her tea and found herself still feeling restless, Piper did what she'd often done in the past to organize her mind—she turned to organizing her dresser drawers.

With high hopes she headed into her bedroom and pulled out her sock drawer, dumping its contents onto her bed. Socks that she hadn't seen since she'd moved in suddenly appeared, and she sorted through them, setting a few aside for pure ugliness—what had she been thinking when she purchased the purple and green striped pair?—some for raggedness, and those few lone socks whose mates had obviously been beamed up by aliens.

That done, she turned to her makeup drawer, tossing out overpriced lipsticks that gave her lips an unfortunate glow-in-the-dark effect and mascaras that made her eyelids itch. Taking a break to fix a mug of coffee, she carried it with her to the bedroom and dug back into her work. Underwear drawer, sweater drawer, and just-plain-junk drawer. She'd worked her way down to the jumblefest that was her jewelry box, refueling with sips of coffee, when something made her stop and stare into space. A recently made casual comment, one that she had every reason to believe, had come to mind. Yet taking that comment as fact meant someone else had lied to her. But why the lie? There was no need, other than . . .

Piper set the jewelry box aside and went to find her phone. She stared at it a few moments, thinking, then made the call. After a brief explanation of the reason for her call, Piper asked some questions. What she heard back was troubling. But was it conclusive enough to point fingers? She didn't think so. What she wanted to do first was get to the hospital. And she wanted to get there soon.

She grabbed her keys, then stopped. What if she was wrong? What if someone was out there waiting to catch her driving alone? She glanced at the clock. It was nearly ten thirty. The roads to the hospital would be as deserted as they'd been that last, harrowing trip. But would having someone with her be protection enough?

Piper immediately called Will, knowing he'd be totally ready to help. The call, however, went to voice mail. Her heart sank. What should she do? Then she remembered Gil Williams, who was bunking out in his bookshop's upper apartment specifically for her sake. Piper knew he'd want her to ask, though she hated to.

She trotted down her steps, however, and walked the short distance to the bookshop, staring upward. All the lights were out. Should she really disturb the older man for what might turn out to be a fool's errand? Then she heard the sound of a car approaching, and tensed. The car slowed, then stopped.

"Piper?" Scott called from the lowered passenger window. "Is that you?"

"Scott!" Piper hurried over. "What are you doing here?"

"I was working late at my office—again. Might as well

be there as sitting in my hotel room, I figure. What are you doing out here?"

"I need a ride to the hospital," Piper said, making up her mind in a hurry. "Can you take me?"

Scott hit the unlock button, and Piper hopped in. "I'll explain on the way," she said and buckled up.

31

~~~~~~~~

The door to the hospital's main lobby was locked, with a sign advising visitors to use the emergency room entrance after ten P.M. Piper led the way there and entered a softly lit waiting room half filled with coughing, feverish children on their parents' laps and adults sporting makeshift bandages.

"How do we find him?" Scott asked, following Piper through the waiting room to the bank of elevators beyond.

"I know where he is."

"And if he's sleeping?" Scott asked.

"We'll wait till he wakes up." The doors of one elevator opened, and Piper picked up her pace as a white-jacketed woman exited, a stethoscope hanging from her neck. Piper held the door for Scott, then pushed the button for an upper floor. "I really appreciate your coming with me. I know it's a huge imposition."

"Not at all," Scott said, then looked at her speculatively. "You know, you've changed."

"I have?"

"Uh-huh. You never used to be so determined or get so involved in other people's problems."

"Maybe that's what small-town living does to a person."

"I guess," Scott said, glancing up at the blinking numbers. "I like it."

The elevator stopped and an orderly got on. The three of them rode silently up one more floor. When it stopped again, the orderly hurried off. Piper and Scott followed and paused at the directional sign on the wall.

"The observation unit is this way," Piper said and turned right.

They walked down a short hall and pushed through double doors that led to a nurses' station. Several yards ahead, Piper spotted someone seated on a metal chair outside one of the rooms; he was wearing a blue auxiliary officer uniform. "There's Ben," she said.

When Ben saw them approaching he stood, dropping the book he'd been reading onto his chair. Piper noticed a thermos on the floor, not surprised to see that Ben had planned ahead.

Frederico's room had a large window, as did the several other rooms on the observation unit. Piper could see Frederico apparently asleep, drip bag lines and monitoring cords still attached, although fewer than on Piper's first visit. The sides of his bed were raised and bolstered with pillows.

"How is he?" she asked Ben.

"Stable and improving, from what I'm hearing. Things have been quiet for the last couple of hours. I guess they'll stay that way until morning."

"Any visitors?"

"A few of his teammates came by. I kept them out with no problem. Being able to see their friend through the window seemed to satisfy them. The only people who get past me are hospital staff. The nurse has been in and out, and a lab person came once to draw blood. I checked her badge before I let her in." Ben paused. "Would you, uh, mind waiting while I take a quick break?" He gestured in the direction of a restroom. "I brought coffee to keep alert, and, well . . ."

"Go ahead."

Ben hurried off gratefully, leaving Piper to wonder what he would have done if she and Scott hadn't appeared. Ben was nothing if not conscientious. That night she fully appreciated it.

When he returned, Piper explained their intention to look in on Don Tucker.

"I heard about what happened," Ben said. "They think it was poison?"

"That's what I've been told." Piper thought about the fruit basket left surreptitiously at her shop and shuddered. Where might she have ended up if she'd tasted that tempting pear?

"We'd better go," Scott said, and Piper nodded.

"Thanks for being here, Ben," she said, and Ben made a brisk head bob. He remained standing, hands on hips and shoulders squared, at least until she glanced back at the double doors.

Since it was only one flight up, Piper and Scott took the stairs instead of the elevator. The door of room 618 was closed, so Piper knocked softly. When there was no answer, she eased it open. The single bed in the room was rumpled but unoccupied.

"He's not here."

"Are you sure?" Scott asked. "Maybe he's in the bathroom." He slipped past Piper into the room and tapped on the closed bathroom door. Getting no response, he cracked it open, showing a darkened room beyond. "Empty."

"Maybe we have the wrong room." Piper went back to the nurses' station. One nurse was on the phone and another deep in conversation with a doctor. Piper waited, her impatience growing until finally the first woman, middle-aged and wearing flower-printed scrubs, hung up her phone.

"We're looking for Mr. Don Tucker," Piper said.

The woman glanced at a list. "Room 618."

"That's where we looked. He's not there. Was he moved? Or taken somewhere for tests?"

"Not at this hour. Are you sure he's not just in the bathroom?"

"We checked."

Apparently that wasn't good enough for the serious-looking woman. She got up to see for herself but was caught by another phone call, which lasted longer than Piper would have liked at that point. Finishing her conversation, the nurse rounded her station to lead the way down the hall to room 618. She made two sharp knocks on the door before pushing it open. Seeing the empty bed, she called, "Mr. Tucker?"

then checked the bathroom. Frowning, she asked, "Have you checked the patients' lounge at the end of the hall?"

"No. At this hour, I doubt—" Piper began but was interrupted by someone calling the woman's name from the desk.

"Excuse me," she said. "Gotta go. The lounge is that way and to the right," she said, pointing to the far end of the hall before scurrying off.

Scott shrugged at Piper and turned that way. Piper had a sinking feeling as she followed him down the hall. Why would someone who'd just gone through what Don Tucker had be wandering around at that time of night? As she'd expected, the patients' lounge was dark and, when Scott switched on the light, empty.

"Let's get back to Frederico's room," Piper said, turning on her heel.

"Shouldn't we keep looking for Tucker?"

"I don't think we'll find him here," she said over her shoulder, picking up her pace. She reached the stairwell and shoved through the door, not waiting for Scott as she trotted briskly down the stairs. When she came out on the fifth floor, the double doors to the observation unit were again closed, but she could see down the hallway through the small windows. Ben Schaeffer was not there.

"Where is he?" she asked, grabbing a nurse who came through the doors at that moment. "Where's the guard for Frederico?"

"Mr. Schaeffer? Oh, he was called away."

"Called away? To where?"

"Why, uh, someone from the sheriff's office called with

a message that Mr. Schaeffer was needed elsewhere. Apparently there was a big accident somewhere near Cloverdale."

The nurse continued on her way, and Piper called, "Come on!" to Scott, who had caught up by then. She pushed through to the long hallway and took off at a run.

Her instant reaction when she reached the room's window was relief. Frederico was okay. A doctor was with him. The white-coated man, who had his back to the window, turned slightly, and Piper saw he was filling a syringe. She also caught sight of part of his face. "It's him!" she cried and rushed into the room. "Stop!"

Don Tucker spun around, holding the filled syringe before him. They locked eyes, and Piper watched a dozen thoughts race through his head as he obviously weighed his options. To erase all but one, Piper said, "It's over, Don. You can't kill Frederico. Just put the syringe down."

Tucker remained motionless—and silent.

"Think of Robin," Piper said.

Tucker's head jerked at the mention of his daughter. Anger and pain shot from his eyes. "You think I haven't been?"

"Hasn't she suffered enough?" Piper asked, as Scott eased in beside her.

"Yes, she's suffered, for years, because of Conti! And I'm not about to leave her alone. So don't think I'm going to meekly hand myself over." Tucker waved his syringe. "Back away, both of you—or the boy gets this." Reading their faces, he added, "You think I won't do it? Try me. With what's in this, believe me, he'll die instantly. It's what I came here to do anyway. But now he gets a chance—if you don't try to be heroes."

Piper eyed the syringe uneasily. "What did he ever do to you?" she asked. "I can understand killing Raffaele Conti. But why Frederico?"

Tucker's eyes narrowed, his expression hard and one Piper had never seen before on the usually genial man. "He saw me leave the hotel desk that night," he said. "Yes, I was on duty, despite what I told you. That is, until Conti called about his flat tire. Now back up! And don't try to sound an alarm. The first person who comes near me gets this." He held up his syringe.

Piper nudged Scott to step away and inched along with him. Tucker edged toward them, holding his deadly needle out menacingly. He gestured toward an electrical cord hanging from a silent, blank monitor. Its excess loops coiled on the floor as the plug end lay unused beneath a wall outlet.

"Pull that out of the monitor and tie her hands behind her with it," he told Scott. "Then your ankles."

"Tucker, you can't—" Scott began.

"Do it!" Tucker ordered. Piper saw Scott's jaw clench tightly. He disconnected the cord from its monitor and reached down for the loops.

Piper felt her wrists being tied. Playing for time, she said, "Robin hasn't been working all these years in Baltimore, has she? I spoke to her myself tonight. She's been getting treatment at Sheppard Pratt. A mental hospital in Baltimore."

"It was his fault," Tucker said, his eyes steely. "Conti's. She was perfect—a gentle, sensitive girl, and happy—until he came along. She fell for his line, when the whole time he'd been laughing at her. It destroyed her."

"It was hard seeing him again at the hotel, wasn't it?" Piper asked, keeping her tone as calm as she could manage.

Tucker snorted bitterly. "He was the same coldhearted monster he'd been thirty years ago, playing the same games with every woman he encountered. I could barely stand it. Then he got stranded out on the highway by Standley's farm. He called the hotel desk and screamed at me, blaming me for getting him a faulty rental. Like I was his menial. The father of the girl he ruined. It was too much. I told him I'd come pick him up, but I stopped at my house first for my gun."

Scott had wound the cord around his ankles, and Tucker reached for the remaining loops. "Give it to me, and hold your hands out."

Scott did, but when Tucker glanced down, Scott thrust his hands upward, catching Tucker's jaw hard and knocking him backward.

"Scott, no!" Piper cried. She saw that Tucker hadn't dropped his syringe, and though he'd fallen against a cart that rolled backward, he was scrambling to regain his balance.

Scott quickly freed his feet and stepped in front of Piper, whose hands were still tied, though not tightly. As she struggled to free them, Tucker rose unsteadily to his feet.

"Watch out!" Piper cried.

"Stay back," Scott ordered her as he snatched one of the pillow bolsters from the side of Frederico's bed and held it in front of him. Tucker lunged, but Scott managed to block the attack. Piper shook off the last of her bindings and glanced worriedly at Frederico, whose bed had been jostled.

"I'll kill you with this if you don't get out of my way," Tucker cried, brandishing his needle.

In response, Scott thrust hard with his bolster, pushing

Tucker toward the wall. He couldn't hope to pin him there, Piper knew. Not without something solid. Something that would keep that deadly needle out of reach of them all. But what? They were in a hospital room, not an armory.

Tucker, leaning backward against the wall, kicked out wildly. He caught one of Scott's knees, knocking him off balance. Taking his advantage, he shoved forward, knocking Scott to the floor.

Seeing Tucker raise his syringe, Piper reached for the monitor whose cord Scott used and hurled it at Tucker. It caught him in the head, hard, and he fell to the side, the two men becoming a tangle of limbs. But Tucker kept hold of his syringe and he twisted toward Scott, ready to strike.

"No!" Piper cried. But the needle sank into Scott's arm.

32

"What's going on here?" two hospital security guards demanded from the doorway, a fleet of nurses and orderlies gathered behind them.

"This man needs help!" Piper cried, pointing to Scott. "Quick! That syringe in his arm. He's been stabbed with something deadly by the man in the white coat. I don't know with what."

Scott looked woozy but alive, thank goodness. But for how long?

The guards acted quickly, rushing in and restraining Don Tucker, who seemed to have run out of fight. Scott, on the other hand, looked, to Piper's eyes, worse by the second. "What did you inject him with?" she begged of Tucker. "Tell me."

Tucker, on his feet with his arms held behind him, looked at her. He said nothing for excruciating seconds, then exhaled, a defeated man. "Thorazine. He'll be okay. It would have killed the soccer player with the sedation that was already in his system. But your friend will sleep it off."

Relief flooded Piper, and she stepped aside as nurses hurried in to attend to Scott and to Frederico. The guards walked Tucker out, and she followed, unanswered questions still nagging at her.

"What did you do with the gun?" she asked when they stopped to lock handcuffs on Tucker's wrists.

"Tossed it in Warren's Pond. Along with Conti's cell phone." He laughed humorlessly. "The phone was a disposable."

Piper remembered Warren's Pond as the location where Denise said Conti had attacked her. Ironic that his murder weapon ended up there.

"I didn't intend to shoot him, you know," Tucker said. "Not at first. I wanted to make him listen as I spelled out exactly what kind of a fiend I thought he was. But when I said Robin's name, I could see he didn't even remember her. He'd wrecked my little girl's life and her name meant nothing to him? That did it. When I took aim, he turned and ran into the dill field. Like the rabbit he really was."

The guards urged him forward, and Piper stayed put. Over his shoulder Tucker said, "Tell Robin I love her."

Piper shook her head, thinking what a horrible, twisted way he had of showing love. She pitied Tucker's daughter, who now had one more thing to deal with in an already unhappy life.

"Robin Tucker was in a mental hospital?" Emma Leahy asked, struggling to wrap her head around the events of the night before. She'd shown up at Piper's Picklings first thing Tuesday morning.

"She started inpatient treatment at Sheppard Pratt in Baltimore," Piper said, "the summer after high school graduation. Don Tucker and his wife told everyone she'd gone off to college early, hoping that would truly be the case in time. Robin told me it was a tougher battle than any of them expected. She also said her problems had begun before Raffaele Conti, but that she'd been in a very vulnerable place when she became involved with him. Her father totally blamed Conti."

Emma drew herself up with a huff, clearly blaming Conti as well. "I had no idea. Joanie, either. The poor thing. And Don and Lois feeling they needed to keep it secret all these years." She shook her head.

"Robin stayed in Baltimore to continue treatment on an outpatient basis and even got a job, so that much was true. But the job was minimum wage, and she needed financial help. She also was mugged on the streets once, ending up in the hospital, which only added to her needs. That might be why Don went back to work after initially retiring. She said her father blamed Conti for the mugging, too, since she wouldn't have been where she was if not for him."

"Don did go down to visit her," Emma said, "but he always claimed Robin's work wouldn't allow her time to come to Cloverdale. We all thought she must be doing some really high-end corporate job. You know, one of those eighteen-hour-a-day, seven-days-a-week careers. When anyone asked for details, Don would just laugh and claim he never understood it well enough to explain. That should have clued us in, right there. Don was a professional man, a pharmacist. He would have understood."

"It was because he was a pharmacist that he was able to fool everyone about being poisoned," Gil Williams said, stepping out of Piper's back room with a fresh mug of coffee. He'd arrived at Piper's Picklings earlier than Emma and already knew the full story. "Don knew what and how much to ingest to make himself sick enough to be taken to the hospital but not sick enough to be incapacitated. Having worked at the hospital, he knew its routines and how to slip around unnoticed."

"Thank heavens you figured it out, Piper, in time to stop Don from committing another murder. I suppose he was the one who caused that boy's terrible accident out on the road?"

"I'm sure he was," Piper said. "Don told me Frederico had seen him leave the hotel desk at the time Conti would have been stranded with his flat tire. Don had lied to me earlier, claiming he hadn't worked the late shift at the hotel the night of the murder. But Phil contradicted that when I spoke to him last night. He said Don had been stuck on that third shift for weeks. Luckily, I managed to connect those two statements in time and catch Don's lie.

"I don't know," she added, "why Frederico would have been in the hotel lobby so late that night—"

"Freddy went down looking for something to eat," Miranda said, having come into the shop at that moment. "He told me so himself."

"How is he?" Piper asked, surprised but pleased to see her.

"Much better. When I heard what happened, I rushed over first thing this morning to check on him myself. Freddy was awake and talking."

"Wonderful!" Emma cried.

"He's still not up to speed," Miranda said. "And he was totally oblivious to what went on in his room last night. But he did know it was Mr. Tucker who tried to kill him on the road. Frederico is a real car buff. He had a long talk with Mr. Tucker, once, about his ten-year-old Dodge Caliber, checking it inside and out. He knew that car."

"That's the second reason Tucker had for getting into the hospital and silencing the young man," Gil said. "Before Frederico could recover enough to tell anyone. I'm sure the sheriff is checking Tucker's car for evidence."

"That must have been why Don was walking everywhere lately," Piper said. "He couldn't take a chance that his car would be identified. Josiah Borkman saw the vehicle that ran Frederico off the road and told me he'd heard a definite whine coming from worn wheel bearings. And I," she said, grimacing, "passed that information on to Tucker."

"Worse than that," Emma said, "I was the one that told Don that Frederico was improving and where he'd been moved to."

"We all trusted him," Piper said. "We had no reason not to."

"Well, it's over now," Miranda said. "And my dad is no longer a suspect, thanks to you, Piper."

"It was a group effort, definitely," Piper said. "If Amy

hadn't tracked down a way to contact Robin . . ." She trailed off, unwilling to voice the awful "might have been." A glance at the others, though, told her they all realized that Frederico would be dead, Gerald Standley might have gone to prison, and who knew how many others Don Tucker would have felt the need to eliminate in order to keep his secret.

Emma, Miranda, and Gil took off, heading their separate ways, but Piper's shop didn't simply settle down to a normal business day. Besides multiple townspeople stopping in for firsthand accounts, Aunt Judy popped in later in the morning, loaded with home-cooked food. Piper had spoken with her aunt and uncle the night before, explaining all that had happened and assuring them she was fine. By the looks of it, her aunt had stayed up the rest of the night cooking. Piper shook her head at the stack of foil-wrapped casserole dishes she carried in with her.

"They're not all for you," Aunt Judy said, laughing. "One is for Gerald and Denise. I was going to drop it at their place, but Denise said they were heading to the hospital to see Frederico. They planned to stop here afterward, so I said I'd leave it with you."

"They're *both* going to the hospital?"

"Yes, isn't that nice? Gerald seems to have unbent with regards to Frederico."

"I'm so glad. Who gets the other casserole?"

"Scott. I checked, and he's in his office. Since it's so nearby—"

"He's at his office?" Piper asked, shocked. "I left him at the hospital last night and thought he'd still be there."

"Oh no. Scott said he got a very good sleep—the sedative, you know—and checked himself out first thing this morning. He grabbed a taxi to get back. He said to tell you he'll pick up his car keys sometime today. Anyway, I thought he might appreciate a little home-cooked food. He certainly deserves much more for what he did last night."

"He acted very courageously," Piper said. "He quite surprised me."

"Have you, um, spoken to Will yet about it all?"

Piper knew what her aunt was asking. How was Will going to feel about Scott getting the chance to play the hero? "Only briefly. We're going to talk more later."

"Oh good. In the meantime, let me take one of these dishes up to your refrigerator. It's one of your favorites. Turkey tetrazzini."

"Thanks, Aunt Judy." Piper gave her aunt a peck on the cheek as she took the dish from her. "I'll do it."

Piper was rearranging things in her refrigerator to make room for Aunt Judy's turkey tetrazzini when she heard familiar voices from downstairs. Denise and Gerald Standley had arrived. Quickly slipping the casserole into the fridge, she hurried back down.

"There she is!" Denise Standley said. Denise looked wonderful, her hair fluffed and the bloom back in her face. She rushed over and threw her arms around Piper. "How can we thank you?"

Gerald joined her, taking Piper's hand and pumping it. "We owe you a great debt."

"Not at all," Piper said, happy to see the deep shadows gone from the dill farmer's eyes. "I'll just be glad to get your lovely dill again. My supply is running low."

"You got it."

"The sheriff's team dragged Warren's Pond this morning," Denise said. "They found the gun. Or, rather, they found *a* gun. They'll have to check to see if it's the one that fired the fatal shot. But Sheriff Carlyle said he can see it hasn't been in the water long. And the serial number will show if it was Don's."

"Excellent!" Aunt Judy cried. "Now you can take down those barricades from your driveway and just get back to your everyday work."

"You don't know how good that sounds," Gerald said. "Getting back to work. I'll never grumble again about getting up at the crack of dawn."

"Oh yes you will," Denise said, laughing, and Gerald joined in. It sounded wonderful to Piper, who not that long ago had witnessed the couple's grim low point.

"I still don't know what happened to my own gun," Gerald said, "which was careless of me in the extreme. I'm determined to find it."

"And when you do, we'll lock it up safely," Denise said.

"How is Frederico doing?" Aunt Judy asked.

"Getting better by the minute," Denise said. Her smile faded. "I can't believe Don Tucker was ready to kill him."

"The boy's been through a lot," Gerald said. "But he's managed to stay positive. I give him a lot of credit."

Well, that's encouraging, Piper thought. A glance at Aunt Judy told her she felt the same.

"He'll need plenty of therapy," Denise added. "We've invited him to stay with us once he's released from the hospital, to continue his recovery."

Even more encouraging.

Gerald nodded but didn't add more. Piper predicted, though, that he'd be kicking a soccer ball around the field with Frederico when the time came. And who knew what would develop after that?

The Standleys left, taking Aunt Judy's casserole and calling out more thanks to both her and Piper.

"I'll take this last dish over to Scott," Aunt Judy said. "It's the smallest because it has to fit in his little office refrigerator." At that point Amy walked in, ready for her regular shift.

Taking Amy's arrival as a sign, Piper said, "Why don't I walk over with you to Scott's, Aunt Judy? Mind watching the shop, Amy? I know you must have plenty of questions about last night, but I'll just be a minute."

"That's fine," Amy said cheerfully. She slipped off her light jacket to hang in the back room.

"Scott needs his car keys," Piper said, dropping them into her pocket, "and I'll get to see his new office, which I've never gotten around to doing, though he's invited me a few times." After what he'd just gone through because of her, Piper felt she owed Scott at least that courtesy. Arriving with her aunt, on the other hand, would keep things a little more . . . what? Casual? Noncommittal? Her thoughts regarding Scott had become a bit confused.

When they walked in a few minutes later, Scott popped up from the small desk in his outer office. "Hey, great! Good to see you!"

"And to see *you*," Aunt Judy said. "I've brought the potato and ham casserole I promised."

"And I brought your keys," Piper said.

"Terrific," Scott said, taking both and setting the dish on the desk. "How do you like the new digs?" he asked.

"Very nice," Piper said and gazed approvingly at the simply but smartly decorated reception area, which still had a fresh-paint-and-new-carpet smell to it.

"More chairs are on their way," Scott said, explaining the relative emptiness. "And this will be my assistant's desk—once I get an assistant. Come see the rest."

He led them to the next room, which held a large cherrywood desk topped with a computer. Two straight, blue-cushioned chairs sat before it, and shelves with the requisite legal books lined the wall along with tall file cabinets. Piper didn't see any papers on the gleaming desktop and presumed the file cabinets were empty.

"Very impressive," she said. "Certainly more attractive than the assistant DA's office in Albany. Have you opened for business?"

"Not quite yet. Still getting settled. But if someone happened to walk in and needed a will looked over . . ."

"Oh, I'm sure there'll be lots of people needing you," Aunt Judy said. "And hopefully for nice quiet things like wills and trusts, not murders. We don't need any more murders in Cloverdale."

"Are you okay?" Piper asked Scott. "I was surprised to hear you came to work so soon."

"I'm fine," Scott said. "Tip-top. What about you? I was too out of it to ask you last night."

"That needle never got near me. But I was terrified when Tucker jabbed you."

"Were you?" Scott held Piper's gaze.

"What you did was very brave," Aunt Judy said. "You had no idea how lethal that syringe was, and you acted anyway to protect Piper and Frederico."

Scott dropped his eyes, and for the first time in Piper's experience he seemed uncomfortable with the praise. "I suppose it was instinct," he said. "What anyone would do. Is Frederico okay? We probably knocked his bed around, not to mention all the noise."

"He's fine and wasn't aware of a thing," Piper said. "Apparently his medications kept him sleeping deeply, which meant Don Tucker's injection of more sedative really would have put him over the edge. And nobody would have suspected."

"Tucker totally fooled me," Scott said. "I'll never underestimate senior citizens again. They're not automatically harmless grannies and grandpops."

Aunt Judy laughed. "No indeed! We're just older versions of the person we've been all our lives. And some manage to hide their darker sides better than others."

"Tell me about it," Scott said, shaking his head. "Well, this whole thing has been a real learning experience, in many ways. I'm really, really glad I could be there for you, Piper."

The look on Scott's face as he said that brought a catch to Piper's breath. She didn't trust herself to speak for a moment. "Thank you, Scott," she finally managed to say. "I'm glad it all worked out and nobody was hurt.

"Well!" she said more briskly, turning to Aunt Judy. We'd better head back to the shop."

"Yes, I suppose we should," Aunt Judy said, explaining to Scott, "Amy's there alone."

"And the place has been a madhouse all morning," Piper added, stepping smartly into the reception area. "I just wanted to pop in for a minute as well as bring you your car keys," she said as she led the way out. "And Aunt Judy's casserole, of course. Love the new office!" And she was out the exit door, Aunt Judy scurrying to keep up.

Once outside, Piper slowed as Aunt Judy made cheery comments on Scott's office setup. But Piper was less concerned with Scott's décor than understanding what had come over her a few moments ago. She'd thought all the warm and fuzzy feelings she once held for her ex-fiancé had died a slow death long ago. What had brought about their sudden reincarnation? If that's what had happened. Or was it temporary insanity?

The short distance back to her shop along with Aunt Judy's kindly chatter didn't allow much time for self-analysis. They came to the pickling shop's front window, and Piper glanced in to see Amy standing at the counter, facing a very familiar figure. Even though his back was to her, Piper knew immediately who it was.

Will.

33

<hr>

Will turned as Piper and her aunt entered the shop. There was a flurry of greetings, then Aunt Judy and Amy seemed to melt away in an instant.

"I was in town so I thought I'd come by," Will explained, then paused. "Actually," he said, "I wanted to see for myself that you were okay." His blue eyes searched her face, and Piper wasn't sure what he was finding there.

"Why don't we get away from here for a bit," she said. "Amy—?" she began, but Amy's voice called from the back room.

"I'll be fine."

Will grinned and took her hand, leading the way out of the shop. Piper spotted two women striding purposefully in their direction and pulled Will the other way.

"Quick," she said, "before they see me." She and Will

hustled off, slowing only when Piper felt confidently out of sight.

"It's been like that all morning," she said. "People showing up to hear firsthand what happened."

"You've become the town wonder—once again. Which is great. But I wish you'd find other ways of achieving that."

"Believe me, so do I."

"What you pulled off, though, was pretty amazing."

Piper looked at Will and saw he truly meant it. She also saw the small reservation in his eyes. "I did try to reach you last night, you know. When I needed to get to the hospital."

"I know. And I kick myself for letting my cell go dead."

"And Scott just happened along as I was making up my mind about whether or not to disturb Gil."

"I totally understand. Doesn't mean I like it any better, but I understand."

They spotted more curious-faced townspeople up ahead and took a second evasive detour into a residential area.

"The thing is," Piper said as they passed a blue-shuttered Cape Cod, "I can't just ignore Scott after all this."

"You can't?"

Piper smiled. "No, I can't. He deserves my gratitude. As a friend."

"Will he take it that way, though? The friend part, I mean? Seems to me he's been trying his best to get things back to the way they were in Albany."

Piper sighed. She knew that. And there was no way she would go back to the way things were between Scott and her those last few months in Albany. But there had been happier times in the early part of their relationship, and

285

apparently certain feelings from that time period had resurfaced—though not at her bidding. She shook her head.

"It's all very confusing. I want to do the right thing—the right thing for all concerned. But I have to get my head straight. That'll take a little time. Can you be patient for a while?" She looked at him.

Will gazed back at her. He was silent for a while but then did an amazing thing. He lifted her hand to his lips and kissed it. "That's the best I can do right now," he explained, "what with half of Cloverdale probably watching us from their windows. I always knew you were a very special person, and what you just said proves it. Take as much time as you need. Just know I'm not going anywhere."

Piper smiled, a lump forming in her throat. "Thank you."

They strolled on in silence awhile longer, then turned back onto Beech Street. As they did, Piper spotted two figures up ahead: Erin and Ben. They were standing, hand in hand, in front of Ben's insurance office.

When Ben saw them, he suddenly looked embarrassed, and Piper guessed it wasn't because of Erin, who, for her part, was looking rather pleased. Piper wondered what was going on. As she and Will drew near, Ben said, "Piper, I feel like such an idiot—"

"No need, Ben," she said, sure of what he was talking about. "How were you to know that message summoning you to an accident was actually left by Don Tucker? He needed to get you away from Frederico."

"Still, I should have double-checked. It's just, I'm used to getting summoned like that a lot, and—"

"Sheriff Carlyle completely understood," Erin said,

jumping in. "He said they should have set up a code word long ago to avoid just such a problem. The important thing is that it all turned out okay. I heard that Francesca Conti and the coach have already left town, by the way."

"That was fast," Will said.

"Perhaps they got tired of the food at the Mariachi," Piper said but then felt a twinge of guilt over the dire things she'd suspected of the two. Carl Ehlers had been under her microscope as well. There wasn't much she could do for the Italian couple to make up for it, but Piper vowed to send as much business Carl's way as she could in the future. She hoped he would get a second chance with Wendy Prizer in time. "What about the rest of Bianconeri?" she asked.

"The bus showed up to carry them off to their next tournament. But not all of them got on it. A few of Frederico's friends decided to stay around awhile. Some grumblings were overheard about the team management in general, and I have a feeling Bianconeri is due for a major shake-up."

"It could probably use it," Will said, and the others nodded.

Erin brightened suddenly and asked, "Did you know that Ben has a new assistant?"

"Yes, I met Leila—" Piper began.

"No, not Leila. Mrs. Spearman." Erin indicated the interior of Ben's office as she stepped aside from the window so Piper and Will could see. A plump, middle-aged woman sat at a desk near the front, typing.

"What happened to Leila?" Will asked.

"Leila got a job offer in Rochester," Ben said. "It came with a much better salary than I could afford, so I urged her to accept it, even though she felt terrible about leaving so soon. Erin found Mrs. Spearman for me right away," he said, smiling at his just-as-pleased-looking girlfriend. "Mrs. Spearman is quite experienced and happened to be between jobs."

"How fortunate!" Piper said. "For everyone."

"Yes, wasn't it lucky?" Erin said. "We were just on our way to lunch, by the way. Want to join us?"

"Thanks," Piper said. "But I should get back to the shop."

Ben nodded, and they all made "another time" noises as the couples said good-bye and went their separate ways. Once they'd gone some distance, Will asked, "Does Erin have relatives in Rochester?"

"I wouldn't be at all surprised," Piper said, her lips twitching upward.

They walked a little farther until Will said, "Think those relatives in Rochester could come up with an opening in the legal profession?"

"I wouldn't know, Will," Piper said, turning to look at him.

Will squinted at a plane passing overhead. Its silvery wings caught the sun briefly before disappearing behind a cloud. "Might be worth checking into," he said, his expression deadpan.

"Might be," Piper agreed.

She left it at that.

Recipes

PEARL ONIONS WITH DILL

MAKES 4 QUARTS

½ cup pickling salt
2 tablespoons sugar
4 cups white vinegar
4 cups water
4 quarts white pickling onions (about 6 pounds), peeled
8 fresh dill heads
4 teaspoons mixed pickling spices
16 peppercorns

Mix salt, sugar, vinegar, and water in a saucepan and bring to a boil. Add onions and simmer for 3 minutes.

Into each of 4 clean, hot, quart jars, put 2 dill heads, 1 teaspoon of mixed pickling spices, and 4 peppercorns. Fill with onions and pour hot brine over, leaving ½" headspace.

Seal and process in a boiling-water bath for 10 minutes.

GREEN TOMATO RELISH

MAKES ABOUT 5 PINT JARS

5 pounds green tomatoes, chopped
12 ounces red bell peppers (about 2 medium), seeded and chopped
10 ounces onions (about 2 small), chopped
¼ cup kosher salt
2 cups white vinegar
1½ cups sugar
1 cinnamon stick
1 teaspoon whole cloves
1 teaspoon whole allspice

Put tomatoes, peppers, and onions in a food processor in batches and pulse to finely chop.

Pour into a 6- to 8-quart preserving pan and stir in salt, then let mixture stand for at least 8 hours.

Bring to a boil and cook for 5 minutes, then, using a

sieve, drain and press out as much liquid as possible from vegetables. Return vegetables to preserving pan.

Mix vinegar, sugar, and spices in a nonreactive pan and bring to a boil, stirring for 5 minutes until sugar is dissolved. Remove spices with a slotted spoon and discard.

Add vinegar mixture to vegetables and bring to a boil, then simmer at lowered heat for 5 minutes, stirring occasionally.

Ladle the hot relish into hot, prepared jars, leaving ½" headspace. Wipe rims with a damp paper towel, then top with prepared lids and rings. Process for 10 minutes in boiling water.

About Dill

Dill is a member of the carrot family along with celery, coriander, fennel, lovage, and parsley. The oil is stored in canals that run along the leaves' veins, so fresh dill needs to be chopped to release its oils.

Fresh dill should be stored in the refrigerator, either wrapped in a damp paper towel and placed in a plastic bag or with its stems placed in a container of water. It can last up to a week.

Dill can be frozen, whole or chopped, in airtight containers, or the leaves frozen in ice cube trays covered with water or stock to add later to soups or stews. Frozen dill weed will darken but will still have more flavor than dried.

During the Middle Ages, people used dill to defend against witchcraft and enchantments. More recently, though, people have used dill seeds and the parts of the plant as medicine for things like loss of appetite, coughs and colds, and sleep disorders.

Dill goes well with many foods, but the flavor is destroyed with heat, so it should be added at the end of cooking.

SUGGESTED USES

Combine dill weed with plain yogurt and chopped cucumber for a delicious cooling dip.

Use dill when cooking fish, especially salmon and trout, as the flavors complement each other very well.

Use dill weed as a garnish for sandwiches.

Since dill seeds were traditionally used to soothe the stomach after meals, place some seeds in a small dish and place it on the dinner table for all to enjoy.

Add dill to your favorite egg salad recipe.

Mix together chopped potatoes, green beans, and plain yogurt, then season with both dill seeds and chopped dill weed.